Ro10805050351

Shifting *Through* *Neutral*

Shifting Through Neutral

BRIDGETT M. DAVIS

AMISTAD
An Imprint of HarperCollins*Publishers*

HarperCollins books may be purchased for educational, business, or sales promotional use. For information, please write: Special Markets Department, HarperCollins Publishers Inc., 10 East 53rd Street, New York, NY 10022.

FIRST EDITION

Designed by Claire Naylon Vaccaro

Printed on acid-free paper

Library of Congress Cataloging-in-Publication Data
Davis, Bridgett M.
Shifting through neutral / Bridgett M. Davis.—1st ed.
p. cm.
ISBN 0-06-057249-3 (alk. paper)
1. African American girls—Fiction. 2. African American families—Fiction.
3. Fathers and daughters—Fiction. 4. Maternal deprivation—Fiction.
5. Motherless families—Fiction. 6. Detroit (Mich.)—Fiction.
7. Runaway wives—Fiction. I. Title.
PS3604.A9556S55 2004
813'.6—dc22   2003065378

04 05 06 07 08 WBC/RRD 10 9 8 7 6 5 4 3 2 1

To the memory of my father,
John T. Davis,
who gave me the gift of unconditional love

Acknowledgments

This novel evolved over time, and along the way an array of people helped me keep the faith. Many thanks to members of Dark Body Writers' Collective past and present, for listening to endless versions of this work; Tom Jenks, for mentoring guidance and incisive instruction; Carol Edgarian, for sage insights offered gently; Bert Baisden, for giving me new ways to approach old material; Amanda Insall and Lizzy Streitz, for being the best writer friends a girl could ever have; John McGregor, for priceless advice offered freely; David Tager, for reading early drafts of an unwieldy manuscript; Michele Blackwell, for unwittingly giving me the courage to write about my hometown; members of Joan Silber's Spring '98 Fiction Workshop, for timely encouragement; my agent, Neil Olson, for his deft blend of literary sensibility and savvy know-how; my editor, Dawn L. Davis, for effusive support coupled with an exacting eye, and her editorial assistant, Darah Smith, for making everything easier; Lula Mae Isom, for helping me to remember; my husband, Rob, for unwavering, long-haul belief in me; my son, Tyler, for inspiration . . .

And to each of my loved ones, for having lived.

Part One

Idling

Driving in Michigan should be a safe and pleasant experience. Be courteous, drive defensively, and prevent tragedy.

Michigan Secretary of State,
What Every Driver Must Know

A fter he returned to me, I slept every night atop Daddy's broad back. He was a soft, wide man, and miraculously he remained still throughout our slumber—never rolled over, never pushed me off. How that sleeping arrangement came to be I do not know, but it felt as natural to me as play. As easy as I'd learned the alphabet I learned to identify the reassuring aromas of maleness that sleeping with a man offered: unshaved face, snoring breath, end-of-the-day genitalia.

Even as a little girl, I knew my father needed me. He was a sick man in near-constant pain from migraines and unable to work. He needed me to fetch his medicine, to make cool compresses for his aching head, to massage his temples with my small hands. And he needed me to help fill his days. He left the house only when it was necessary to go to doctor's appointments, to buy food, to cash his pension check. Otherwise, he stayed close to home, not bothering to strike up friendly conversations with the neighbors. My father felt out of sync with these men, who walked out of their front doors each morning dressed in starched shirts and skinny ties, to civil jobs in government offices, their kinky hair kept low. He preferred to wear his hair in defiant waves like Cab Calloway, lie across his sofa bed dressed in elegant silky underwear, and watch daytime TV—his ears perked for the sound of us schoolchildren walking home along Birchcrest Road, our high, pebbly voices drifting into his open window. Other days, he read hard-luck paperbacks by the light of a naked bulb stuck in an old, shade-less lamp as a transistor radio tossed the blues into the room. He might sometimes drive his sleek gray Cutlass Supreme Oldsmobile to Mr. Alfred's auto body shop, where he'd shoot the breeze. But by the time I skipped up the walkway, book bag slung across my shoulder, face flush from conquering a new cursive letter or the secret to multiplying by nine, he was standing on the porch waiting to greet me. Together we wound through our evening of dinner, cards, TV, close sleep.

This is how Daddy remained alive for me all those years—by settling into a life of simple actions, slow movements, perpetual rest. Speed brought throbbing headaches, and so he paced himself. When doing nothing still made his head hurt, he mitigated the pain with loose aspirin and later, sleep-inducing injections of Demerol—eking out as many extra years as he could to embed himself, like a fossil, into my psyche. As a result, I formed myself out of the five o'clock shadow of his maleness.

He hadn't always been sick. The migraines didn't appear until he was thirty-two. Before then, his hypertension was symptom-free, allowing him to spend his young manhood like many migrated southern black men—gratefully working overtime at factory jobs, eating neck bones and greens slow-cooked by wide-hipped women, playing hard every Friday night after payday.

But I only knew Daddy one way, apart from a few old photographs and scattered stories about his past—as a doting father worn down by pain. It's the image I savor, the one I prefer. If he'd been a virile, healthy man when I entered his life, who is to say whether he would've stayed at home, giving so much of that life to me?

Daddy knew he was living on borrowed time. In four short years he went from experiencing monthly to weekly migraines—the kind that lurked behind a low-grade headache, encroaching toward a blunt, excruciating throb that pulsed through his entire body for hours, leaving him nearly weeping and weak with exhaustion—to daily ones. He was only thirty-six when granted disability from General Motors' assembly lines—the youngest man in the auto company's history to do so. It must have seemed a financially prudent gesture on his employer's part, given that the company doctor diagnosed his condition as "extreme." It was surely a blow to his ego, finding himself stripped of a livelihood, facing mortality, still so young.

I was the one who over the years convinced myself his hypertension was a health quirk, an inconvenience to be put up with like a sinus condition or a heart murmur. One day as he drove us home from the doctor's office, when I was no longer a child, I asked Daddy, "Just how high is your blood pressure?" We were cruising along Livernois Avenue, past the neon signs of gas stations and the waving flags of car dealerships that added primary color to Detroit's main streets.

"I can't say, exactly," he answered.

"Why doesn't Dr. Corey ever take your pressure anymore?" I wanted to know, remembering a time when his doctor used to roll out the pressure monitor with the big name. The sphygmomanometer. We called it the spiggy. He'd wrap the cuff around Daddy's arm, pump air through the tube, frown as he studied the dial closely.

Daddy shrugged. "He can't. Numbers on the spiggy don't go high enough." And then he chuckled. "How's that for the puniness of modern medicine?"

I laughed too, believing he could beat it.

M y parents, Vy and JD, met at a raucous card party when Mama was twenty-four and the single mother of a five-year-old girl named Kimmie. She told him she was divorced. He didn't care one way or the other, liking how she played bid whist—bidding high even when she knew she couldn't win. He took her again and again to roaming cabarets, where they slow-danced to Sam Cooke tunes—doing the social, as they called it—while he sang into her ear of what a wonderful world it would be, causing tiny goose bumps to erupt down her neck.   7

She was his kind of woman, high-class *and* good-looking. A woman who could transport him far away from a shameful childhood, a place where he once found a strange man lying across the doorway, satiated inside of his drunken mother. Vy could help him wipe away that haggard image from his mind: the sight of his ma's flabby thighs, that bastard's dusty black ass. She could brush a coat of respect onto his up-from-the-South, hardscrabble Motor City life. At least that's what he envisioned, eyeing her in the amber light of the Twenty Grand Club, where she perched knowingly on a bar stool, puffing on a filter tip, her long legs crossed just so.

In my father, Mama saw a respite. She too was running from a ragged past: a teenage mother who left her as a baby on the steps of an orphanage and a father who six years later appeared, convincing his girlfriend-of-the-moment to go retrieve his daughter. That girlfriend raised Mama as her own child, even after my grandfather had moved on to other women. Years passed before Mama learned about her birth mother—a flighty gal with mental lapses who had three other wild children living on the east side of town in a bulging frame house. Children who, as they grew, embarrassed Mama in school, yelling her business out across the playground. "Hey, I know who you are! You my sister. We gave you away 'cause you too ugly!" They called her Trash Can Baby.

Mama's adopted mother didn't exactly love her in the affectionate, lots-of-hugs sort of way, but she did teach her three key things in life: how to make money taking in other people's money, the importance of a king-sized bed, and a love of pretty men. Her own father had been pretty. This she learned when they all lived together briefly, so briefly it was cruel, like witnessing a caterpillar as it undulates into a butterfly, then seeing it squished under a sadistic shoe, wings wasted. What she remembered most about her illusive father was that he was always coming and going, coming and going. He wore a fedora. And he sang to himself constantly. In a beautiful voice that made his young daughter long for him even before he disappeared—a haunting and mournful voice of high, sad notes that quivered in a room after he walked out of

8

it. When he left them, he left completely, leaving no trace of himself behind. Not even a dent in the tube of toothpaste.

Mama matured under the not-so-watchful eye of her adoptive mother, soon found a man as pretty as her father, and had his baby. But the man already had a wife. It took Mama a few more years to find her own husband. Daddy, it turned out, was handsome if not pretty, had a good-paying job at the General Motors plant, and didn't mind a ready-made family. JD was a witty guy with sweet ways and smooth moves. Plus he could sing. How could she not fall in love? I only heard my father sing twice: Once, on the day when my big sister, Kimmie, left for good, he sang to me in a lilting falsetto that burnished my pain. And then again, much later, near the end. At his funeral, I couldn't bear the thought of a sentimental rendition of "Amazing Grace" or "Up Yonder." I chose that famous country tune by Ray Charles, Daddy's favorite singer, the one he named me after. When Ray cried out from the little boom box in the back of the funeral parlor room, *"I can't stop lovvvving youuuuu, no matter how much I tryyyyy,"* his plaintive wail, the pleading for what cannot be and the resolve to accept it, to *"live my life in dreams of days gone by,"* it made even Daddy's doctor weep.

By the time they married, Mama was four months pregnant. Daddy was thrilled, so ready to grab on to something he could call his own. Mama too wanted "a real family"—to drown out gossipy whispers from neighborhood busybodies who called her a "woman on the side" with a bastard child. But my parents' first baby was born premature and still-born, the fetus falling amid gushing blood in the toilet as Mama had a miscarriage. Horrified, she screamed for Daddy to come quick. He scooped the tiny life out of the water, cut the umbilical cord, felt for a pulse, found none. They dug a grave for him in the backyard, beneath the apple tree. That misfortune was like a pothole on a dark road. An old clunker could charge right through it, but a new car, its axle untested, never rides the same again. Mama changed her mind about Daddy adopting Kimmie—as though his paternity could no longer be counted on—and out of hurt feelings he withdrew from his stepdaughter. Daddy

9

wanted his own child, but Mama thought it would be tempting fate to try again. They slid. She into mood swings inherited from that flighty gal of a mother, and he into deep doubts over what he could really offer her. Their fragile, new marriage imploded. She stayed depressed, and he stopped singing. By their first anniversary, Mama had found someone else via phonograph records whose voice gave her chills, and both of them had sought other lovers. She returning to Kimmie's father in interstate roadside trysts, and he falling for the sweet young clerk at the Social Security benefits office.

In the midst of that mutual dalliance, I got born. As the early weeks of my life passed, Daddy noticed my eyes were just like Kimmie's, the color of a muted, blue-gray sky. He assumed I wasn't his, kept his distance. His headaches had begun but were no more than monthly ordeals that laid him out for a few hours at a time. He felt good, good enough to have other interests across town. He must have savored his situation at first—a high-class wife in one place, a sweet-loving girlfriend in another. But years passed, and in that time both the headaches and the thoughts of leaving us encroached. Finally, on a searing July morning when I was four he pushed his Olds from the curb, pushed it all the way to the corner so as not to create the sound effects of departure—the jingling keys, the running motor, the slamming car door— got in, and drove off. Now I'd done the same thing thirteen years later, only I gunned the engine of my new car because there was no one to sneak away from. I just pulled out of the driveway of our family home on Birchcrest, Daddy's obituary tucked into a Samsonite bag beside the appointment card for my abortion, and headed west.

10

After Daddy took his last breath, I closed the door of his private room, entered the lavatory, and gathered soap, a washcloth, and warm water in a plastic basin. Returning to his bedside, I gingerly removed his hospital gown. There, his flesh lay before me. Carefully, methodically, I bathed each part of him, beginning with his left arm, retracing the scars on it, following this road map to his past as the soap glided across his fevered skin. When I was a child, long after he had returned to me, Daddy showed me his scars. On one of our many nights together, after we'd eaten his special "zoup" (creamed potatoes, lots of butter, and milk) with fried liver swimming in onions and gravy, Daddy pointed to each scar one by one and told the story behind it. This one he got while hoboing his way north on the Tennessee Valley railroads, that one from a freak accident on the assembly line, and this one, the one over his knuckles, came when he beat a man silly for saying the wrong thing to Vy.

"You love Mama?" I asked.

He paused. "Like a sister."

This answer seemed fine to me, as I had a sister and couldn't imagine any love better than that. "Tell me about this one," I said as I ran my finger over the rubbery smooth scar on Daddy's left thumb.

He belched softly from his Pepsi-Cola. "When you're older, I'll tell you."

"I'm a big girl now," I reminded him. "In school, Miss Felton says I'm advanced for my age. I'm in Group Three; that's for the best readers."

He looked at me, head cocked to one side, one eye open. "You *sure* you old enough to handle things I tell you?"

"Daddy," I said, trying to sound exasperated. "I'm gonna be seven years old on my birthday!"

He chuckled, put me on his lap. "Wow! Seven, huh? You getting up there, almost ready to leave home." I giggled as he held me close. "Well, you may not totally understand this now, but I suppose it's something you should know . . ." He told me about my big brother who died because he was born too soon. "And this here scar come from the shovel I used to bury his little body," he said.

I was fascinated by the idea of a baby being born too soon. How did that happen? Was the baby in too much of a hurry? Suddenly, I missed my brother. "What was his name?" I asked.

"Joseph," Daddy whispered. "After me."

Now sitting next to his lifeless body, I massaged that thumb scar with my own thumb and thought about my life of phantom siblings, about the power of absence—how intensely someone who is not physically there, but can be conjured, informs your life. I bathed Daddy's pendulous breasts as they hung above his huge, wide belly with its cavernous button that I so loved. I then soaped along his skin-darkened thighs, flesh sagging, and moved on to the strong knees and shapely legs, retracing my path to his limp, shriveled penis. "Men who suffer from hypertension often suffer from impotence," said a book I once read on the disease, back when I was still self-deceiving and vowed to "do something" about his condition. Back when I arrogantly tried to make him give up pork and those thrice-weekly Demerol injections. Back when I railed against Dr. Corey for keeping Daddy supplied like some pusher man out of a crude Blaxploitation movie.

12

I confronted him once in his office. I was there because I was fifteen, still a virgin, my period mysteriously gone. "It happens sometimes," Dr. Corey said. "You start out being irregular, skip a few months, then as you get a little older, things settle into a pattern. Don't worry." He patted my hand, smiled that gentle, crinkly-eyed smile. He was still the most handsome man I knew, with his crisp white doctor's coat and his silken brown skin. A *Black Is Beautiful* Marcus Welby, M.D. When I was five and he'd given me my vaccination shot, he kept apologizing because Daddy insisted I get it in my hip ("No sense messing up a girl's arm with that ugly scar") and afterward I couldn't walk. Dr. Corey had handed me multicolored lollipops as Daddy carried me out of his office.

"How's your father?" he asked.

"High all the time," I said, hopping down from the examining table, where he had just pushed a cold metal instrument up my vagina. "Like an addict."

He cleared his throat. "Well, he's on some pretty strong pain medication."

"And who's responsible for that?" I asked.

He folded his arms across his body. "Your father lives every day in pain, Rae. You know that. Without medication, he couldn't function."

I didn't really believe that. I believed the headaches would stop as soon as Daddy stopped doing whatever caused them.

"But he can't keep taking that stuff forever," I said from my high horse. "You could help him find the willpower to—"

"Willpower?" Dr. Corey looked perplexed. Then he shook his index finger at my face. "He's a medical miracle, young lady, and you need to recognize just how lucky you are to still have him around." He calmly turned his back to me. "You can get dressed now," he said over his shoulder, closing the door behind him with force. As I left his office I lifted a pad of blank prescriptions from the sign-in desk when Ilene, his office manager, wasn't looking. Just for spite. And just in case.

After that, I stopped going to Dr. Corey. He had pricked my denial, and I preferred to believe he was yet another crack doctor with a ghetto

13

office preying on the poor and uninformed, making a living off of comeback dollars. I wasn't ready to face anything as complicated as the truth.

Later, when I began having unprotected sex, I never even considered going to Dr. Corey for a pregnancy test. I went straight to the Women's Health Clinic in the suburbs, where teen girls of every hue could come and go flagrantly without parental knowledge, be given soft-pedal counseling and complete privacy. I went there the first time I got caught, and I would go there again, this time. I knew the routine: *Sit in the little stainless steel examining room, dressed in a royal blue paper gown, matching blue paper house shoes, and a blue plastic shower cap, then wait for my name to be called. After the injection, wait for everything to go dark until a nurse looms over me in the recovery room, shaking me back into consciousness from a place where I am laughing at Daddy's wit: "Rae? Rae Dodson?" says the nurse. "Can you hear me? I need for you to wake up now."*

"Daddy?"

"Sit up for me, okay? Put this napkin between your legs, okay?"

"What?"

"Here's a prescription for pain. Take this instruction sheet and read it over, okay?"

Look grateful.

I knew the routine.

After my father chose to distance himself from me, Mama put Kimmie in charge of my care. In fact, I have no conscious memory of my parents during that time, as I thought Kimmie was my mother. Eight years old at my birth, she was still a child herself, caring for me with gusto and ignorance. My first memories are of playing Go Fish. "Do you have a two?" I'd ask, believing in Kimmie. "Nope, Rae Rae. Gotta go fish," she'd say. Into the pile of cards splayed across the carpet I'd go, looking for a two. We played and played away the years while Mama waited for her lover to come and whisk her away, us girls in tow. She waited and waited. And then, in 1967—during that summer when the smell of violence permeated our open windows as brown-skinned men with no jobs roamed the streets looking for excuses to release their rage while a heat wave bore down on their better judgments—Mama lost her mind. She couldn't handle the responsibility of a not-yet-potty-trained child, a restless preteen, an unwanted husband, *and* a looming race riot. She broke down, and Kimmie was soon sent to live with her father, the very man who wouldn't come.

On the day she left, I sat on the carpeted stairs of our house eyeing Kimmie through the banister, my pudgy hands grasping the railings, a jailbird in soiled underpants. She eased her thin arms through the spaces and hugged me, oval travel bag dangling off her shoulder, tears lining her eyes, swirled metal between us. And then my big sister was gone: a cool air hitting my legs, the door closing. Out of the echo of her disappearance, Daddy scooped me into his arms and carried me up the stairs. My face rested against his foreign one, the stubble from his unshaved chin tickling my wet cheek, rough and reassuring, the Temptations singing "You're My Everything" somewhere outside a window as he gently placed me on my parents' bed, where I would sleep each night between them as consolation.

I was told Kimmie had gone to a mysterious place called Louisiana, where she had safe roads to walk and her own papa to care for her. I missed her terribly and didn't understand why I couldn't be with her, as she was the only one who fed me affection and love alongside my buttery sweet oatmeal, the only one who shared my secret world of hiding places, and the only one who kept me from being afraid of the dark. I wanted desperately to follow her to Louisiana with its multiple syllables and musical vowels, my body aching for the unknown highways that would get me there.

Still, I found rich comfort in that brief span of days following her departure, lying between Mama and Daddy in their huge bed, feeling the combined warmth of their bodies as I hung my leg over his thigh, rested my hand on her shoulder. My mother and father, who had been strangers to me, suddenly felt like solid bookends of protection. Not once did I wet the bed during the night. Kimmie's disappearance had just begun to lose its sting when, curled between my parents dreaming about Captain Kangaroo, I suddenly awakened to a rush of cold air and a strange, outdoor sound; I sat up, found Daddy gone. I climbed out of bed, tiptoed to the open window, and looked down, where I saw Daddy's silvery new Olds creeping along the street. The driver's door was open, and a figure was working the steering wheel and walking the car, guiding it forward. When the car reached the corner, I saw Daddy get in, heard him slam the door, turn the motor, and drive off, lightly screeching the tires. I didn't understand how he got away without awakening me, hadn't yet realized parents could be sneaky. I turned to

16

look at Mama. She was wide awake, her eyes hardened, her big lips tight. She knew more than I did. "Get back in the bed," she said.

I climbed back in, clinging to her, wrestling with the edge of sleep. Again I awakened abruptly—this time to a loud firecracker boom and an orange light ripping the darkness outside my parents' bedroom window. I sat up. More loud shots. Mama bolted up, grabbed me roughly, and dragged me out of the bed onto the floor, where we crouched beneath the window. "Stay down!" she whispered harshly. "Stay down and don't move!" I smelled smoke. And then I heard the sound of sirens. Disobeying Mama, I rose on my knees, peeked out the window. The house across the street, Mean Mr. Green's house, was burning furiously. Cottony gold flames consumed the huge oak tree in front of it, and its thick branches danced like headless puppets in the early-morning sky. Firefighters blasted their water hoses at the house, the tree. I started to cry, certain Daddy was out there escaping and wanting him here, at home—to be the other half of my protection. I had no faith that Mama, whom I barely knew, could handle me without assistance. I grabbed the hem of her nightgown. "Where's Daddy?" I screamed. "Where's Daddy?!"

She must have been as startled by my outburst as she was by the spread of the riot onto our street. "We're safe inside the house," she offered, shakiness crouching beneath her words. "Come on, get away from that window." But I was suddenly hysterical, uncontrollable in my fear that she wasn't enough. "But where's Daddy? Where is he?!"

"Stop screaming, Rae," she hissed, fumbling with the nightstand lamp until it crashed to the floor. "I can't take it. Really. You're working my nerves."

Mama grabbed her flowered telephone book, nervously lit a cigarette, and called Mr. Alfred, Daddy's closest friend, demanding that he tell her where Daddy was "with that fat bitch."

She wasn't fat. She was plump and buxom. When she showed up at Daddy's funeral, I knew who she was immediately. She sat quietly in the back row. Dressed in a tidy white suit. Beechnut skin radiant beneath a tasteful white hat. Looking like the kind of woman a man should run away with. When she went to view the body, she leaned over Daddy, opened the button of her jacket, pulled a small gardenia out of her bosom, and placed it in the lapel of his white suit. There they were in matching outfits, this flower ritual shared between them from a love life long ago interrupted. I felt we should all turn away from such an intimate moment. And I was oddly proud that the last time she got to see him, Daddy looked good—his mustache trimmed, his taut face smooth and pain-free.

For two whole days and nights, Mama cared for me with an intense focus she would never again muster up on my behalf. I remember so well those days, how it felt to discover that this woman was my mother, that I was her child. Suddenly, she became important to me, to my survival, and I watched her carefully for signs of escape. If one parent could sneak away, so could another.

That first day she was right on top of me, saying, "Stay where I can see you" and "Please don't do anything crazy, okay?" She didn't really know what kind of little girl I was, having left me in Kimmie's hands for so long; and now she had to figure out on the spot what I was capable of, what I wasn't. This while a riot raged somewhere beyond our door and unknown dangers floated overhead like an ominous Goodyear blimp.

I obeyed Mama, in part because I was an obedient child, and in part because I felt sorry for her. She had to concentrate mightily to stay on top of everything—to feed me and lock the back door and remember where the fire extinguisher was kept. This four-bedroom house was suddenly so big to her. I knew every room and drafty crevice—from attic cubbyhole to basement playroom—as Kimmie and I had explored them thoroughly together. I knew where to hide if the need arose, and I sensed that Mama did not. She seemed lost in her own home. Fueled by empathy, I secretly hid my smelly training pants and went to the toilet on my own for the first time—so as not to give my mother more to worry about.

That night we watched fed-up black, brown, and yellow men clash with white police as we sat in our nightgowns before the den's floor-model Magnavox television. Mama kept her arm tightly around me. I was shocked by the shoving and pushing and anger spewing from the screen. "Are they coming after us too?" I asked, terrified of those navy blue uniforms, those billy clubs.

"Of course not," said Mama. "Those people there, they have nothing to lose. But we're different. We have this house." She paused. "You remember that. It's important to have something you're not willing to lose."

Her words comforted me. That was the only piece of advice my mother ever gave me, and over the years, I clung to that advice, used it as a way of justifying my bouts of selfishness—and as a way of rationalizing hers. No matter where she goes, I told myself, she won't abandon this house.

When my grandmother politely died in her sleep after Mama's eighteenth birthday, she left her adopted daughter with a modest estate garnered from years of number-running and poker-party proceeds: a family home and rental property. Three duplexes peppered around the city's neighborhoods closest to the Detroit River and the Canadian border. Mama didn't want to live on that side of town, where tough memories taunted her like those half brothers and half sisters she was running from, and she couldn't wait to sell the house in which she'd grown up. With the proceeds, she purchased a spacious colonial brick in an upscale neighborhood on the west side, where white flight had left behind lovely homes of doctors and lawyers and businessmen who with their families had soared across Eight Mile Road to untainted suburban retreats. A house of solid structure with leaded-glass windows, stucco walls, high ceilings, and a big backyard. A house that would endure. Here she was, not even twenty, my mother, handling the intricacies of

20

post-death financial details. An inheritance. Selling property. Buying a home. It's no wonder that she soon had a baby. A real house conjures up the need to fill it with a real family.

She kept the house ablaze with light and played the hi-fi even as the television blared. "I want them to know there's life going on in here," she said, the Motown Sound commingling with Walter Cronkite's stern voice as we crawled on our hands and knees from room to room, below the windows and out of the range of errant bullets. I felt a skewed mixture of excitement and fear at the prospect of facing danger with my mother nearby. That first night as we prepared to climb into bed together, I confessed, uncertain what my bladder might do under the excitable circumstances. "Kimmie usually has me wear a blanket to bed," I admitted.

"What?" Mama didn't immediately understand, but when she saw the receiving blanket and giant diaper pins that had been my nightly attire, she looked devastated. In that moment, I am sure she saw the depth of her own depression and its swirling offshoots—neglect and denial. "Tonight will be the last time you'll need this, okay?" she whispered. I nodded, suddenly aware that I loved this woman.

On day two, Mama swiftly potty-trained me. "When you feel that urge, you run to the bathroom, okay?" Things were eerily quiet, the streets deserted apart from remnants of ash and smoke clinging to the air. Mr. Green's house across the street was a blackened carcass of itself. I was inexplicably happy. "Mama's going to let the water run in the sink to help you pee-pee," she told me. By mid-afternoon, men atop huge armored tanks, guns drawn, rolled down our street, yelling orders from megaphones. "Stay inside. Do not come out. This is the National Guard! Obey the curfew. You are forbidden to leave your homes." Even with the doors and windows closed, their voices penetrated, creating a fear that crept up on me. I crawled into Mama's slender arms.

"They see we're cooperating, they'll leave," she said. "All we have to do is cooperate. And stay down."

Her assurances kept me calm, but it turns out, *she* was beside herself   21 with panic. Not over the riots, rather over the prospect of single mother-hood. There'd been several near misses with her and Kimmie in those five years before Daddy appeared in her life. Times when she forgot to pick up Kimmie from school, lost her at the supermarket, dropped her off at the wrong corner. She never liked shouldering obligation single-handedly. It made her desperate. But she knew how to hide it. Mostly.

"Where's Daddy?" I finally asked, envisioning a tank rolling away with him inside as we sat cross-legged on the kitchen linoleum, me eat-ing Cheerios out of the box, Mama sipping instant coffee. I assumed he had left to join the effort, like a man off to war, and my question was now born of curiosity rather than concern. I felt safe.

"He's gone," said Mama. She gripped the cup tightly with both hands. "And we're here."

I nodded, trusting my mother. Just an hour before, she had gotten Daddy on the phone and pushed against her pride, begging him to come back. She had offered a proposition: *Help me raise our daughter. Let's give her two parents. Every child deserves that. And then once she's older and can handle things, you and I can go our separate ways.* He said he didn't see how he could do that. Not now. There was someone else to consider. *Please,* she begged. *She's your daughter, JD. She is. She's yours.*

What Mama did next as we sat together in the kitchen was what she'd come to do throughout the overwhelming moments of her life. After her breakdown three weeks before, she'd been prescribed an onslaught of Valium to be taken as needed. This was the first time I saw her take one. And I suppose she did it as much for me as for herself.

"What's that?" I asked when she popped it into her mouth.

"A vitamin," she said.

"What's it for?"

She took a sip of coffee. "My nerves," she said. "They're bad."

"Does it make them good?" I asked.

Mama smiled. "Makes them behave."

"Then you're happy?"

22

She thought for a moment. "I will be in about five minutes."

And she was. Like magic, she changed. She became calmer, less paranoid. She let me play outside of her purview in the backyard on the swing set. Out there alone, I pumped and pumped, swinging higher and higher, trying to kick the sky. When I let go, the momentum propelled me through the air until I landed hard on the itchy grass. I was bruised *and* happy.

In the evening after a TV dinner, I was right behind Mama as she crawled to the living room and flipped through the handful of albums stacked inside the hi-fi cabinet. She selected one by Little Stevie Wonder, sitting back on her heels as she dropped the LP onto the turntable. His earnest, high voice tumbled out of the built-in speakers, singing earnestly to a friend that the answer was blowing in the wind. Mama hugged herself as she hummed along, still on her knees.

It was the saddest song I'd ever heard, and I wanted it to stop.

"Mama?"

"Hmm?"

"Will you play Go Fish with me?" I was suddenly missing Kimmie, not because this new life with Mama didn't satisfy, but because it did and I wanted to blend something into it from my life with Kimmie, to enrich and confirm it. She'd only been gone for days, but that was already a different time.

Mama shook her head. "I'll do you one better. Crawl upstairs and get my pocketbook. And come right back."

Mama lay on the carpet beside the stereo, her limbs stretched out, ear close to the speaker. She dug through her purse, pulling out a deck of cards and her cigarette case. "I'm going to teach you how to play Tunk," she said as she placed a cigarette between her lips. "It's easy." She shuffled the deck, creating an elaborate waterfall in her cupped hands. It was so lovely, the flutter and blur of the cards, their uniformity, like tiny birds' wings in motion. Little Stevie's harmonica electrified the room. It was one of those childhood moments that stay with

23

you forever: the flash of the cards, the drift of the smoke, the beat of the song. I remember how lucky I felt to be there, arched across the carpet on my elbows, so close to Mama I could smell her smoky breath.

Playing cards, it turned out, was another kind of nerve pill for my mother. As was listening to Stevie Wonder's music. And smoking Kool menthols. And humming. After she left me, whenever I was missing her mightily, wanting to invoke her presence, I relied on music, cards, and cigarettes.

"The object is to be the first to have the smallest numbers in your hand," she said, dealing us each a pile of five cards. "You draw from this deck, throw away high cards, keep the low ones. Work fast." Luckily, I could already count to thirty. Mama peeked at each card before she pulled it from the deck. We played five times before I got the hang of it, before I could settle the anxiousness that welled up in me, my palms sweaty as I rushed to draw low cards before Mama did. Finally, by the sixth hand, I too was taking solace in the slick stiffness of the cards, the repetition of their red and black colors and finite numbers. Time flew.

"I wish he was my son," Mama said suddenly, nodding toward the hi-fi.

"Little Stevie Wonder?" I asked. Still at the age where famous people on television and on records lived inside the electronic box their image or voice came out of, I hadn't imagined them with mothers.

Mama smiled, drew her next card, tossed off a queen of spades. "His mother lives right on Cherrylawn. Now there's a lucky woman! She travels. To all kinds of places—Las Vegas and California and Hawaii." I didn't know these places, but the way Mama spoke of them made me certain they were all a stretch of highway away, near Louisiana. "Motown folks live all around here," she went on, pride in her voice. "Up the street, around the corner, in those big, fine houses along Palmer Woods." She paused. "But some are starting to move away. Go places."

The National Guard rolled off of our block, their megaphone-loud voices growing fainter. Mama drew a new card, tossed it off.

"Tunk," I said, laying down my hand. I'd quietly added it up with my fingers and toes, and it totaled nineteen. I thought that was pretty hard to beat, and I was proud of myself.

Mama studied the spread for several moments, sighed. "Someday we'll do that," she said.

"Do what?" She didn't answer at first. "Do what?" I asked again.

She scooped up the cards, wiping out my winning hand, and began shuffling the deck. "Go places," she said against the whir of the blue and white checkered plastic. "Travel. See things."

She was supposed to have traveled after high school. Her adoptive mother had left her enough money to do that—take a train ride across country perhaps or venture on a trek to the motherland like other Negroes were doing at the time. See an African country liberate itself into independence. But instead she'd enrolled in Marygrove College on Six Mile Road, taken an English course from the Creole man with the pretty-boy face. And after that, after she became his mistress, the farthest she'd gotten was Louisiana, to his hometown and then New Orleans. And so, that became her world away, with its French manners and tropical heat and spiced foods and illicit love. There lay possibilities for a life different from the one she lived in Detroit, where factory smoke drifted across the skyline and February lasted forever.

That night as Mama and I lay side by side, I wished that soon we would all, Kimmie included, be headed off to a new place where we would see new things, far away from angry men in riot gear. It was the perfect wish for a lonely child, and I held on to it all night and then into future nights—long after I'd outgrown it.

On the third day, Daddy returned looking tired and spent, like the looted shops along Twelfth Street—having survived an ordeal but not without cost. "You're back?" I asked, shocked when he swung open the front door. I never expected to see him again.

"Gotta take care of my little girl, now, don't I?" he said, lifting my chin with his finger, looking at me for several heartbeats. In those moments he noticed what he hadn't bothered to notice before—that my eyes had changed, had become the color of new pennies. He hugged me with relief. "Hey, Brown Eyes," he said, chuckling. "Hey."

I was stunned by his hug, he who had largely ignored me before. But something in his voice, in the way he said my new nickname, teased my heart, and I felt a brand-new feeling, a painful one I couldn't identify. Which parent to love, now that they both seemed to want me?

Mama, it turns out, was so exhausted from caring for me alone, that she didn't leave her bedroom for a week, and Daddy was forced out of necessity to take over. And from that point on my parents no longer pretended to be in a real marriage. While Mama slept in their bed upstairs, Daddy slept downstairs, in the little den off the living room. With me.

On one level, I adjusted well to yet another shift in the parenting constellation, not unlike a foster child moving from hand to hand, but with a twist—each hand within the same household, part of the same family. Already I was adaptable and resilient, and I didn't expect Daddy's love to become the centerpiece of my existence. I had no way of knowing my eyes had changed colors. I assumed Mama would take over again when she woke up, and things would be as they had been between us during the riots. I half expected Daddy to push his car to the curb again one night and take off.

But that never happened. Mama stayed away from us. She had no qualms about Daddy and me sleeping together. As far as she was concerned, it was the way it should be—a father caring for his daughter. Still, she was secretly furious with Daddy for at first abandoning her, and resentful that he had someone somewhere else who wanted him. The fat bitch with her little east-side shack. Meanwhile, the man Mama wanted didn't want her. So this was her life. Living upstairs while Daddy and I lived down.

Suddenly, this woman whom I had fallen in love with over those couple of riotous days was distant and mysterious again. I was like a jilted lover after a two-night stand: why didn't she want to see me?

Every morning as soon as he opened his eyes, the migraine was there, pushing against his temples, waiting for him, hinting at the pain to come. He held his head carefully, stiffly, as he watched me eat my cereal, brush my own hair. Next he sent me upstairs—"Look in on your mama"—where I bathed and dressed, then crept quietly into her bedroom and kissed her cheek. Sometimes she'd awaken, a soft sleeper, and look up into my eyes, startled for a second or two beyond recognition. "You okay, Rae?" she'd ask, her forehead wrinkled. I'd whisper *yes*, and she'd nod, drift back to sleep. Sometimes she didn't wake at all, and I stole a touch, letting the back of my hand rub against her smooth face, trail off at her chin. I relished a chance to show her affection when

27

she couldn't reject it—delicately, surreptitiously. Always, standing guard on her nightstand were twin bottles of pills. *Mama's naughty nerves,* I secretly called my mother's affliction.

I'd leave Mama, run to the kitchen, grab a bottle of Pepsi-Cola from the refrigerator, pop the metal cap, and carry the cold drink back to the den. There, where the headache sat perched between his eyes, Daddy would take one of many double-pack Stanbacks from his end table drawer and gently pull the little red string that released the protective plastic. Next he'd unwrap the navy blue packaging, open the neatly folded wax paper, and expertly guide the loose medicine into his mouth, head back, powder piling on top of his tongue. And then he would take his Pepsi and wash it all down, grimacing slightly from the cola's fizz coupled with the aspirin's bitter flavor. He'd repeat the ritual with the second packet—pouring, drinking, grimacing—then sit quietly and wait for relief to kick in. Some days it kicked in better than others.

One day, a year or so after Daddy's return, I entered my own room, which was more a guest room, and found Mama sleeping in my bed like Goldilocks. I tiptoed close to her, leaned into her face. She smelled so different from Daddy. Flowery sweet, yet bed sweaty. I kissed her cheek. She awakened.

"Good morning, Rae," she said, still groggy. "Sleep all right?" I nodded, secretly exuberant over her interest, chest thumping.

"Good. Let's see him try to slip out with *you* on his back," she said, then turned over, done with me for the day. I was devastated by the sight of her back, and in that moment I stopped waiting for things between us to return to what they'd been like before; I decided to throw all my love Daddy's way, stop saving some for a mother who didn't seem to need it. I was five.

She wanted me to be Daddy's watchdog because she worried that he might tire of their agreement and run back to his lover. Mama, living above us, completely missed what was happening below—that Daddy was already too involved to ever abandon me. Not noticing that would cost her a lot later. Meanwhile, having transferred my loyalties whole

28

cloth, I became wildly afraid of Daddy's leaving after Mama said those words—"let's see him try to slip out with *you* on his back"—and I began a brief but urgent habit of grabbing onto his leg whenever he tried to leave the house.

Daddy was tickled by my leg grabbing. Evenings when his friend Mr. Alfred waited for him in the vestibule, they'd laugh together about it, unfazed by the depth of my panic. "You sho' don't have to worry about 'Mama's baby, Daddy's maybe' with that one," Mr. Alfred said, chuckling.

Daddy disentangled himself from me, laughing, shaking his head, kissing the top of mine. "Yeah, she's a Daddy's girl, all right."

In the evenings, he cooked my dinner and gave me warnings. Over pork chops and Jiffy's cornbread one night and Polish sausages on white bread with mustard and sliced tomatoes another, he'd tell me harsh stories of his sad mother, a woman "weak for men and alcohol." He'd tell me about a dirty, no-good stepfather who drowned Daddy's two little brothers in a water-filled quarry, drowned them for the piddling insurance money his mother had taken out on them. And how she died from heartbreak. "Her being weak for men, that's what did it," Daddy explained, shaking his head. I listened carefully, learning early that weakness for men leads to death. I passed from kindergarten to first grade to second grade to third this way—learning some useful skills at school and learning life lessons at home.

One evening, our bellies full from fried chicken and cream-style corn, Daddy said, "Get your sweater, Brown Eyes. We're going for a little ride."

Together we climbed into the front seat of Oldie, our nickname for Daddy's car, and we rode down to Six Mile Road, made a left turn, and headed east. On Woodward Avenue we passed the golf course with the big chain-link fence, then glided along the busy street, car windows down, a ubiquitous Ray Charles tape in the eight-track player.

29

We passed buildings with huge, neon signs, the letters M-O-T-E-L flashing in hot, fluorescent colors. I hung my bare arm out the open window, the thick night air draping my skin like sheer gauze. Before long we were downtown, in the area boasting Art Deco–style structures and so different from the gutted-out landscape a few blocks east. "That there is the main public library," said Daddy. "Prettiest place I ever been inside. Majestic. And over there is the art museum. Got a fresco by a man named Diego Rivera that'll make your heart stop. And I believe that one there is . . . hell, I don't know what that one is." He turned the music down. "When your mama and I first got together, I wanted to move over in here, but she pitched a you-know-what, saying nobody who was worth a red cent lived downtown or on the east side. Started talking about that damn Motor Town Revue and how the musicians did all their recording and everything on the west side." Daddy chuckled. "That woman thinks if you wanna live like the famous, all you got to do is live by 'em."

All I knew was that I had seen very little beyond the few blocks between home and school. These rides with Daddy taught me that there was a whole world out there I didn't know. Blocks and blocks of it. "I want a bicycle for my birthday," I blurted out.

"We'll have to see about that," Daddy said. "Bicycles can be dangerous." He made a turn onto a narrow street and parked in front of one of the houses. It was much smaller than ours, with light blue aluminum siding and a white door. Flowers bloomed all along the walkway and in boxes at the windows. "Ain't that a sweet-looking place?" Daddy said, excited. He gripped the steering wheel as he peered through the windshield at the house. I nodded. It was pretty. Gingerbread style.

He rang the doorbell, and she answered. She had long black hair curling on her shoulders and a moist, open face. We went inside, sat together in the living room, with its rose-patterned sofa and matching pillows. The thick pink shag carpet felt bouncy beneath my Pro-Keds. Our house's decor was basic and dark, nothing like this tangle of color.

I don't remember much more about that visit, only that I was allowed to play with another child's toys in the backyard: a swing set with a swirling slide, a wooden Paddle Ball, a red-and-white jump rope. I remember she and Daddy stood holding hands as they watched me play from the back porch steps.

It was my job every night to grab a fresh Pepsi from the kitchen as Daddy repeated his Stanback ritual. Always, he saved the last swig of pop for me. He'd then lie down carefully, stretched across the den's sofa bed, exhausted from getting through the day. On cue, I'd run to the powder room, dampen a washcloth with cool water, fold it into a rectangle, and, returning to Daddy's side, place it across his forehead, gently applying pressure. After several minutes, once I heard light snoring sounds, I'd remove the cloth, quietly tiptoe away and into my pajamas, brush my teeth. I'd then return to the den and crawl on top of Daddy's back.

Some nights when I wasn't yet sleepy, I'd sit beneath the dining room table and draw pictures of moving vehicles. I'd imagine myself in the driver's seat of a big car or truck on a highway, zooming. Occasionally, I'd see the long legs of my mother, her feet clad in pastel nylon slippers, walking soundlessly to the kitchen; I'd keep very still as she passed back by, up the stairway, out of sight. I studied those beautiful legs and fantasized about grabbing onto one, refusing to let go. How far would she drag me?

While I spent my nights with Daddy, I did spend some rare mornings with Mama. She would summon me to her room by calling downstairs from her private telephone line and say to Daddy when he picked up: "Tell Rae to come here for a minute." I'd run up the stairs, my long limbs taking them two at a time, and enter as though crossing the threshold of a queen's lair. There she'd be, on her throne, and there I'd be, so small in comparison, so grateful. She never really wanted anything, just my silent company as she held court from that giant king-sized bed, which was always covered with piles of stuff: newspaper   31 clippings and bills and mail-order catalogs and receipts. These piles were part of her spring-cleaning ritual, which happened year-round. "I'm sorting through the clutter," she'd explain to me. "Getting my things in order." I never saw any progress she made, but it helped her pass the time during those empty years. I would rummage through the piles as I sat perched on the edge of her bed, looking for clues to who she was.

Mama slept a lot. She could sleep through an entire day and then stay awake all night, prowling the upstairs like a sleepwalker. To get through those wee hours, she often played solitaire, smoking in bed with the window thrown open for relief—no matter what the season. By the time I came into the room to kiss her good-bye before school, she was just settling into slumber. I often caught her humming herself to sleep as a Little Stevie Wonder album spun on the red record player Daddy had given me for Christmas, volume down low. If she was still awake when I entered, she might point to the whirling LP and whisper, "This is his latest one. His mother gave me an advance copy."

I noticed that the Motown singer's rich voice was no longer high. And he now sang of not letting sorrow hurt him, of never having a dream come true. As I remember it, like Mama's twin bottles of pills that stood guard, Little Stevie's songs became more and more haunting over those years—and ever more pervasive.

Mama went few places. Her major exception was the monthly card parties she attended with a small group of friends who'd known her since those early, hopeful days with Daddy. These parties were hosted on rotation at each card member's house, but Mama had never hosted one at our place to my knowledge. Paradoxically, it was when she left home for these parties that I got to know her better. For a solid two hours at least, before Daddy would wonder where I was, I could rummage through Mama's room. It was something I did every month during those five years before I turned nine. I had it down to a system. I'd begin with the smaller things first—her lingerie drawers with their soft nylon panties in pastels and lacy Olga bras, and her vanity table with its cacophony of cosmetics and powders arranged atop a brass tray, coordinating hairbrush nearby. I'd reserve the majority of my limited time, however, for her closets.

She had two of them, one on either end of the bedroom, and they were so deep they had windows that looked out onto the side of each next-door neighbor's house. I thought of them as identical little toy houses, both Rae-sized and filled with Mama-clues. In one she kept her stacks of shoeboxes, even more shoes sloped across the wall with matching purses on the shelf above, and beside that an array of octagonal hatboxes. In the other were all her hanging clothes: the pantsuits and summer shifts and dreamy mink cape. I played dress up, of course, trying on her size-nine shoes, slipping a sequined cocktail dress over my rail-thin body. I felt my mother's presence profoundly in those closets, as they were so intimate and filled, everything permeating with the strong flowery smell of Jungle Gardenia perfume. Just before leaving, I'd grab an armful of her hanging clothes and bring them to my nose, inhaling deeply. It wasn't the next best thing to having Mama there—it was better. If she'd been there, I'd never have been able to get that close to her. I wouldn't know where to enter.

And even though Daddy was a different story, I sometimes felt so guilty about the time spent singularly indulging in Mama's inner sanctum that afterward, I would run downstairs to the hall closet, swing open its door, and leap into the darkness, grabbing hold of Daddy's hanging coats and pants and jackets as I tumbled atop the cushion of clothes on the closet floor—all the while filling my lungs with the faint animal scent trapped inside.

My opportunities to forage through Mama's things were rare because apart from those parties she seldom left home—her social life and mail-order shopping conducted on the telephone with its long cord snaking through the hallway, following her even to the bathroom. She was devoted to catalog purchases, found solace in buying what someone

33

else had already selected and coordinated. My mother would buy not only a dress, but the shoes and accessories a model was wearing. The whole outfit. Daddy once told me that when Mama selected new living room furniture, she bought the store's entire floor display, right down to the vase filled with dried flowers on the coffee table. She seemed to believe this method gave her a modicum of control—as though making the right purchases could somehow stave off life's capriciousness.

I inherited some of that belief. Long before I began exclusively wearing hand-me-downs, I can remember once wearing a soft yellow knit ensemble Mama had mail-ordered for me. Because it was Daddy's birthday, I wanted to look pretty for him. But the day turned ugly, as by the end of it both Mama and Daddy hovered before the Magnavox TV. At first, seeing them together excited me. But I soon saw their stricken faces. Mama moaned and Daddy kept shaking his head as the anchorman spoke of Dr. King's assassination. "He was the same age as me," said Daddy. "That man was the same age as me." Watching my parents' sadness, I regretted how brightly dressed I was. In my child's mind, that celebratory outfit was somehow implicated in the turn of events.

I remember too my first day of school, wearing a navy blue sailor dress, this one from the JC Penney's Back-to-School catalog. When Daddy left me in the classroom, I cried hot tears, worried throughout story hour and snack time and what should have been nap time that he wasn't coming back. My crisp new dress was, I was certain, a portent of bad news. By that afternoon Daddy was miraculously there—waiting to walk me home. Yet in his absence I had feverishly pulled the dress's little white dickey from my throat, had ripped off its matching bow, scratched my thighs red from its itchy synthetic fabric.

Over those years, Mama and Daddy only talked to each other through me. There was little to talk about. Not about the housework. Miss Queenie, the day worker, cleaned our home from top to

34

bottom and did the laundry and bought the groceries once a week. Not about the neighbors. We barely knew ours. And never about me. Never about me. Only about money, which Mama always seemed to have a drawer full of thanks to her rental properties and which Daddy never had enough of thanks to his meager disability check. "Go ask your mama to loan me forty dollars till the first," Daddy might say one night. Up the stairs I'd go. "Tell him I need my money!" Mama might say a week later. Down the stairs I'd go. If he'd ventured out to play poker that weekend and won, he'd hand me the money he owed her. And if he hadn't, he'd say, "Tell your mama I'll take care of her after the first. I promise."

This power dance around money taught me that women control things. Men take what they can get. I was awed by Mama's personal wealth for a long time. She wielded cash in bundles, turning presidents' faces in the same direction as she counted out bills rapidly, before tucking the wad into a nightstand drawer. And it wasn't just the money that kept me in respectful admiration; it was also her engaged laughter and animated tones on the telephone, showing more enthusiasm for whoever was on the other line than she'd ever exerted for her own little family. Then there was her sophisticated illness—bad nerves—that kept her shielded from too much interaction with us. Daddy fed this aura of mystery surrounding Mama by often insisting I be careful around her, not do anything that would upset her because her nerves were "delicate." He spoke of her in revered terms too, more than once telling me what a mighty fine mama I had, how lucky we were to have her in our lives. "I don't rightly deserve her," he'd say. She dressed fine, had flown on airplanes, gone to college. She was sophisticated. "She had options, coulda made some different choices, and she chose us," he pointed out to me. I felt duly appreciative.

My parents, one striving to middle-class status, the other striving to just get by, inhabited our house accordingly. Mama believed certain behavior was way beneath certain people, and she couldn't bear to see it: broken things "nigger rigged" rather than properly repaired (like the   35 time Daddy used pliers to turn on and off the kitchen faucet rather than call a plumber), or meals eaten on snack trays in the living room, or cheap floral sofa covers tossed over worn-out couches. Our furniture was covered in fitted plastic. Worst of all were any telltale signs of low-class living on the outside of the house, the greatest offense being car parts strewn across a back lawn. Mama was very conscious of the responsibility of living next to white folks, even after most of those who'd been our neighbors had moved away. Daddy, on the other hand, used things until they were worn out, or "lived in," as he called it. The stuffing was coming out of the arm of his sofa bed, he wore old shoes with the backs down, turning them into makeshift slippers, and he had an array of "do rags" for his hair, collected from frayed remnants of old silky T-shirts.

For the chance to enter Mama's mysterious world even just a bit, and in order to stay in good stead within Daddy's, I acted as the go-between for my parents. I was the weight that kept both sides of the seesaw balanced. Up. Down. Neither ever considered whether I minded this role. And I never considered whether it was fair. It was just the way it was.

Things began to change a June day in 1972 when Mama ventured out for her monthly card party. She came down the stairs that evening dressed in a sharp turquoise polyester pantsuit bought from a B. Siegel's catalog, her purse in the crook of her arm, lips red. Only this time she didn't wait on the porch for her ride—a mysterious-looking white Mach II Ford that usually pulled up to the curb—but rather started walking the one block to Seven Mile Road. Daddy said she must've been catching the Hamilton bus. Mama didn't drive. She'd learned once but was so afraid of oncoming cars that she refused to make left turns. After a while, she tired of trying to figure out whether a destination could be gotten to with all right turns.

She didn't come back that entire night. And even I knew that card parties couldn't last that long.

"Where's Mama?" I asked Daddy around noon the next day.

"She probably decided to hang out with her friend Johnnie Mae," he said, peering up the street from his perch in front of the den window. "That's her running buddy when she chooses to run." I'd never thought of my mother as the one escaping until Daddy and I saw her later that evening, being dropped off by her card buddy Lyla, who, it turns out, owned the mysterious Mach II. I noticed Mama had a head-held-high stride, but no packages.

He'd come to Detroit, her former lover, after five years of nothing, and they'd spent a wistful night together. She'd kept in regular, secret contact with Kimmie over those years, and Kimmie in return had kept her abreast of his love life. He was still married, and there were other women too. But on this night, when she should have been at her card party, he made an announcement: his wife was leaving *him*. With this revelation, Mama started hoping. She came home the next day looking for a sign. That night, I fell off the den radiator and gave her one.

I'd put a milk crate on top of it, then climbed onto that so I could reach the windows. I loved them because they were tall and narrow with small square panes. I was convinced they were the exact windows that existed in castles. I could, if I stood on tiptoe, peek through the triangle of colored stained glass at the top. Blue, pink, and yellow. I imagined this was how the world looked to Mama when she took one of her pills—warm and tinted. My goal was to quickly peek through the colored panes, then open the window and let in the smell of apple blossoms growing on the tree in our front yard. But the window was stuck, so I pulled on the latch with all my might until it opened suddenly, its pointy corner jabbing me in the face, right next to my eye. I stumbled and fell off the milk crate, landing on my back. I could hear the faint traces of Little Stevie's disapproving voice drifting down from Mama's open bedroom window. *Mary wants to be a Superwooooman but is that really in her head?* I cried as much out of fear as pain.

Daddy rushed into the den, grabbed me off the floor, and examined my eye. I couldn't stop screaming.

"Shhhhh!!! Let me see, let me see. There's just a little blood, Brown Eyes. It's okay. It just scared you, that's all. Shhhh. Now tell me what you were doing up there."

My screams turned to sobs as I tried to explain myself. "I. Was. Trying. To. Open. The. Window. And. Then. I. Fell."

"You know you shouldn't have climbed up there like that, don't you?"

I nodded my head.

"Are you all right, Rae?" Her voice came from nowhere, like the principal's voice at school, suddenly booming across the loudspeaker, silencing all homeroom chatter. There she was in the den doorway, framed by the glass French doors, looking down at us, nightgown flowing to her ankles.

"She's fine," said Daddy. "More scared than anything." He looked over at me as if to say, "Get up, show your mother no harm can come to you when I'm nearby." I didn't move, as I was stunned by the fact that my parents were in the same room together.

"You can't put all your weight on something that's unstable to begin with," Mama explained to me. "Of course you fell." For a few seconds she said nothing else. I could feel her studying me, assessing our lot. Danger, she realized, could follow you into the house. Perhaps that was the moment she decided for sure it was time to leave it.

Finally, Mama spoke, hands on hips. "It's high time she learned to sleep on her own back!" she hissed. Then she turned on her heels, her gown creating an arc of chiffon behind her.

The next morning, my ninth birthday, Daddy said, "Hurry home after school, Brown Eyes. Got a surprise for you."

That afternoon, I ran the entire five blocks to Birchcrest. My eye barely hurt anymore. I didn't even stop to play Scramble with penny candy on the corner alongside the other kids and Terrance Golightly, whom I adored with his lopsided Afro and snaggletoothed grin. Yet, as I ran up the walkway to our front porch, my heart stop-started like Oldie's motor on a cold day. Daddy was not waiting there to greet me. Mama was.

She stood in the doorway with her arms hugging each other. She looked young and thin, wearing deftly applied makeup and a navy sailor's blazer with white pants. Dark, short wig. Very mod. Like she looked on the evenings she went to her card parties. Only I knew this wasn't a card party night. It was too early in the day. And it wasn't the weekend. When I think about it now, it's hard to believe my mother was already thirty-six.

39

"Hi, Rae," she said.

"Hey," I answered, breathless.

"Hey? Well aren't we a grown-up something!" She laughed, as though laughter was something we always enjoyed between us.

"Where's Daddy?" I asked, suddenly scared.

Mama squatted to my level, grabbed onto my shoulders, and looked me in the eye, her perfume so powerful and sweet I almost choked.

"He's sleep. Now listen to me." She inched closer. "I've been waiting for someone, for something," she said, her voice low, as though we were playmates sharing a secret at recess. "And now what I was waiting for is here." She paused, her grip tight on my shoulders. "And it has changed everything. We're going to be . . . we're going to be happy."

"But I thought your pills made you happy," I said, never assuming she needed people for that.

She slowly shook her head from side to side, a triumphant smile forming at the corners of her mouth. "I don't need those anymore," she said. "Now we're going to have the real kind of happiness. The kind that lasts." She tenderly lifted my chin with her finger, tilted my head up to hers. Her touch made me dizzy. "Wouldn't you like that, Rae?"

I looked my mother in her hopeful eyes and nodded my head slowly. I wanted *her* to be happy.

She kissed my cheek, stood, smoothed out her white linen pants. "We're going to do things together like a family!" she promised as we walked hand in hand through the front door, past the vestibule, and into the living room. There, both standing so lovely and new in the middle of the floor, were a banana-seated bicycle and my big sister, Kimmie, come home.

Taking Off

When you are driving, unexpected events can happen very quickly with little time for you to react. Plan ahead.

WHAT EVERY DRIVER MUST KNOW

She was stunning. Seventeen and exotic, with long wavy black hair and Crayola-gold skin and funny-colored eyes that danced in their sockets.

"Wow, Rae Rae, you're such a big girl!" Kimmie said, her voice cool and sweet, like 7-Up over ice cream. "Just let me hug you!" She came at me, her arms flung wide. She smelled like baby powder and fresh rain and wore a crinkly peasant sundress that tied shoelace-style at each delicate shoulder. She had a nervous energy to her that must have come from years of attention getting, a wary confidence reserved for girls who are told repeatedly how pretty they are but never fully believe it.

I was so startled by her presence that I dared not move. I thought I would worship Mama forever for this ninth-birthday present.

"Hmmm, Hmmm, look at you," Kimmie cooed as she held me at arm's length, checking me out. "It's been so long!" I couldn't believe how tall she was, how long her hair was, how mature she looked.

"You're here," I whispered. "You're here." Kimmie nodded, smiling. I clung to her elbows.

Just then the toilet flushed, and I worried it might be Daddy unaware—dressed only in his silky underwear—when suddenly a tall, beige-colored man entered the living room. He had metal gray eyes, the color of Oldie, and he winked at Mama, grabbed Kimmie into his arms, and—*smooooch!*—loudly kissed her forehead. Kimmie giggled. Dressed in a plaid flannel shirt and blue jeans, he looked outdoors healthy, like Big John on the Beans 'N Fixin's can.

"Best be getting back on the road," he said, his voice deep and scratchy. "Long drive ahead." He looked at me. "And I'll bet you're what they call Rae Rae."

I nodded, wondering how *he* figured into this happiness that Mama had promised.

"Heard a whole heap about you," he said. "Cute as a buzzing bee, too."

"This is my papa," explained Kimmie. "He drove me up here from Louisiana."

Even though I'd instantly decided not to like this man, I had to ask, "What's that like?"

"What, Chicken?"

"Louisiana." I said it slowly, so as not to stumble over the syllables.

"Oh, it's a fine place. Mighty fine. Maybe one day I'll take you there to see it, okay?"

"Okay," I said, envisioning a magic kingdom with a gated entrance, scripted words above the archway announcing the destination, this Papa as the gatekeeper.

"Cyril, let me walk you out," said Mama in a voice I hadn't heard before. Light, girly. Straining for a second chance. "You sure you don't need some food before you get on the road?"

"Well, if you want to go with me to that little diner I passed up the street, I'd be much obliged," he answered, eyes twinkling.

Mama glanced at Kimmie, who said, "You should go on. You know how Papa hates to eat alone."

"But you just got here, Sweetie. I could stay—"

"Vy, I'm not going anywhere, okay?" Kimmie smiled at me. "Don't worry. Rae Rae and I will be right here when you get back."

"I cannot get used to you calling me Vy," said Mama as she grabbed her purse. "It sounds too . . . grown. Cyril, what'd you do to my little girl down there?"

Cyril chuckled. "Kept her out of trouble, like you told me to do, that's what."

"Yeah, and everyone knows I'm just trouble waiting to happen," said Kimmie, her smile tight.

It was blasphemous to me that Kimmie called Mama by her first name. I thought everyone was in equal awe of my mother. I glanced at the den door. "Where's Daddy?" I asked, unclear why he was not here to say happy birthday and stop Cyril from taking Mama away.

"Shhhh! I told you before, he's asleep," said Mama.

"So, how *is* Daddy Joe?" asked Kimmie. "Does he still make that yummy zoup soup?" She followed my glance, walked across the living room, peered into the den's glass French doors. "Wow. He's knocked out. Is he okay?"

"Depends on what you mean by okay," said Mama. She and Kimmie exchanged a quick glance, and I noticed that despite Mama's dark-chocolate skin and Kimmie's fair complexion, they looked almost exactly alike. Same little nose, same high cheekbones, same full mouth. Different eyes. I didn't look like anyone. Except that Mama and I both had brown eyes.

"I'll be back soon," said Mama. I wanted to announce that *she* was the one who slept all day, but I kept quiet.

"Bye, Papa!" said Kimmie. "I'll miss you. . . . Drive safely!"

"You bet I will, Sweet Pea," he said. "You be a good girl up here in Detroit." He said it in a way I'd never heard—stressing the *D*. Then Mama and Cyril left, and he slammed the front door hard, the way Daddy hated for people to do.

From that moment of that door slam there was a shift, a rush of light wind in the motionless air of our family life. And it didn't let up all summer. This breeze rather brought with it a whirl of activity to the house—rustling the heavy curtains and our lives, disturbing the precarious balance Daddy, Mama, and I had managed to create.

45

I've tried often to imagine what it must have been like for Kimmie to return after all those years, after Mama had sent her away against her will but after she'd been gone long enough to think of that other place as home, the place where she groped motherless through her early teens. Did she think long and hard about what to wear to see her little sister and mother for the first time in five years? I still remember that baby powder and rain smell. Did she make her papa pause at a rest stop along I-75 just south of the city, in Toledo perhaps, so she could splash water on her face, pour talcum down her chest, change clothes, dry her wet hair? I imagine she was nervously excited standing in our crowded living room introducing her father to me with her stepfather a few paces away, watching her parents go off together, knowing they'd go to a motel, maybe even one advertising its services in Day-Glo neon on the highway she and her papa had just exited.

K immie and I watched as the sporty red Volvo tore away from the curb. "Papa's new car is the best. You wouldn't believe how smooth it rides," she said. "I slept all the way here once we hit Kentucky. And his sound system has like four speakers!"

I thought about Daddy's Olds, still gray, no longer shiny. The muffler had fallen off the week before, and he'd tied it back on with a rag. I wondered what it would be like to ride in a cool, brand-new car.

"Come on," she said, leading me upstairs, straight to the spare bedroom—which I now remembered had been *her* room—where I watched her unpack. Out from her many suitcases came mounds of stylish clothes, a cornucopia of schizophrenic seventies fashions: demure high-neck granny dresses and plunging V-neck wrapped ones; skirts in a stunning array of lengths from micromini to maxi; Indian-style suede fringed vests and crocheted ponchos; bell-bottom pants in mod designs; gauzy and tank and tube tops in frenetic colors. Hanging from belts and necklaces and bracelets were all kinds of beads and patches and feathers. Pairs and pairs of shoes—towering creations on wedged and platform heels—occupied their own luggage. I watched in awe when suddenly with a flourish Kimmie handed me a pair of purple hot pants with a matching halter top. "These are for you," she said. "Happy birthday."

As I held the clothes, feeling tingly and light-headed, she said, "Try them on. I want to see how they look on you. You can model for me." Then Kimmie pushed me, affectionately. "Go on, Rae Rae."

I stumbled a little and quickly slipped out of my pedal pushers and tank top, nervously scurrying into the new clothes. The sound of her young, exuberant voice, a new sound in the house, made me giddy, so giddy that I lost my balance trying to direct one foot into the hot pants while standing on the other. When I fell, Kimmie's laughter tumbled over me, warm and reassuring, like fresh towels straight from the dryer.

I modeled for her, turning around and around in my pure-cotton outfit, which I knew would never be found in a Penney's catalog. Kimmie nodded her approval, and I ached with joy.

"Hey, how nosy are the neighbors around here?" she asked, slipping out of her sundress into a fresh pair of hip huggers.

"We don't really know our neighbors," I said.

Kimmie cut her dancing eyes at me. "You don't? That's weird. I knew all our neighbors when I lived here. Same thing in Louisiana with Papa. Everybody knows everybody down there."

"Did your papa live here before?" I asked, imagining Daddy kicking him out, pushing him down the back porch steps perhaps.

Kimmie laughed. "No. That was . . . let's just say that was impossible at the time. Besides, he would never live in this house." Kimmie ran her hand along the bedroom wall. It needed fresh paint. "Papa's got his own taste. Contemporary, he calls it. You should see our house. It's split-level with a patio and sliding glass doors and a sunken living room. Papa had it built. Very *Brady Bunch*."

I changed the subject back to our neighbors. "I forgot, there is Mean Mr. Green," I offered, not wanting her to think we were *that* weird, not when she'd just gotten here. She might leave again.

47

"Oh, I remember him! Lives in that two-family across the street, sits on his upstairs porch all the time, watches everything and everybody?"

I nodded. "His house burned down, but they rebuilt it."

"I definitely didn't like him. Is he still nosy as sin?"

"Yes!" I offered, relishing the chance to connect my life to Kimmie's again. "He told on me once when I ran across the street by myself."

"Oh yeah? I hate a tattletale." She paused, thinking. "Guess we'll just have to sit on the back porch, where his greedy little eyes can't see us, won't we?"

Kimmie grabbed my hand and led me down the stairs, through the hall, and out the kitchen door. She plopped down on the back steps and pulled a cigarette out of the breast pocket of her midriff top, slipped two fingers down the slit of her hip huggers, produced a book of matches, and lit up, all in one grown-up motion. "This is our little secret, okay?" she said. "Papa hates smoking inside the house."

"I don't think Mama will mind," I said. "She smokes."

Kimmie puffed. "Yeah, but just the same let's keep this to ourselves, Rae Rae."

I sat on the bottom step and studied Kimmie's face. I noticed the way her cheeks sucked in each time she inhaled and the way she closed her eyes, tilted her head back, exhaled. Our next-door neighbor had just cut his lawn, and that fresh, grassy scent beneath my nose was so promising of a golden summer unfolding, that I reached out and touched Kimmie's cheek just to be sure she was really part of it.

"Hey, watch this," she said, pushing her mouth into an *O* shape. Suddenly, little oval smoke rings glided from between her lips. They were so perfect I grasped at one. It disappeared in my hand.

She smashed her cigarette out with her sandal, picked it up, flicked it across the neighbor's fence, and turned to me. "How about we go for a ride on that new bike of yours?"

The thought of Daddy alone in the den popped into my head. This was the beginning of a crushing sense of divided loyalties that I would suffer with that entire summer. But Kimmie grabbed my hand and led me back through the house to the living room, where my new bike was waiting, kickstand erect. We eased the bike out the front door ("Leave the door unlocked 'cause I don't have a key yet," she said), and together we carried it down the porch. Kimmie let me ride with her on the banana seat, and we took off. She immediately left the sidewalk and glided into the street as I leaned back against her chest. Pink and purple streamers hanging on the ends of the handlebars fluttered in the breeze as we rode down Birchcrest, over to Margarita. "God, it's all coming back to me now," said Kimmie as we flew by houses with dense green lawns and curvy walkways. The sky was like a blue-white sheet stretched out to dry. "I had a lot of fun back then," she announced.

"Are you having fun now?" I asked as we turned onto Curtis, my bearings deliriously lost.

"You betcha by golly wow I am." Her breath tickled my ear. She stopped peddling, and we glided downhill, thanks to a big dip in the street. We coasted, passing by Greenlawn, Northlawn, Roselawn, Cherrylawn, completely silent and close. *Maybe we can just keep riding,* I thought. *Send Daddy and Mama postcards from the road.*

Just as we reached the main intersection at Wyoming, we saw Terrance Golightly riding toward us on a grown-up bike. He was pedaling so hard uphill that the bike swayed low to each side, pedals scraping the pavement.

"Heyyyy, Rae of Sun!!!" he yelled as he passed by us.

"You know him?" Kimmie asked.

I nodded. "That's just a boy at my school."

"He likes you," she said. "I can tell."

"How can you tell?" I asked, puppy love for Terrance heating my face.

"Has he tried to hit you yet?"

"He tripped me once. And another time, he pushed me."

"I knew it." Kimmie turned down a side street, her words snatched

49

by the wind before returning to me in a gush. "Boys and their love taps."

As I held on tighter to Kimmie's waist, I assumed that was a good thing—love taps. Much later, with my boyfriend Derek, I endured pushes, slaps, and assorted abuses because I thought that was what togetherness wrought—love taps run amuck.

D addy's feet were clean. He'd just washed them the day before entering the hospital. They were smooth and soft and now, all for naught. I hated the waste.

How many times had I watched his foot-washing ritual? Watched him spread newspapers all around the den floor, plunge his feet one at a time into a mop bucket of soapy water, let the roughness soak away. "I say, I say, my brothers and sisters, cleanliness of feet is next to Godliness," he used to joke as he brandished a razor between deft fingers, about to attack the crusty white skin on his heels. "What did Jesus do when he had free time? Washed the feet of his disciples. Say Amen!" He scraped and sliced, and I watched enthralled, as the peelings fell like petals onto the paper. Once done, he slathered on Johnson & Johnson's green-colored foot cream, the smell of menthol dominating the tiny den.

Now, I regretted that I could not lift my father's lifeless body, roll him over, and wash his beautiful broad back. I ached to see it one more time. Instead, I massaged each clean foot for good measure.

Once I had asked him to scrape my feet too. He chuckled. "Feel this," he said, holding up the sole of his foot. I did. It was rugged, the skin cracked and split in places, worn slick in others. "Now feel the bottom of yours," he said. It was pink and supple. "That's the difference between a girl and a man," he said. "Dead skin." He smiled his thin-lipped smile. "You remember that when you get into a hurry to be grown."

The only thing I was in a hurry to do was drive. Years later, on my fifteenth birthday, I enrolled in a driver's education course. An interminable waiting period with a learner's permit followed, and then I finally got my license. "This won't be long," I told Daddy when we pulled up in front of the license bureau. "I'm going to fly through the road test!" And I did. Afterward, I was so excited, so anxious to legally drive home, I bumped right into a boy. We apologized in unison. Feeling independent with a temporary license in hand, I gave him my number. Back outside, I found Daddy waiting. He looked at me, smiled, and handed me the car keys.

The boy, Derek, spotted us as he was leaving the building with his father, and he winked at me. By the time my permanent license arrived, Derek and I were no longer virgins. His father, an executive at the GM Proving Ground, had given him an ocean green Pontiac Sunbird as a birthday present, and in the tiny, leather-upholstered backseat of that absurd little car we had sex. As awkward and cramped as it was, we prevailed.

Many things led to the end of Derek and me, but none so disturbing as what I once witnessed him do to that car. We were returning from Cedar Point Amusement Park in Sandusky, Ohio, when the poorly made Sunbird overheated. We pulled over, and Derek walked the mile or so to a gas station, gripping a tin can upon his return. He lifted the hood of his car and leaned under as though he knew what he was doing. I watched him closely. He poured the motor oil into the antifreeze spout.

A year later, for my road trip west, I had Mr. Alfred do a complete tune-up. I didn't want to take any chances that some ignorant soul at a fly-by-night service station might pour the wrong liquid down the wrong hole of my sensuous new car.

On our first bicycle ride together, Kimmie and I rode and rode until the streetlights popped on. That seemed to trigger our appetites.

"Hungry?" Kimmie asked.

"I'm starving," I said, just realizing it.

"Me too."

We picked up speed, and everything Kimmie had pointed out to me got revisited in a blur: houses where her elementary school classmates lived, the candy store where she bought Tootsie Rolls and Mary Janes after school every day, and the alley where a boy first kissed her.

As we eased the bike back into the house, it was eerily quiet. I knew it was nearly time for Daddy's Pepsi and Stanback, his cool compress. But I wasn't ready to leave Kimmie and didn't know how to do both—stay with Kimmie and attend to Daddy. I headed upstairs with her.

"Let me take a quick shower, and then we can fix ourselves some dinner, okay?" said Kimmie.

I nodded, right at her heels as she entered the bathroom, watching as she peeled out of her clothes. Her yellow panties said "Saturday." Her bra was like a bikini top, bursting with colors all swished together. I could see now that she was tanned, that the skin beneath her underwear was creamier, like custard.

"Want to take a shower with me?" she asked. "It'll be quicker."

"I don't know how to use the shower," I admitted.

"Really?" She ran the bathwater, tested the temperature, turned the middle nozzle. Shower water sprayed into the tub like a burst of good news.

"Daddy always has me take baths."

"I love showers," said Kimmie, slipping out of her weekend panties and psychedelic bra. I bit my lip because I'd never seen a big girl's body before—not even Mama's. Kimmie had breasts shaped like scoops of butterscotch ice cream and a patch of hair in her triangle where mine was smooth. I couldn't stop looking at her, even though something about it felt dangerous.

"What are you waiting for?" she said. "Take your clothes off."

"I can't." I pictured myself in the shower, water hitting my hair, wetting it. I imagined how wild and tangled it would be once it dried and the mess it would be in for days and days before Miss Queenie came around to comb it out. Mama never combed my hair. "I can't deal with her crying," she'd say to Miss Queenie, handing over the wire-bristled brush. "It's too much on my nerves." I didn't want Kimmie to see me like that, wild haired and compromised. I wanted her to adore me as she had when I was four and she couldn't bear to leave me.

"What's wrong, Rae Rae?"

"My hair." I covered it with my hands.

"Oh, I know what to do about that. Come on, get in."

I stripped and stepped into the tub. Kimmie maneuvered me behind her so the water hit her first, soaped her body, rinsed, handed me the huge pink bar of Lifebuoy. I lathered my flat body, and then Kimmie guided me in front of the showerhead so the spray missed my hair entirely. The water felt like a thousand little kisses.

When we stepped out of the tub, I ran to the linen closet and grabbed two big towels. We rubbed ourselves dry. I'd never felt so clean. Or grown-up. We dressed quickly. Kimmie changed into cut-off

54

jeans and a gauzy *Made in India* shirt, but I wanted to put back on my new hot pants and halter-top. "They're not dirty yet," I explained.

"Okay, Rae Rae. Hurry up. I'm starving!"

We agreed on grilled cheese sandwiches. After I pulled out the skillet, the butter, the Velveeta cheese, and the Wonder bread, Kimmie took over.

"The key is to let them cook nice and slow," she said. "So the cheese really melts."

When they were ready, we ate our sandwiches with tall glasses of cherry Kool-Aid on ice. I didn't think about Daddy.

Later we sat cross-legged on the beige carpet, our knees touching. Kimmie held the cards in the palm of her hand, her eyes closed. After several seconds, she looked at me. "I was exchanging energy with the cards," she said, holding the deck out. These cards were nothing like the ones Mama and I used to play Tunk. They were more frightening, with their beautiful medieval images, dramatic size, and power to tell the future. They reminded me of the gypsy booth I'd been drawn to at the Michigan State Fair, and I knew these cards were the kind of thing you keep hidden in your top drawer, beneath your panties.

"Okay, cut with your left hand," said Kimmie. I picked up half the deck and placed it on the carpet, and she placed the other half on top. "Okay, think carefully about what you want to know," she said. "You get three questions. Remember, the question has to be one where the answer is just yes or no." Her hand rested on the deck.

I didn't have to think about the first question. "Will you be staying this time?" I asked.

Kimmie looked up at me, her fingers frozen on the top card. "That's your question?"

I nodded.

"Oh, Rae Rae, you don't need the cards to tell you that one. I can tell you, I'll be here for the whole summer."

55

"And then what?" Suddenly, I heard the jingle of a key in the front door and I jumped up, as though I'd been caught at something.

"Hey, relax," said Kimmie, just as Mama stepped into the living room, her red lipstick brighter than when she left.

"What are you two up to?" she asked, tossing her purse on the landing of the steps. She plopped down on the floor between us in her wrinkled white linen pants, crossed her legs, and waited, the way Markita Stoddart always waited to be let into a game of jacks on the school playground. Patiently, with her chin in her hands. She smelled like her signature scent mixed with the outside world. Her eyes shone. "Hmmmm, tarot cards! I haven't seen these in years," she said. "Since the last time I was in New Orleans."

She and Kimmie used to go there often to see Cyril, back when Kimmie was a little girl and Mama an unwed but cunning mother with a wedding band on her finger and a modest bank account. She spent too much of the money her adopted mother had bequeathed her on those trips, on illicit nights of drink and jazz in Bourbon Street clubs with Cyril at her side and Kimmie alone at the inn, where she always got her own room. Having dropped out of college, Mama used those trips as her advanced education—those secretive visits where the biggest thing she learned was not what she found in the French Quarter but how to take your love for a man and pull it out of your pocketbook, express it, fold it away for long stretches, take it out again, express it. Wait for the next time.

"Have fun?" asked Kimmie.

Mama gave her a demure smile. "Your papa says he'll call to let you know he arrived okay."

"Good." Kimmie nodded in my direction. "Go ahead. Ask your next question."

"Yeah, Rae, ask your question," said Mama. "And after you, I'll go."

I just blurted it out. "Why were you gone so long, Kimmie?" Now that she was back, it felt cruel to have been without her for five whole years.

"That's not a question that can be answered by a yes or no," said Kimmie. "Remember what I told you?"

"Because it wasn't the right time," said Mama. "And now it is."

"Yeah." Kimmie laughed nervously. "Now that I'm grown."

"Not yet, you're not," said Mama, defiant. "It wasn't that long ago, Missy, that I took you downtown to Hudson's to get your first training bra."

Kimmie stuck out her blossoming chest. "Now look at me."

"Yes, just look at you," said Mama, wistfully.

She'd missed Kimmie all those years. And she wanted to make up for them. She wanted things to be like they had been during their visits to Louisiana—the three of them eating family-style at a touristy spot where candles burned, Mardi Gras beads hung from Kimmie's little wrist, and Cyril's wife stayed away.

Kimmie drummed her fingers lightly atop the deck of cards.

"You know what I remember most about back then?" she said to Mama, picking up on a conversation the two of them didn't need to begin, so embedded was it in their delicate past, like gnarled roots of a fragile ficus tree.

"Hmmm?" said Mama, stifling a yawn.

"The way you'd let me sleep with you on the nights Papa couldn't get away."

Mama looked up at Kimmie. "Yeah? But you got to sleep with me at home sometimes."

"I know, but somehow it was different when we were in New Orleans. It was more special."

Mama thought for a moment. "I guess that's true," she said. "It was."

I knew then that I was the odd one out. Even though I'd had Mama with me in this house for several years, Kimmie was the one who had slipped off with her into the southern nights. Kimmie was everything: love child, prodigal daughter, beautiful progeny. Their complicated, fierce connection was as impenetrable as it was bruised, and even a nine-year-old girl could see that.

57

Mama closed her eyes, stretched out across the carpet, and curled up her knees. "So glad you're back, Sweetie," she mumbled.

"Me too," whispered Kimmie.

Then Mama fell asleep.

Kimmie placed her tarot cards back into the little velvet pouch they'd come out of.

I grabbed at her hands. "But what about my future? My other question?"

"We'll do it another day, Rae Rae," she said. "I promise." She looked at Mama, full of sympathy. "She's so thin. Has she been doing all right?"

I had no idea how to answer that question. "She stays in her room a lot," I said, shrugging.

Kimmie looked at me. "Doing what?"

"I don't know." I was getting nervous, feeling as though I'd been a bad daughter for not paying better attention to our mother, not watching her closely enough for signs of breakage. "She listens to Little Stevie Wonder a lot."

Kimmie laughed, that sparkling giggle that I'd already come to crave like cream-filled cupcakes.

"Well, that's a promising sign! She's still got good taste in music." She looked over at Mama, the furrow gone from her brow, love bouncing off her face. "Should we leave her here to sleep?"

"Well, she never sleeps downstairs."

"Oh. I guess not." Kimmie shrugged. "Okay, then help me get her up."

We nudged Mama so she could at least walk with our help—me holding one arm, Kimmie the other—as we led her up the stairs. I thought I heard Daddy's footsteps below, but I couldn't be sure. We got Mama to her room; Kimmie slipped shoes off her feet, eased legs onto the bed, and guided her to lie down. That done, Kimmie stepped back, brushed her hands together. "There. She can get undressed if she wakes up." She sighed, a heavy sigh. "I think I overdid it today, what with the drive up here and that bike ride and all." She looked over at Mama. "It's been a long time coming, today. And it's been a long day."

I followed Kimmie's gaze and watched as Mama coiled into a ball, easing her hands under her cheek, a bit of a smile on her face. As I turned to leave, I noticed too that the twin bottles of pills were gone from her nightstand, no longer standing guard. We stepped into the hallway, and Kimmie walked to her room—her room!—waved at me, then closed the door. I stood staring at her bedroom door. And then fast as I could, I ran downstairs to the den.

D espite myself, I was mad at Daddy. I hadn't seen him all day, and I couldn't believe he'd slept through *everything*. It was strange for him to sleep during the day. That was Mama's thing. I pretended I was mad at him for missing my birthday, but it was really for being too fat to wear blue jeans and a plaid shirt, for having headaches that kept him from driving the highways from North to South and back. I wished that I could join Kimmie upstairs in her room and spend the night with her. But I felt too guilty just thinking about it, and so I reluctantly entered the den.

He was sitting upright, one arm lying nonchalantly across the back of the sofa. On the radio, Bill Withers sang for somebody to lean on. Daddy wore one of Mama's old nylon stockings stretched across his forehead, tied tightly as he often did to fight back the migraine. He looked like a has-been pirate. I regretted that I hadn't brought a cool washcloth with me.

"You have fun out there, Brown Eyes?"

"Uh huh."

"Nice being with your sister again, I bet."

I nodded. "She gave me this outfit for my birthday." I paused. "Thanks for the bike, Daddy."

He smiled. "You like it?"

"I love it! Kimmie and I went riding on it and . . ."

59

"I got you something else, too." He pointed his head in the direction of the little end table, where a cake sat waiting for me. Not just any cake, but a bustlike replica of my own face, with black icing for my hair and brown icing for my skin.

"Wowww!" I said, dazzled by the odd beauty of the cake, its strong resemblance to me. Beside it sat a small carton of ice cream that had begun to melt.

"You'll never guess the name of that ice cream," said Daddy. "Rae's Sunshine Swirl." He winked at me. "How 'bout that? Rae's Sunshine Swirl."

Daddy cut a piece of cake, slicing right through a section of the face and hair to the chocolate beneath, then scooped out a hunk of the ice cream; he served it to me on a little party plate, then set me on his lap; I dipped my finger into the brown and black icing and licked it away. Nothing had ever been so yummy.

"Me and your mama are getting a divorce," said Daddy, just as I'd put a tiny piece of cake into my mouth. "You know what that word means, *divorce?*'"

I struggled to swallow and shook my head no. I'd never heard that one in Miss Wheeler's third-grade class. It sounded sharp and dangerous.

"It means your mama and me won't be married anymore," he said. "And I'll be gettin' up out of here."

This news made me cry. I wanted to ask if the divorce was because of Kimmie's arrival, but I didn't. He said nothing more, just rocked me in his arms as I thought about my new, banana-seated bicycle and wondered, would I get to take it with me when Daddy and I left? In silence, Daddy scooped the melting ice cream and fed me, the taste of salt from my tears mixing with the caramel sweetness of Rae's Sunshine Swirl.

In the early days of Kimmie's return, a shot of normalcy injected itself into our familial vein: Kimmie, Mama, and me together in the breakfast nook each morning, eating toast and scrambled eggs served on yellow floral-patterned china rescued from the attic. We clinked our silverware against our plates and asked each other to pass the butter and the jelly and moved through the motions of a small family used to this daily ritual, rather than what we were: a mother with two daughters who'd been kept apart for years. I'd asked Daddy to join us, thinking maybe his presence at the table would change his mind about the divorce. I didn't want to leave, certainly not now when I only had Kimmie for the summer. Detroit summers never lasted as long as its winters.

"I ain't never been much for eating first thing in the morning. You know that, Brown Eyes," Daddy offered as an excuse. "All I need is a piece of bread to put a little something on my stomach before I take my Stanback."

One evening Kimmie walked in on us as Daddy and I were watching *The Flip Wilson Show*. It was the best part of the show—when the comedian swished across the room in a psychedelic pink and purple dress and high heels, saying, "What you see is what you get, sucker!"

Daddy and I loved when he played Geraldine, and Kimmie caught us both in mid-laughter.

"Hey, Daddy Joe," she said.

"Hey there, young lady." Daddy wiped a tear from his eye with a knuckle. "Look at you, all grown up."

She came closer, leaned over, politely kissed him on the cheek.

"Glad to be back?" asked Daddy.

"Yeah, I am." Kimmie paused. "I hope you don't mind."

"Why would I mind?"

She laughed nervously. "I know I caused you some grief back in the day."

He shook his head. "Nah. Grief was already up in this house. You just caused us to deal with it."

Kimmie nodded. "Well," she said, looking around the den, "things are different, aren't they?"

"You been gone a long time."

"But I remember it all like it was yesterday."

"Oh yeah?"

"Yeah. I remember you always dashing out of the house with that hat you wore everywhere, jumping into your cool blue Mustang, zooming down the street. You always had somewhere to go."

Daddy chuckled. "That car was more trouble than it was worth. Couldn't drive it to work. If I'd a pulled up to the gates of GM's plant in a Ford, they woulda directed me to the nearest unemployment office." He shook his head, tickled by his own gall.

Kimmie shifted her weight, looked at him. "It's good to see you, Daddy Joe."

He winked at her. "You too, Kimmie. You too."

"You had a Mustang?" I asked as she backed out of the room.

"In another life," said Daddy, whose attention had already returned to the tail end of Flip Wilson's Geraldine skit.

For the next few weeks, Kimmie and Daddy formed a comfortable reacquaintance. Sometimes she would run into him in the kitchen, and they'd banter easily with each other, talking about old times. She remembered all sorts of fun things about him unbeknownst to me—that he could sing and dance and tell dirty jokes. I couldn't get used to this phenomenon, the realization that Kimmie knew Daddy before I did, that *he* was her father before she went to live with her real one. I envied their history.

Mama started cooking dinner, venturing into the kitchen every evening with Kimmie's help. Together they fried things—eggplant, catfish, green tomatoes, cornbread. Kimmie showed Mama how to make various types of batter with egg or cornmeal or breadcrumb or some combination of the three. As it turned out, Cyril was a good cook, and Kimmie had learned this one culinary trick from him.

And so there they were, Kimmie and Mama, leaning into each other's ear, laughing at jokes that all began with "Remember when . . ." Other times, they were together in the living room, Mama between Kimmie's legs as Kimmie bent over her, scratching the dandruff from her scalp. I'd get close enough to see the dirty white flakes land on Kimmie's golden arm, the sight making my mouth water as I longed for dandruff of my own.

"Shhh," Mama said once as she saw me peeking around the den corner. "Little pitchers have big ears." They stopped talking until I left the living room, treating me like a spy. In truth, Mama was afraid I'd tell her business to Daddy, ruin her plan. That was when I began to understand the equation: Kimmie was for Mama, Daddy for me. No intersection. And so I accepted the pairing off and waited for those occasions when Mama and Daddy were distracted and Kimmie and I could sneak away and be together.

Meanwhile, Mama put her heart into the kitchen—practicing for the soon-to-be single Cyril?—the way a new wife aims to prove herself

63

worthy of the role. Never mind the rest of the house. She didn't plant flowers or dust tables. She simply cooked. And she was rusty—burned the chicken sometimes, put too much Lawry's seasoning salt on everything, left her cigarette burning on the Formica counter until it fell and singed the linoleum.

As my mother and sister forged a new dynamic, my life with Daddy didn't change. He stayed in the den. I still rubbed his forehead with a cool compress every night; he still let me have the last swig of Pepsi after he took his medicine. I still slept on his back.

Whatever Mama had prepared each evening, Daddy and I ate together on snack trays in the den while Kimmie and Mama had their dinner at the breakfast nook. I could hear them talking and laughing, the little black-and-white television on the kitchen counter blaring Archie Bunker's bark or Tom Jones's croon or Mary Tyler Moore's whine, TV voices mixing in with theirs.

"Come eat with us," Mama said once, shocking me as I headed toward the den. I stood there, balancing the plates in both hands. "It's not going to kill him if you eat with us for a change, Rae," she urged. And so, hungry for inclusion, I did.

"Not interested in eating dinner with your boring old daddy no more, huh?" he said later, smiling as the hurt poured from his eyes. "Guess you girls got things to talk about."

The next day when Mama beckoned, I shook my head no. She sighed, dismissed me with a flip of her hand. "Go on, then. Be with your daddy, if that's who you prefer."

When I entered the den, Daddy was eating potted meat and mayonnaise slapped on white bread, washing it down with ice-cold pop. "Can you make me one of those?" I asked, pointing to his sandwich.

"*You* need to go on in there, eat what your mama cooked," he said. "Growing girl needs vegetables."

"What vegetables?" I asked. "Everything has cornmeal sticking to

64

it." Daddy laughed until the extra flesh on his belly jiggled, and I breathed easier, knowing we were okay again.

There were other rejections by me over the years, none of them conscious. Slights more than anything else. Times when he wanted me with him and in my teenage fecklessness I chose instead parties or trips to the new mall or Derek's backseat. Choices that haunt.

65

I walked quickly to Daddy's hospital room, my senses assaulted by the smell of alcohol, the sight of those polished white floors, and the silent footsteps of nurses and orderlies striding in rubber soles down the long, narrow hallways. Entering the room, I was startled by what I saw: Daddy propped up against the pillows, covered by a feeble white sheet. The tubes and IVs didn't disturb me. It was seeing him in a bed flat on his back. Daddy always slept on his stomach, a sight that had comforted me. His prostrate position made me think of that floating, meaningless euphemism "laid to rest."

He popped open his eyes. He took a few seconds to focus, and once he recognized me, held out his hand. I moved to grab it, leaned in, kissed his lips. They were dry, chapped.

"I'm worried about you," I whispered, reaching in my bag for my lip balm.

"It's not as bad as it looks," he said as I dug my finger into the Chap-Stick, dabbed it across his parched mouth.

"How's your head?"

"Hurtin'."

Instinctively I rose, entered the bathroom and wet a washcloth with cool water, returned to his bedside, placed it across his forehead.

"You're going to be all right," I said.

"No, I'm not."

I took a deep breath, and it hurt, as though a tiny straight pin was lodged in my chest. "They give you anything for the pain yet?"

"Suppose to, but they haven't."

"I'll get the nurse," I said, ready to bolt out the door, do something concrete.

"Nah, just sit here with me a spell. You know how this place is— they liable to make me wait all night."

"But if I say something to them—"

"On your way out you can do that, okay?"

I nodded and pressed the washcloth into his forehead. Excess water escaped, creating rivulets down Daddy's cheeks. "What else can I do for you?" I asked.

He looked up at me, his face mocking deep thought. "Oh, I don't know. Hold my big toe?"

A lump gathered rakishly in my throat, and I gulped it down before trying to speak. "You know I will if you want me to."

He'd done that for me once. It was the night after Mama announced that it was time for me to sleep on my own, the night before Kimmie returned. I couldn't fall asleep. I rolled off Daddy's back, cuddled against him on the sofa, and shook him awake. "Daddy? Daddy?"

"Yeah, Brown Eyes?" He was groggy.

I swung my leg over his torso. "Would you hold my big toe?"

He grabbed it, half sleep, and held on.

After a few seconds I asked, "Daddy?"

"Uh huh?"

"Could you make sure it doesn't touch the bed?"

And so he held it up. Moments went by. His arm finally got tired. "Well, I will be damned!" he said.

"What?"

"You something else, you know that? Got me holding your big toe. And like a fool, I'm doing it!"

I could tell he wasn't angry, could hear in fact the pride in his voice.   67

I felt empowered by his rough hand around my foot. Feeling anchored, I drifted off to sleep.

Now he smiled. "I know you would hold my toe, Brown Eyes. I'm just teasing."

I held on to his hand instead.

O n one of the final days, Wendy, the morning-shift nurse with the tired, kind face, pushed her stethoscope into Daddy's chest and said, "Heartbeat's getting fainter. We're real close." Harboring no illusions about miracles, I didn't pray, knowing the unthinkable could happen because it already had in my life. Helpless, I sat there and watched Daddy slip away, remembering a childhood day. I am playing alone in the yard while Daddy watches me from the back door threshold. I decide it would be fun to dig to China using my little sandbox shovel, and choose a spot under the apple tree. "Stop that!" he yells. "Don't you never dig in that spot. I mean never!" He didn't say it was the very spot where my brother was buried. It wasn't until now, as he lay dying, that I figured it out. What was that like, to know what lay in your backyard, beneath the topsoil, mingling with roots and worms and eternity? Children, it seemed to me, were a source of continuous, ongoing pain, a pain worse than a migraine—the kind that offered no warning, no Stanback relief, no way out.

After Daddy first told me about his lost son, I didn't think about my brother for years. Not until I was in high school researching a persuasive argument for speech class on "The Health Risks of Childbirth Versus Abortion." In my research, I read that all miscarriages are *spontaneous abortions*. When little Joseph fell from Mama's womb into the toilet, it was because her body made a rash decision to expel him. This insight later made me grateful for the chance to control my own destiny, to decide with my mind what my body would do. I was relieved that everything had been arranged: rest at the clinic in the back room on a

68

cot for a few hours after the procedure, and in the evening hit the road, drive west through the whistling night wind, guided by bright headlights and sound judgment. I wasn't nervous about going through the abortion alone, having done it before.

I knew the routine.

A couple weeks after Kimmie's return, Mama decided to throw a Welcome Home/Fourth of July party for her. I had secretly hoped Kimmie and I could go see the fireworks at Edgewater Park. Instead, there was this party.

"But I don't have any friends in Detroit to invite," Kimmie said.

"I do," said Mama. "It'll be fun."

It was a major undertaking for our mother. She made several lists as she sat at the kitchen table, smoking her Kools and sipping instant coffee: the guest list, the grocery list, the liquor list, the menu, the what-to-wear list.

One evening when Mama and Kimmie were bent over those lists, Daddy said, "Get your sweater, Brown Eyes. We're going for a little ride."

It had been a long time since last we pulled up to the pretty blue house with the white door.

"JD?" Her voice asked the question, but her face showed no doubt.

"The one and only," he said.

Her fingers flew to her chest. "I wish I'd known you were coming."

Daddy shrugged. "Didn't set no plan to it. Got the urge, that's all." He put his arm around me. "I wanted you to see how my little girl has grown."

She looked at him with nervous eyes. "Well, come on in," she said. "And excuse the house."

We followed her as Daddy kept his arm around my shoulder. "Have a seat while I get you something to drink." She gestured to the living room. "Lemonade sound good?"

We moved toward the rose-patterned sofa, but Daddy stopped abruptly.

"Whose are those?" he asked, pointing to a pair of man's work boots sitting by the closet in the doorway.

She looked at the shoes and then looked at Daddy as she held on to the lemonade, sweat from the glasses dripping onto her hands. When he'd left that July day five years before to return home to me, she hadn't ended their affair right away. But in time she did. Told him she couldn't live like that anymore. And then she had lapsed, as women in love do. All those nights when Daddy claimed to be playing poker, he was here. She broke it off again, and they hadn't seen each other in two summers. We sat in silence as I sipped my cold drink. Finally, she turned to me.

"Would you like to meet my little girl?" she asked. "She's in her room playing." I set my glass down on the coffee table, looked over at Daddy. He nodded, and I followed her back to where a girl a year or so older than I was sitting on her bed.

"Josie," she said. "This is Rae. She's gonna play with you for a while, okay?"

"Okay," she said, her face a cool mask of detachment. She was playing with three Barbie dolls, each dressed for the wrong weather in winter coat, leggings, and hat. A radio sat on her dresser, playing a song I'd never heard before. The singer sounded white. I perched on the edge of the bed.

"Leave the door open," she said as her mother went to close it.

"You wanna play?" she asked once we were alone.

I shrugged. I had a couple of baby dolls at home, didn't know exactly how to play with these hard-bodied adult ones.

My uncertainty must have annoyed her. With her arm she swept all   71

the Barbies off the bed. They tumbled one at a time, landing in contorted angles on the carpet. We both stared at their tossed bodies. I was
nervous. Suddenly, she began to sing along to the radio. She knew all
the words. *And the sailor said, Brandy, you're a fine girl, what a gooood
wife you would be, but my life, my love, and my lady is the sea.* I watched
her carefully, noting for the first time in my life that a song could tell a
real story, and through her lips I became engrossed in the tale of this
sad girl Brandy who when the bars close down walks through a silent
town *and loves a man who's not around.*

"I got an idea," she said, song over. She reached into a dresser
drawer, pulled out a string, and began making string designs with both
hands. She showed me how to do the Cup-and-Saucer, Cat's Cradle,
Jacob's Ladder, and finally Crow's Feet. She was fast and smooth. It
took a while for me to catch on, and in that time we eavesdropped on
the adults' conversation, hearing snatches of it, so small was their
house.

"All those years . . ."

". . . A man's gotta do things a certain way . . ."

"And I waited . . ."

". . . Just shouldn't have gone off and done that."

"She needed . . . we needed somebody."

". . . 'Cause I'm ready now . . ."

". . . I can't . . ."

Silence was followed by muffled sobs and then more silence.

"Stick your hand in here," said Josie, who'd formed an intricate diamond pattern with the string. I pushed my fist through the center. She
brought her hands together, then pulled, magically freeing my fist. "I
know who you are," she said.

"What?" I asked, certain only that I had missed something. She
didn't answer, and in the next moment, her mother stuck her head into
the room. "Your father is ready to leave now, Rae."

"Wait! Take our picture, Mommy!" said Josie, running to get a
Polaroid Instamatic camera out of her closet.

"Pumpkin, I don't know if this is the—"

"Why'd you buy it for me if you never let me use it?"

"Okay, okay," said her mother, cutting off the tantrum at its onset. She took the camera. "You two stand together."

We put our arms around each other, and she snapped. Waiting for the picture to develop was like waiting for a cake to rise while peeking through the little window of my Easy Bake Oven. I wanted to hold on to that feeling of expectation. As Josie gently peeled back the black paper, like a thin scab off an old wound, and unveiled the picture of us, she insisted upon keeping it. I was happy to ask her mother to take another one for me. Fanning my wet Polaroid, I joined Daddy at the front door.

"Why, that's a real nice picture," he said, studying it for a few moments.

"It's for you," I said, handing it to him. He blew on it before slipping it into his back pocket. "Well," he said to Josie's mother. "Well."

"Bye, JD," she said. "You take care." Then she looked at me. "Can I have a hug?"

I nodded, and she took me into her arms and squeezed. My face fell into her big chest and sunk into its cuddly warmth. I loved it when Daddy hugged me, but his chest was different, stronger and unmoving. Mama's was small, her grasp always urgent and tight. Josie's mom's was as soft as new pillows. A faint sweet smell like that of apple-flavored Now&Laters—or was it penny wine candy?—drifted down to me, and I wasn't ready for her to let go when she did.

Josie appeared from her room, walked over, and whispered something to Daddy before she leaned into his open arms. He hugged her with his eyes squeezed shut. Then he kissed her on the forehead.

"Bye Bye, sweet girl," he said as he stared into her mother's eyes.

And then we were gone, back in Oldie, back up Woodward Avenue, back toward the den.

Daddy said nothing the whole ride home, not even bothering to punch on the eight-track player. Just pushed his thumb against the

73

space between his eyes. I don't know how much of his plight I understood. He'd done what Mama had asked, left Josie's mom to come back home to raise me, and now that Mama was freeing him, it was too late for them. People move on. That much I understood.

"Your head hurt?" I asked.

He nodded.

"We'll be home soon," I said. "And I'll take real good care of you."

K immie, Mama, and I went grocery shopping the morning of the party, catching the Hamilton bus on the corner. It was the first time I'd seen my mother in a supermarket, and she strolled each aisle with a hunger born of too many years spent buying things sight unseen over the phone. She filled three carts—grabbing foods that made you hum theme songs, foods that came out of cans and cartons and plastic bags like Birds Eye black-eyed peas and Shake 'n Bake chicken and French-style string beans. (*Ho, Ho, Ho, Greeeeen Giant!!*) She made up for lost opportunity as she ravaged the household cleanser isle, devoting one entire cart to paper items. "Papa and I always get that brand," Kimmie said offhandedly as Mama stood transfixed before the variety of toilet paper. "It's squeezably soft." She tossed Kimmie's recommendation into a cart, then moved on, stunned by the choices of two-ply paper towels. We went next to the liquor store, where Mama pointed to gleaming bottles of bourbon and rum and Scotch whiskey that stood on shelves behind the cash register. By the time we got home, it was all being delivered to our back door.

Miss Queenie came over to clean, or "give us a day," as Mama called it. She dipped snuff, ate lunch in the basement next to the dirty laundry, and cleaned the whole house to a sparkling Mr. Clean and Murphy Oil Soap shine. Before she left, Miss Queenie brutally combed my hair—I cried through the whole process—and put it in two ponytails with rubber bands so tight they gave me bloodshot, Chinese eyes. Mama set up a card table gotten from the garage and placed a brand-new pack of red ACE playing cards in the center of it. I helped Kimmie create a little makeshift bar with the TV stand and a snack tray, complete with lemon juice, Coca-Cola, little stirrers, and coasters advertising Cedar Point, the very same place where I would eventually go for sex and roller coaster rides with Derek, witness him violate his car.

"You need an ice bucket," Kimmie told Mama. "Silver or maybe even a wooden one."

"I do, don't I?" Mama looked crestfallen. "Should we run out and get one?"

"No, that's okay." Kimmie patted Mama's shoulders. "We can use a plastic bowl today. But you should get one at some point."

Mama pressed her lips. "There are a lot of things I need. And I've been doing without them for a long time." She said it as though it had just occurred to her. And I suppose it had. Daddy, despite his chronic pain, was the one who'd always gone to Kresge's and bought new dish towels and cereal bowls. Daddy was the one who had Elgernon from down the street clean the windows in the spring. And Daddy was the one who made sure there was plenty of soap and toilet paper in the bathrooms. But Mama was like a newly awake coma patient, acutely aware of what she'd missed in her life and wanting to catch up with Godspeed.

I begged Daddy to come to the party. Why not? I whined. Why not?

"I don't have the head for that right now," he said. While we prepared, he stayed out with Mr. Alfred doing whatever middle-aged, been-there-done-that black men did back then on a Saturday afternoon. Usually, on first-of-the-month Saturdays I went with him to the check-cashing place, to the doctor's office, to the corner drugstore, to Mr. Alfred's body shop. But this first-of-the-month Saturday was different. As I watched Daddy leave, I felt a pang of fear that Josie's mom would take him back—and I secretly crossed my fingers by way of protection.

76

Mama was nervous as she dressed for the party. This was her coming out, after all those years of existing in this house but not really living in it, certainly not entertaining in it. Kimmie and I helped her apply her makeup, testing lipstick and eye shadow shades on the back of our hands. I brushed her Naomi Sims wig, and Kimmie helped Mama slip it over her thin, cotton-soft hair. When Kimmie noticed the striped knit pantsuit Mama had laid out to wear, she protested.

"People aren't wearing things like that now that the sixties are over," she said before going to her room and returning with a suede fringed vest and crepe palazzo pants. "This is brand-new," she said. "Papa bought it for me." I was surprised to see my mother and sister wore the same pant size. Then Kimmie gave Mama a pair of elaborately designed silver and turquoise hoop earrings. "I got these in New Mexico," she said. "They go just right with the vest."

"Do you have anything for me?" I asked Kimmie, wanting to be part of their little clique.

"Let me see." Kimmie rummaged through her stuffed jewelry box, not finding the right thing. Finally, she unclasped the silver charm bracelet she was wearing, little elephants and giraffes and tigers hanging from it. "Here, put this on," she said. "Don't lose it. Pueblo Indians made it."

"I could use a little something for my nerves right now," said Mama, who'd been trying all that time to slip a huge hoop through her pierced ear. Little pearls of sweat had formed at her temple.

"I have a good idea," said Kimmie, disappearing from the room.

I helped Mama get the earring in, sitting beside her on the bed. She hugged me, and I slipped my arm around her waist. "Having fun?" she asked. I nodded. I was enjoying myself. "Good. We're going to do more things like this too," she said. "You'll see."

Kimmie returned with a pre-party drink of dark liquid amid lemon, 77 a red maraschino cherry on top. Mama slipped her arm from around me, reached for the glass, took a gulp.

"How is it?" asked Kimmie.

"Perfect," said Mama.

"Papa taught me how to make those. The secret is egg whites."

"When did he start drinking these?" Mama looked at the glass in her hand. "Gin and Rose's lime juice used to be his drink."

"Marva got him into whiskey sours a while back," said Kimmie.

Mama sipped. Moments passed. "You two do a lot together?" she asked.

Kimmie shrugged. "The typical things. We'd go downtown to shop. Or out to dinner. Sometimes she'd drive me to parties. Nothing major."

Mama nodded, and we all sat in silence as she drained her glass. We heard Daddy's key open the door, listened as his heavy footsteps crossed the living room, as the doors to the den whined themselves close. I uncrossed my fingers. Mama stood up, moved to the vanity, and sat before the mirror. The dresser was covered with jars and tubes with women's names on them: Estée Lauder, Helena Rubenstein, Flori Roberts, Marcella Borghese.

"How do I look?" she asked us, her false eyelashes spread wide, exotic as little Oriental fans.

"Like a famous person," I said. Mama smiled at me.

"A lot prettier than Marva with her gobs of makeup," said Kimmie. "That's for sure."

Mama's eyes caught Kimmie's in the mirror. "I'm not worried about her," she said to Kimmie's reflection. "Because no matter what, I'm your mother. She's not."

The doorbell chimed, and Mama stood, smoothed out her pants, slipped her arm through Kimmie's, and together they walked to the front door. I followed, the charms on my new bracelet jingling together like those forgotten, beat-up wind chimes hanging above the back porch.

The party guests consisted of exactly four people. There was Romey, who had thick eyeglasses and an older, white-haired boyfriend named Ernesto; and Lyla, who wore go-go boots, a wet-look miniskirt, a blond wig, heavy white eye shadow, and a younger face than the others. Then there was Johnnie Mae. I thought she might be Little Stevie's mom, but I couldn't be sure. She didn't look at all how I thought the mother of a famous singer would look. She had a deep voice along with a big chest and wore lots of diamond rings on her puffy fingers.

Up-tempo jazz played as Mama held a Kool's and a fresh whiskey sour in the same hand, her smooth skin crinkling a bit at the corners of her eyes from the smoke. She and her guests sat around the card table—except for Ernesto, who sat alone on the sofa, his legs crossed, a big drink in his delicate hand. Kimmie played hostess, refilling glasses, passing around a tray of pigs-in-a-blanket. I sat on the landing of the stairway, just close enough to hear and see everything. I was wearing my purple hot pants, content to be around grown-up conversation, be near Kimmie, and witness my hip mother having fun, an entire staircase away from her throne, nerves behaving.

"Honey, you look good," said Johnnie Mae. "Don't Vy look good?"

"She sure do," said Lyla. "You just glowing, girl!"

Mama smiled faintly. "I feel better than I have in a while."

Romey shuffled the deck with thick hands, his style functional and without beauty. "She's got her girls back together again," he said. "A mother's coup." He started to deal. "Must be real nice for you, Kimmie. Being back home."

Kimmie nodded, balancing her drink tray with one hand. She looked perfect in a crocheted miniskirt and halter top. "It is nice, Mr. Johnson," she said, owning sophistication just in the way she set the drink at his elbow. "Thank you for asking."

"Well, being away from this Murder Capital sure didn't hurt your manners, now, did it?" Romey dealt methodically as the cards landed in front of each player. "I can barely get those rug rats I teach to call me Mr. Whatchamacallit, let alone by my actual name."

Kimmie nodded. "Everybody's polite in the South. Papa says it's a good thing I left Detroit when I did, or I'd have a lot of bad habits by now."

"Now tell me again, just why did you leave?" asked Romey. "I forget."

"My mother felt it was best," said Kimmie.

"The city was no place for a twelve-year-old girl," said Mama, quickly. "You all remember what it was like that summer. Nobody was safe."

"But it was okay for a four-year-old?"

Once Kimmie asked that question, the moment hung suspended, and even I knew that a line of some sort had been crossed, borrowed fringe vest or no. Kimmie's hands flew to her mouth.

Mama looked at her, eyes asking, *Why'd you have to spoil this for me? Why?*

Kimmie tried to clean it up. "I don't know why I said that. I mean, you know, I just . . . wish I could've stayed here with everybody, with my family." She sighed. "That's all I meant."

Mama didn't look at her, rather scooped up her cards and neatly folded them into her hands, her silence dripping over us. She fanned the cards out in front of her, inspecting them carefully, shifted a couple around, folded them all, then fanned them out again. "You got first bid, Johnnie Mae," she noted calmly.

"I pass," said Johnnie Mae, the words gushing out because she, like the rest of us, had been holding her breath. Kimmie grabbed Mama's glass, refilled it. Johnnie Mae chattered on. "Ain't nothing in this hand to speak of. You must've forgot my black ass when you dealt out the goodies, Romey."

"No, I didn't forget," said Romey. "I gave them all to myself and my partner. And do watch your mouth, Madame." He looked over at me on the staircase. I stared back at him through the banister.

Lyla seized the light moment to stick up for her friend. "Southern living has never hurt nobody," she said. "I know if I could, I'd go back down home myself."

"Why don't you?" said Romey, something naughty happening with his lips as he gathered the cards in front of him.

"Why you think? I make good money at Ford's. Just to stand around and put left doors on cars? Shoot, don't nobody wanna pay you what you worth in the South. No unions, no overtime pay. Slave labor."

"You could get yourself some education," said Romey. "That way you could at least oversee the slaves."

"Ha ha," said Lyla as she grabbed another drink off Kimmie's tray. "Very funny, Romey. Ha ha."

Johnnie Mae laughed. "Your highfalutin ass got enough education for all of us, Romey."

Mama studied her hand intently. "I'm going to say . . . a four special."

Romey nodded his approval. "Education is not that hard to come by, you know. At Wayne County Community College, you can get a degree in two years." He swished the ice in his glass with his finger, licked it. "In between shifts at the plant, of course."

"I hated school when it was free," said Lyla. "Guess what I think   81 about paying for it." She shook her head. "Shoot, I gotta say a five, Vy. You leave me no choice."

"What are you coming in?" asked Mama.

"Heck if I know."

"Well, you made that bid without consulting your partner, so don't look here for no damn help," said Johnnie Mae.

"Hey! No talking across the board," said Romey. "And not that anyone seems to care, but I pass also." He looked over his glasses at Lyla. "What will be trumps?"

"Hearts. Uptown."

"That figures," said Johnnie Mae, who gulped down the last of her bourbon, held it up for Kimmie. "Wet this again for me, will you, Honey Bun?"

"I'd like to go back to school one day, finish my degree," said Mama, shifting a few cards around in her hand. "I was very good in my English lit courses."

"Yeah, and a certain Creole member of the esteemed faculty at Marygrove apparently thought you were good too," said Romey. "Very good."

Mama glared at him. He winked at her as he flipped over several cards he'd set aside during his deal. "The gods have shown kindly on you," he said, sliding the pile over to Lyla.

"Ooh, now that's what I call a kitty!" said Lyla, who grabbed at the sea of red cards.

Johnnie Mae shook her head. "What they gotta get to set us? Three books? Shit, hope you got a whole lotta hearts in your hand, Lyla, cause I—"

"Johnnie Mae, you really have to stop all that yapping," said Romey. "The idea is for your opponents to *not* know what's in your hand. Get it?"

"Negro, please. I was playing bid whist before your fairy ass was swishing around town. And for all you know, I could be bluffing."

"Watch your mouth!" said Mama. This time, she was the one who cut her eyes over at me. I held *her* gaze, brazen behind my banister.

82   "No respect for minors," said Romey.

"It ain't minors I was talking to," said Johnnie Mae. "Far as I'm concerned, *minors* ought to be in the bed by now." I rolled my eyes. Kimmie handed Johnnie Mae a fresh drink. "And hell, what's wrong with calling a spade a spade?"

"See what a couple trips to Hollywood have done?" said Romey. "Made you *overt*. Discretion is the first sign of valor, Madame."

"Oh, hell, you and your big-ass words." Johnnie Mae studied her hand. "Nothing wrong with Hollywood. Prettiest place I done ever seen. Got palm trees on the freeway! And the sun shines every day. You hear me? Every day!"

"I don't want to be any place where it never snows," said Romey. "Shoveling snow builds character."

Johnnie Mae sucked her teeth. "Well, I don't like snow." She pushed a fist into her side, elbow jutting out. "And if Motown can move to California, I know I can damn well go there."

"You mean it's true?" said Mama. "Motown's leaving?"

"Damn near done left." Johnnie Mae shook her head. "Everybody knows that, Honey."

"I thought it was a rumor." Mama looked wounded. "But why?"

"Because they'll do anything to keep Stevie happy, and he made it clear he did not want to live here no more," said Johnnie Mae.

Mama nodded. "Well, I guess I do understand that. This is a place to leave."

"All due respect, Madame, but I heard a slightly different story," said Romey. "Berry Gordy himself, if rumor serves me correctly, had to hightail it out the back door because the mob pushed its way through the front one." He leaned back, satisfied. "That proves that fame and fortune corrupt."

"How would *you* know anything about fame and fortune?" asked Johnnie Mae.

Everyone laughed at this, even Ernesto-on-the-Couch, and Mama, whom I'd never seen laugh out loud before. Her teeth were small, white, glistening. Johnnie Mae was so tickled she clutched her chest.   83

"I won't dignify that low blow with a response because I like Little Stevie's music too much," said Romey. He looked over his glasses at Lyla. "It's on you, I believe."

"He ain't Little Stevie no more, Baby," said Lyla as she tossed out an ace of hearts. "He's a man now."

They played for hours, the music of jazz horns and pianos on the hi-fi accentuated by the staccato sound of cards slammed down on the table, like percussive exclamation points.

At one point, when Romey and Mama were apparently losing miserably, he turned toward Kimmie, who was rifling through records piled on the console, and leaned in her direction. "Bet you miss your dad already."

Mama looked at Romey, but he ignored her.

"It's okay. I'll be seeing him soon," said Kimmie.

"Is that right?" said Romey, peering over the top of his glasses at Kimmie.

"Yeah, we're going there just as soon as . . ."

"Rae!" said Mama, startling me off my spot on the stairway. "Be a good girl and go in the kitchen and put some more ice in that bowl, will you?"

I did, but first I stood quietly by the dining room entrance, where they couldn't see me, and eavesdropped—a little pitcher with big ears.

"Kimmie, it's better not to say anything in front of her. I told you how she is about her daddy."

"Sorry," I heard Kimmie say. "I forgot."

"And how is JD these days?" Romey again. "Have you got him locked up in the attic tonight?"

"He's in the den," said Mama.

"Well, aren't you going to ask him to come out and say hello to your guests? I like Daddy Joe."

"I'm warning you, Romey!" said Mama, her voice low, but not that low. "Keep your big mouth shut, you hear me?"

"You need to be watching the board," said Lyla. "Y'all don't have a single book yet."

I listened to the sound of ice tinkling against glass as I stood there, letting the plastic bowl grow colder in my hands. I looked down into the frozen cubes and saw the situation clearly. I told myself to start packing right away, so I'd be ready when Daddy decided it was time for *us* to go.

Just as I stepped back in the room with the ice, Johnnie Mae yelled, "Well, I'll be damned! Lyla Honey, we done run a Boston on these knuckleheads!"

"We? I'm the one had all the trumps!"

"Excuse me, but I do believe both my ace and king of clubs turned two of those books!"

Lyla giggled. "You right, Johnnie Mae, you right." She held her palm out. "Give me five! We whooped their butts!!"

Lyla and Johnnie Mae slapped each other's hand, and this ended the card playing. They pushed the table to the side; Romey took a seat on the sofa next to Ernesto, and the others sat in the dark green, high-back chairs. Except Mama. She lounged across the carpet like a teenage girl would do, legs crossed at her ankles, back against the wall, whiskey sour at her side. Kimmie handled the music.

"Don't you have anything here that's newer than 1967?" she asked Mama.

"Ain't nothing been made worth listening to since then," said Johnnie Mae. "'Cept for Stevie's music."

Kimmie sighed and settled on a few hit Motown tunes—by the Supremes, Four Tops, Miracles—piling the 45s on top of one another and holding them in place with the arm of the record player. When she finally succumbed and played "Signed, Sealed, Delivered I'm Yours," Johnnie Mae said, "Good choice!" as Mama jumped up to dance in the middle of the living room, drink in her hand.

"Ooh, Vy, I didn't know you could dance like that," squealed Lyla. "You do that camel walk, girl!"

She did it perfectly, moving across the floor like a swan cum robot. She snapped her fingers as she danced, and Romey called out, "Well, all right! Well, all *right*, now!" On cue, Kimmie jumped up and joined Mama, imitating her camel walk in a funny way that made her look like an ostrich. They danced together, snapping their fingers in unison.

Later, the night winding down, Romey eyed me on the landing of the stairway and beckoned me to come to him. I did. He grabbed my hand. His was hairy. "How old are you now?" I told him. "And how's school?" I mumbled an okay. "And so when do you plan to stop sleeping with your daddy?" He laughed, in a throaty kind of mean grown-up way. Kimmie laughed too, which hurt. I shrugged my shoulders. They all made me sick. "On my next birthday," I whispered.

"Negro, leave that chile alone," said Johnnie Mae, her rings bouncing light off her glass of liquor. "What she do in her own house is none of your never-mind."

"Ain't that the truth," said Lyla.

"I'm just asking. Nothing wrong with that," said Romey. He looked over at Mama. "Right?"

"You don't know how to keep your damn mouth shut, do you?" said Mama as she looked over at me. I looked down.

"Romey, you ought to quit," said Ernesto, soft-like, yet fatherly.

I wanted to get away from all of them, but I was trapped. My sister saved me.

"I'm going to bed now," said Kimmie. "It's been a long day."

"Okay." Mama stretched out her arms to her. "Come give me a big, big hug." She squeezed her hard, closing her eyes; then she opened them abruptly, releasing Kimmie. "Time for *you* to go to bed too," she said to me, for the first time in my life. "Come here."

Kimmie said good-bye to Mama's friends, climbed the stairs to her bedroom. I went to receive my mother's embrace, tight and brief as ever, then walked across the room and entered the den. I was certain I

86

heard Romey's loud snickers trailing behind me, and someone saying "Shhhh," but I ignored them. I drifted off to sleep thinking about the part of my mother I'd met tonight—the part that drank whiskey sours and did the camel walk and liked college English. I dreamed she and Kimmie left me behind, pushing the white Mach II to the curb, the engine silent. Later that night, I awakened to the feeling of eyes upon me. Crowded around the French doors, peeping in through the glass, were Romey, Mr. Ernesto, Lyla, Johnnie Mae, and Mama. Staring at me as Daddy's heavy breathing caused my little body to rise and fall, rise and fall.

I never got to see Daddy's back again after he walked through the hospital's emergency room doors, days before he died. I couldn't turn him over in his bed when I came to visit him; certainly couldn't after he took his last breath, life drained from his hefty frame. All I could do was remember, remember the comfort gotten from the smooth, enduring flesh beneath me when I was a little girl and slept peacefully each night in the small curve of that back, a shoulder blade my pillow.

When the doorbell chimes rang—*dinggg, donggg, dinggg*—the deep serious sound of them startled me.

"I'll get it," said Kimmie. "Don't smudge your nails!" she yelled over her shoulder as the chimes rang again. *Dinggg, donggg, dinggg.* She'd just given me a manicure with her new chalky yellow nail polish. I ran behind Kimmie, feeling the chimes' vibrations under my feet as I leaped from the bottom landing of the staircase, fingers spread out to dry.

"Heyyyy!!!!" said Kimmie to the girl standing there. "Come on in."

She had short, brick-red hair with black parts peeking through. Her eyes looked out from heavy eyeliner and frosty blue eye shadow. She wore a hot pink tube top with tie-dyed jeans and white clogs. I'd never seen clogs, and I instantly loved them. She was holding a bottle of Faygo grape pop.

"God, you look the same!!!!" said Kimmie.

"You the one, girl! You the one!!! Still got that long pretty hair!"

"*Your* hair is too sharp. I love the color!!"

"You do? I'm always experimenting with it, drives my mom crazy."

"This is Rhonda," said Kimmie. She threw an arm toward me. "And you remember my little sister, Rae Rae."

She put her hand to her mouth, then let it drop. "Wow, that's Rae

Rae?" She smiled. "You don't remember me, but I remember you. You were a baby last time I saw you!"

"Really?" I never thought of myself as having been a baby—especially since there were no baby pictures of me anywhere.

"Yeah, for real! You were so small, and Kimmie used to pick you up, carry you everywhere, like you were her own little doll. I remember that."

Hearing that made me realize my life went back farther than I had imagined.

"Rhonda and I were best friends in elementary school," Kimmie explained. "Right up until I left."

"Sure were. Remember sixth-grade graduation?" said Rhonda.

"Do I? You wore this lemon yellow ensemble with a cool Nehru collar . . ."

"You had one on too, remember? I think yours was light blue."

"Yeah, yours was sharp, but mine was mail-order brocade," said Kimmie. "Looked like I stole somebody's draperies!" They both laughed. "God, we thought we were so grown up!"

"So much was going on . . . remember how crazy the ceremony was?"

"Oh, man, Matthew Conyers running across the stage!" screamed Kimmie. Both she and Rhonda balled their fists, raised their arms in the air, and yelled, "R-E-S-P-E-C-T! Find out what it means to me! R-E-S-P-E-C-T! Take care of TCB! Sock it to me, sock it to me, sock it to me!"

"Hey, you girls keep it down in there," said Daddy, his voice coming at us from behind the open den doors. "Or take it outside."

"Sorry!" Kimmie called out before beckoning to her friend. "Let's go out back," she whispered.

They headed toward the back door, and then Kimmie stopped, looked at me. "Come on, Rae Rae. You can join us."

"Just a minute," I said, ducking into the den. "Daddy, how's your head?" I asked, trying to sound casual.

He had turned on the TV and was watching an episode of *The Mod*   89

Squad with the sound low. He yawned, long and wide. "I'm fine. You go on, have yourself some fun with your sister."

"Are you sure?" Shadows hung under his eyes.

"What'd I say, Brown Eyes?" He shooed me with his hand. "Go on now."

I nodded with gratitude, pecked him on the forehead, never saw him flinch in pain as I ran and joined them on the back porch, catching Rhonda in mid-sentence.

". . . I mean that was just a wild summer."

"Tell me about it," said Kimmie.

"The riots and all . . ."

"Spook getting shot . . ."

"Candy Thompson gettting pregnant."

"Stinker OD'ing in his mother's basement."

"And you running away." Rhonda said it so matter-of-factly, yet the pause that followed was overbearing. What did my sister run away from? I wondered.

Kimmie shrugged. "Well, you made sure that didn't work out."

"You never did understand that I *had* to tell," said Rhonda.

"No, I didn't understand, because I was your best friend, and I asked you not to."

"I was scared for you. I mean, if something had happen—"

"I told you I'd call you when I got where I was going, so you didn't need to worry."

Rhonda shook her head. "Girl, please! We were like twelve years old! Your mother called the police. They were talking about sending out a search party and everything."

Kimmie shrugged. "You did what you felt you had to do. And I got to go live with my father anyway." She smirked. "All's well that ends well."

Rhonda took in Kimmie's words along with a swig of her Faygo pop. "So the man in that room in there is your . . . ?"

90

"Stepfather."

"Oh. I never knew that." She seemed embarrassed for not knowing. "When you left, I didn't know where you'd gone. I mean, you didn't say good-bye or anything. You didn't write."

"I was mad at you."

"You shoulda thanked me."

"Yeah? Thanks," said Kimmie. "Friend."

Rhonda wore her hurt like a heavy backpack as she stood. "I gotta go," she said quietly.

Kimmie reached for Rhonda's hand, pulled her back down onto the porch steps. "You want a cigarette?" She eased two Virginia Slims out of her breast pocket, offered them to Rhonda.

Both were solemn as Rhonda took one, leaned in as Kimmie produced matches. They each puffed, exhaled slowly in unison before Rhonda spoke.

"How come you never came back?"

"Because you get somewhere and that's your life. And before you know it, years go by."

"So why now?"

"Everybody thought it would be a good time for me to come. So here I am."

"Wow. Heavy."

Kimmie blew a series of smoke rings. "Actually, it was now or never. Next year I'm going to be too busy finishing high school and getting the hell out of Louisiana."

"You going to college?"

Kimmie nodded. "Definitely. I'm not sure where yet, but it'll be somewhere different. I'm thinking about Albuquerque."

"Where's that?" asked Rhonda.

"New Mexico."

"Don't you have to speak Spanish there?"

"No, silly rabbit. It's part of the United States. They speak English.

91

And there's a lot of Indians living on reservations. I visited there once when my papa took us all on a cross-country trip."

"In a car?" I asked.

"That's the only way to go," said Kimmie. "The desert is a little boring because it's endless, but it's a great trip. Rocky Mountains, Grand Canyon. I can't even begin to describe how beautiful it all is."

"I'm going to drive cross-country when I grow up," I said.

"Maybe you don't have to wait that long," offered Kimmie.

"Far as I'm going is Mercy College," said Rhonda. "Right on Livernois and Six Mile. Study nursing. At least that's my plan right now. My dad's a foreman at Chrysler, and he says they're hiring. Training ladies to be crane operators!"

"Don't do that," said Kimmie. "Go to college."

Rhonda shrugged. "I don't know; we'll see."

"Can I have a sip?" Kimmie held her hand out for some of Rhonda's pop, took a big swig, handed it back. Burped lightly. "My father is going through a little thing right now. He and my stepmother broke up after, I don't know, a hundred years, and he wasn't used to being like a single parent. He started getting, like, really strict. One day he tells me, 'I do not need no boy-crazy teenager to look after right now. I got too much to deal with.'" Kimmie took out another two cigarettes, lit them both, handed one to Rhonda. "Like all I do is think about boys."

"That's all I think about," said Rhonda. They looked at each other and broke into naughty laughter.

"Well, I'm not going to say I don't think about boys *most* of the time," offered Kimmie.

I used the moment to grab my Paddle Ball on the porch steps. I'd gotten so good I could hit the paddle with the rubber ball a hundred times without missing if I concentrated. I could do it either way—with the string long or short.

"Speaking of boys, guess who has gone and grown up and is looking all fine now and is having a party on Saturday?" said Rhonda.

Kimmie blew a smoke ring. I missed after fifteen short bats. "Who?"

"Toby Jenkins."

"Toby Jenkins? Wait, let me think. Not that little short guy with the stupid grin and the squeaky voice?"

"He ain't short no more, girl. He is about six feet tall, and he's a football player, and he's got this deep voice and this nice little mustache. The grin is sexy now."

"Nooooo!!! He was such a gump!!!"

"Well, wait till you see him. He's cool. You gotta come to his jam with me on Saturday night. It's a pool party! His mama moved downtown to one of those high-rise apartment complexes. Lafayette Towers. Got a rec room, an indoor pool, everything. They say it's outta sight!"

"Oh, shoot," said Kimmie. "I've got to get a new bikini then."

I stopped batting my ball. "Can I go shopping with you?"

"Sure, Rae Rae. We'll go downtown Saturday morning. Get on the bus early. Maybe get Boston Coolers at Sanders. Ooh, I haven't had Sanders's French vanilla ice cream in ages! And don't even try to get Vernor's ginger ale in Louisiana. Forget that." She nudged Rhonda. "You should come with us."

Rhonda shook her head no. "I'm working Saturday. Got a job at the Dairy Queen on Curtis. It's a drag, but it pays. And since I got a car now, I got to keep gas in it, you know?"

"Wow, you got a new car?!" I asked.

"It's not hardly new. It's my mama's old one. Sixty-nine Riviera. But it gets me around."

"Can you believe I don't even know how to drive?" said Kimmie.

"Oh, I'll teach you," promised Rhonda. "It's easy once you get the hang of it. Especially with my car. It's an automatic."

"That would be very cool." Kimmie paused. "If I could say I really accomplished *something* this summer."

They watched me for a while as I played with my Paddle Ball, long-string style. I stood with my legs spread apart, my free arm out to the side for balance, showing off. Then the string popped, and the tiny red ball flew over the fence into the neighbor's freshly cut yard, leaving me behind gripping the paddle so tight, I smudged every one of my brand-new, yellow-painted fingernails.

On his final night in the hospital, Daddy woke up and barked, "Go get her!" He looked right at me. In a clear, unslurred voice, he boomed: "Go get her. She's right outside, waiting for me. Right outside."

Stunned that he could talk at all, I tried to reassure him that no one was there, tried to calm him down. "Go, goddamn it!" he insisted.

"Okay, okay," I said, getting up and walking out the room, where I stood in the hallway. "He's talking!" I whispered to myself. "That's a good sign." I walked toward the pay phone with newfound, ludicrous hope, thinking I'd call Mr. Alfred and ask him to get in touch with her. As I passed the nurses' station and the closed doors of dying people, I made elaborate plans in my head that involved my role as a kind of Nurse Nightingale, with Daddy back home, returning to an optimum health he'd never had. But I got all the way to the pay phone and picked up the receiver before realizing I didn't have Mr. Alfred's telephone number with me.

When I reentered the room, Daddy said, "I gotta go. She's waiting for me." And then he looked out past me. "Oh, I can't walk," he said, shaking his head. "I can't walk, and she's waiting for me."

All night in the chair beside him, I watched his bedsheet quiver from his breathing as a riot of moonlight barged past the heavy curtains and shimmered atop his huge, still hands. Those same hands had once built a tree house for me; built because I'd asked for one, just as I'd asked for a pony and a trip to Disneyland. I never expected to get any of those requests, but there he was one day in the backyard, not far from the apple tree, with hammer and nails and two-by-fours and plywood and a saw. Mr. Alfred had given him an old tire to be transformed into a swing. The lawn was strewn with junkyard salvages, looking exactly like Mama had always fought against: cluttered and low-class and alive.

Because of his shaky health, Daddy never did finish the tree house. As winter approached, it remained on the back lawn, half done. A few steps had been hammered into the tree trunk and a three-sided frame erected. But it looked forlorn and abandoned, vulnerable to the elements. Over the years it got weather beaten and faded. When feeling low and lonely, I saw that unfinished tree house as the embodiment of our biggest problem as a small family—trying to remain whole in a house so nakedly incomplete.

For a while, when I was fourteen, I decided there was little that house on Birchcrest could do for me. I tried to stay out of it as much as possible, preferring the house of my friend Lisa LaBerrie, whose home looked majestic with its white columns and stone facade. Inside, the living room was always cool and ever inviting with its blue sectional couch, blue carpet, blue walls. I loved the piano in the corner and the wood-carved dining room sideboard, which showcased a genuine silver tea set. Pictures of Lisa and her sister on Communion Day sat atop the mantel. Sometimes, their fireplace roared. Lisa lived with both of her parents, and when I stayed over for dinner, we all sat around the table together, eating gumbo or étouffée dishes that revealed her mother's Louisiana roots. That added fact—that her parents were from the place with the multiple syllables and vowels—convinced me the LaBerries were the kind of family to have. A real one.

Lisa and I stayed in the streets. We were maturing alongside the city's own adolescence, watching it go from resentful and surly child of white forces to a wild and excited youth of black power. We added another running buddy—Angie Stoddard—and became a threesome. Lisa and I knew each other from our Girl Scout days. But Angie was something new, a fast girl who wore Quiana dresses over her developed body, had boys she was seeing ("Steven and I go together!"), and already knew the intricacies of French-kissing. She had stolen her sexy young mother's birth control pills out of the medicine cabinet and had already done "It," describing all the wondrous details to Lisa and me. It sounded frightening and dangerous and worth trying.

But Angie apparently did something wrong in taking her mom's pills because she became pregnant and was sent down South to have the baby. When we saw her again at the beginning of eleventh grade, she was a changed woman. Withdrawn and repentant. Born again. Childbirth, she said, was horrible, sparing us nothing as she relayed the details of gushing blood and excruciating pain and a ripped pussy. Lisa and I sat riveted by her tale, the way we once sat listening to ghost stories before a campfire during our Girl Scouting days. Terrified and thrilled.

Angie concluded that she wanted no part of sex again. Wanted to ignore everything "down there" from here on out. Lisa and I decided that we absolutely did not want to have babies and promised each other that we never ever would. To seal our pact, we hooked our forefingers together and whispered in unison, "Girl Scout's honor! Girl Scout's honor!"

Even now, before taking off, I was determined to be true to my oath.

Accelerating

Michigan's Basic Speed Law means you must
drive at a "careful and prudent" speed, considering
all driving conditions. . . . Anticipate trouble ahead.
Be ready to stop.

WHAT EVERY DRIVER MUST KNOW

On that Saturday morning of the pool party, Daddy got up early and took his Stanback for the last time, bathed, shaved. I sat on the toilet lid in the pink powder room and watched as he completed his out-in-the-world ritual. First, he wet his fingers under the faucet and ran them through his hair till it was wet, next raking through it with his skinny, fine-toothed comb. The back part near his neck was the kinkiest, from where he'd slept on it. He dipped his comb in Vaseline and ran that through his hair, over and over. Dip, comb, dip, comb. Soon his hair turned soft and wavy. Good-looking.

"Where are you going, Daddy?" I asked.

"To Dr. Corey's."

"But it's not the first of the month."

"Couldn't wait. You wanna come?"

I really wanted to go downtown with Kimmie, help her shop for a new bikini to wear to the pool party. I wanted to get Boston Coolers with her at Sanders Bakery. Yet I looked up at Daddy's strained face and nodded.

"Okay. Go get dressed. And hurry up, Rae Rae. I don't wanna be in that doctor's office all day, not in this heat."

I took the stairs two at a time to my room. At first, I forgot why I was there. This often happened. I stood in the middle of the floor, a bit startled, not really knowing much about my bedroom because I never spent any nights in it. Or much time during the day. I knew nothing about how cones of light bounced dust particles across the room on sunny days or how the trees outside my window scratched against the leaded pane at night. And I had no idea where the sweet spot of my bed's mattress lay. All my possessions were there, true—my books, my clothes, my toys—but it was like secretly investigating a mysterious twin sister's room, perhaps the wild-haired girl who fantasized about kissing Terrance Golightly. I always had the feeling of spying, rummaging through someone else's things. It didn't matter that that someone was I.

Dressed in culottes and a tube top, I joined Daddy in the front vestibule. The air was humid, July day already hot. Daddy drove carefully as always to Dr. Corey's office. The car's air conditioner hummed as we flowed smoothly in the traffic along Livernois Avenue, Daddy having adjusted his speed so that we hit all the green lights. "You been having a good time with Kimmie," announced Daddy. "That's good to see."

These were separate relationships I had with Kimmie and Daddy, and it made me a little possessive whenever one mentioned the other. I didn't want to share either of them. I was silent.

Daddy flipped down the visor against the mid-morning sun. "I think you're gonna be happy being with her and your mama, don't you?"

"What?"

"When I leave, it'll be okay 'cause you'll have your big sister."

I gripped the dashboard. When he'd sat me on his lap and told me about the divorce, this wasn't why I'd shed tears into my ice cream. "But I thought I was coming to live with you." Would I have to run away like Kimmie to be with my father too?

"You can come over and spend the night with me whenever you want, Brown Eyes. Whenever."

"But you said I could come live with you!" I whined. "You said so!"

"I don't rightly remember saying that."

I tried another tack. "Well, Mama and Kimmie are leaving anyway, and they don't want me to come with them."

"They're leaving? When?"

"End of the summer."

"You sure about that?"

I nodded. Daddy slowed to a crawl, getting caught at a red light. The giant pair of foam dice hanging from the rearview mirror bounced around with vigor. "You know, I can't give you all the things your mama can," he said. "She's in a better position to do for you. You understand what I'm saying?"

"You don't want me with you?"

"It's not that. You know it's not that."

I flopped back against the seat, arms folded. "I already started packing."

Daddy turned to me. "You did?"

"Yes." I had thrown some clothes, my rock collection, and a few Trixie Belden Mystery books into my purple suitcase, shoved it under my unused bed.

"Well, I'll be damned," said Daddy as he hit the accelerator and sped off, dice dancing a jig. "You something else, Brown Eyes. You know that? You something else."

I smiled, pleased that I'd won, barely aware of what I'd given up.

Inside the doctor's office, nearly every seat in the waiting room was taken.

"Hey there, Mr. Dodson," said Ilene. "How you feeling today?

"I been better, that's for sure."

She nodded. "We're gonna get you right in, I promise." She turned to me. "And you doing all right, Rae?"

"Yes, thank you."

"Growing like a weed with your cute self." She smiled, her bulbous

103

lips spreading across her wide freckled face, divulging dimples. "Have a seat, and I'll tell Dr. Corey you're here."

I sat on his lap. He smelled Daddy-fresh—that mixture of Old Spice aftershave, Vaseline, and Jergen's lotion. I rested my head in the crook of his neck, closed my eyes. Soon Ilene poked her head out a back door and beckoned to us.

Daddy sat on the examining table, and within seconds Dr. Corey entered, holding Daddy's chart against his chest.

"Morning," he said. He washed his hands as he talked, still youthful, not yet gray at the temples, unbelievably handsome. "See you got your little girl with you today."

"Gotta do something about these headaches," said Daddy as he rolled up a sleeve. "Nothing's working. Stanbacks might as well be orange-flavored children's aspirin." It suddenly hit me that Daddy had been splayed across his sofa bed a lot more lately. Why hadn't I noticed?

Dr. Corey wheeled over the spiggy. He tied a wide black cuff around Daddy's arm, pumped the rubber ball, and watched the numbers rise. "Two twenty over one ten . . . no, it's higher than that." He frowned. "You may want Rae to wait outside."

"It's okay. She knows about my condition."

Dr. Corey shook his head. "Pressure's real high, JD."

"Hell, my pressure's always high."

"I know that, but this is higher than usual. Even for you." He took the band off, wheeled the spiggy out of the way. He looked down at Daddy. "You been taking it easy?"

"That's all I can do, Vernon."

"Have you been under undue stress?"

"What stress is ever due?

"Help me out here, JD. What's going on at home?"

"Nothing 'cept I'm starting to look for me a place."

"Well now, that's a pretty big thing, I'd say. What's got you doing that?"

"Things."

"Well, *things* can hurt a man with blood pressure as high as yours. I'm calling the hospital now to—"

"No!" Daddy barked. "Just give me something."

"Nothing I give you is going to bring that pressure down."

"I'm talking about bringing some relief."

"We've discussed this, JD. I don't think it's a good idea to just deal with the symptoms—"

"Yeah, well, I'm begging."

Dr. Corey put his hand on Daddy's shoulder. "Be reasonable."

Daddy looked at the floor. "Vernon, how long we known each other?"

"I'm obligated to warn you . . ."

"Rae Rae, wait for me outside," said Daddy.

"Why?" I whined. "Are you gonna be okay?"

"Do as your daddy says now. Wait for me outside."

I pushed out my bottom lip as I left the room. Dr. Corey closed the door behind me. I sat in the waiting room, swinging my legs back and forth, counting each swing.

I can imagine what Daddy said to Dr. Corey, convincing him to administer that first dosage of Demerol, the narcotic pill he would swallow daily for the next three years, before graduating to a more potent form. He told his buddy from high school that he needed to function well enough to take care of his little girl. And then for sure, once we were all settled into the new place, he'd admit himself into the hospital for a complete workup. Sure thing. Right away.

When Daddy finally came out—two hundred and twelve leg swings later—he was holding a white square of paper. He grabbed my hand with his free one, and I swung our arms, relieved to be going home. Dr. Corey stuck his head out the back door. "Take care, JD," he said loudly. "And don't forget what I said."

"I done heard you the first three times, Vernon." Daddy held the door for me. "See you next time, Ilene."

"You take care, Mr. Dodson," she said, waving us off. "You too, Rae." 105

Back in the car, I asked Daddy if we could get Boston Coolers at Miss Ann's. I knew he wouldn't feel up to driving downtown to Sanders.

"I don't see why not," he answered, pulling up to the pharmacy on Ewald Circle. We went inside and waited while the pharmacist filled his prescription. I flipped through the August issue of *Young Miss* magazine, getting more anxious with each passing page.

During the drive to Miss Ann's, the little white paper bag sat between us on the front seat. I finally asked what I'd been thinking but holding in through five traffic lights.

"Daddy, are those pills in that bag?"

He nodded.

"Why did the Stanbacks stop working?"

He looked over at me. "I just need a little something more, Brown Eyes. Something stronger."

We rode for several blocks, passing the Pontiac car dealership, Dot & Etta's Shrimp Shack, and the rickety railroad track where trains hardly ever crossed. "So, now you're going to be just like Mama before she threw away her pills? Sleeping all day?"

Daddy made a right turn. He idled the car at a red light and rubbed his hand down his face, from hairline to chin, the way he did sometimes when he was just waking up. "I'm taking these pills 'cause I'm trying to get rid of my pain." He looked over at me. "Your mama takes her pills 'cause she's trying to get rid of her problems."

The light changed, and Daddy took off faster than usual. I scooted up under him as he laid his hand on my thigh. "So now," he said. "How 'bout we go get a couple of them Boston Coolers?"

That night of the pool party, when Rhonda rang the door chimes, Kimmie ran down the stairs wearing cut-off jeans with embroidered patterns sewn into the hip pocket and a red wet-look bikini top. "See you later, Rae Rae!" she called over her shoulder as she rushed out the house. I ran to the den window. Daddy was already there, leaning his elbows on the ledge, gazing out at the street. The twisted strain was gone from his face. He smiled when he saw me, a cottony, dry-mouth smile that I would come to know well over the next several years.

"Can you believe Rhonda's got a car the same color as the sky?" I said, leaning my own elbows onto the ledge beside him.

"Custom-color," said Daddy. "Look like she got matching interior too. No, it's white. White is nice."

"It used to be her mother's car," I said. We watched as the Riviera took off down the street.

"That right? She must have a young mama, that girl. Only a young woman would special-order a car like that." He moved away from the window, headed out the room. "Right nice color for a lady, too. Baby blue."

I joined Daddy in the kitchen, and together we made a dinner of liverwurst and Colby cheese on Saltine crackers with hot sauce, and as an afterthought, sliced tomatoes on iceberg lettuce. That night was like old times, with Mama upstairs sorting through her things, Kimmie gone, and Daddy and me together. After dinner we played Chinese checkers. Then Daddy pulled out the round white tabletop he kept propped against the wall. He placed it on the folded-out sofa bed, grabbed his worn deck of cards, and with deliberate concentration dealt our first hand of gin rummy. I kept score. Daddy liked the three-of-a-kind spreads, while I preferred the sequential ones. Usually, he was good for about twenty minutes before he'd have to rest. This time we played all the way to five hundred points. I was winning by a narrow margin when Daddy dealt me a king and queen and jack of diamonds. I held the spread until I'd gotten rid of all my other cards, and then I laid it down with a flourish and yelled, "Gin!!"

"Didn't see that one coming." He shook his head, caught with face cards and an ace worth fifteen points in his hand. "You something else, Brown Eyes, you know that? You something else."

107

After gin rummy, we watched *Sanford and Son*. Every time Redd Foxx grabbed his chest and said, "Elizabeth, I'm comin' to join you!" Daddy laughed till tiny tears squeezed out the corners of his eyes.

Later we cuddled together on the sofa bed, and Daddy showed me a couple of ads in the *Michigan Chronicle* that he'd circled with my orange crayon. One read: *Furnished, 2 bdrm; bsmt; washer & dryer, $110, utils. paid*. The other read: *Upper flat, sharp, 2 bdrm, appliances. Kids & pets OK. $100*.

"I figured I'd get the furnished one, even though it's a bit more money," he said. "You can still make a place feel like yours, even if it's got somebody else's things in it. Add your own little touches."

"Daddy, you're doing better, right?"

"Better than I been in a while. Now I can focus on us getting up outta here."

"Those new pills really work, huh?"

He squeezed me to him. "Think I mighta turned a corner, Brown Eyes. Feelin' like my old self, damn near."

We both slept well that night, the smelly heat of Daddy's breath rising to greet me in the face, his steady snores my lullaby.

The next night, a Karmann Ghia driven by some guy pulled up to the curb. The driver tooted the Marx Brothers horn, and Kimmie flew out the front door, running down the walkway, peace sign patch dangling off the butt of her jeans. Daddy and I watched from the den window as the VW idled loudly and then backfired a bit as they took off.

"Don't trust those little imports worth a damn," said Daddy. "Especially something with the engine in the rear. You have an accident in that, you don't stand a chance." He shook his head. "You just can't trust those foreign cars . . . and you sho' can't trust nobody who drives one."

Upstairs, Mama was peering out her bedroom window, also watching Kimmie leave. She saw her own young self, slipping into Cyril's new VW Beetle and tearing off into the night, into possibility and trouble. She envied Kimmie; and she feared for her. Anxious and jittery, she wanted to pull the pill bottle out from under her mattress and swallow two Valiums dry, but she didn't. Instead, she lay across the bed with a premonition forming about this nameless guy Kimmie had just met, about their liaison disrupting her carefully laid plans.

R honda never did teach Kimmie how to drive that summer. After she started seeing the Karmann Ghia guy, who was slit-eyed with an arrogant smile and a penchant for Stroh's beer, she decided to take lessons from him instead. His name was Nolan, and he and Kimmie had been out on endless dates in the three weeks since meeting at that pool party—where he tossed her into the deep end without knowing if she could swim. Looking back, I'm certain they had sex on the first date. She was so swiftly obsessed with him.

Those long July days lumbered by in one sticky red blob, like a pregnant Irish setter trying to get to the corner. Kimmie launched into a frenzied series of driving lessons, Mama sorted and boxed her possessions, and Daddy and I sat in front of the oscillating fan drinking Pepsi—mine on ice, his from a chilled bottle.

The first of the month, he and I rode together in Oldie to cash his disability check at the check-cashing storefront. I stood in line for him. When I returned with a wad of money, he took out two crisp one-hundred-dollar bills and handed them back to me. "Here, you tuck this away somewhere safe, okay? That's our get-outta-Dodge money. Whatever you do, don't lose it."

Next, we went to Miss Ann's diner for grits and eggs and fried chicken. And then, to Mr. Alfred's body shop, where I reveled in the smells of exhaust and motor oil and Mr. Alfred's cigar as the two men perched on folding chairs beneath the open garage door.

"Yeah, I tried some of that new unleaded gas. Car knocked so bad I could barely make it back to the shop!" said Mr. Alfred. "And the stuff cost a whole five cents more a gallon than regular!"

Daddy whistled. "Glad my car is good on gas. I could drive it four hundred miles if I wanted, wouldn't have to fill it up but once." 109

"Your car is five years old, JD. It can't hardly get that far on one tank of gas. Used to. Not now."

"Ain't that what I pay you for?"

Mr. Alfred chuckled. "I'm a mechanic, not a magician." He rose, grabbed a hubcap. "Now what you ought-a do is get yourself a new car. Ford's making some nice ones now. Not too much."

It was Daddy's turn to chuckle. "Uh huh, I think I'll go get me one of them Pintos, so the first time somebody bump into the back of me, it can explode, burn my black ass to a crisp."

Both men laughed out loud as Mr. Alfred placed the hubcap on a jacked-up car tire's rim. The laughter settled; he pulled the cigar from his lips. "So how's the search going?"

Daddy sighed. "Found a nice two-bedroom, a flat, over on Petoskey. Might go ahead, take that one."

"How much flats over there going for?"

"One ten with heat included."

It was Mr. Alfred's turn to whistle. "Kinda high, aint' it?"

"Not for no two-bedroom in a good neighborhood. Gotta live somewhere decent for my baby's sake."

"I hear that," said Mr. Alfred. "I hear that."

Can I ride with you? Please, please!" I begged Kimmie one day, hating that her summer romance was stealing away our precious time together.

"Okay, Rae Rae, but you have to sit quietly in the backseat," she ordered.

I gave her my Girl Scout's promise and followed her out to Nolan's egg-yellow VW, climbing into the car's miniature-sized backseat.

"You don't look like sisters," said Nolan, checking me out in his rearview mirror. Kimmie giggled nervously, but I found nothing funny.

We took off, the car farting loud engine sounds as he revved it and drove to Mayflower Church's parking lot a few blocks away. Nolan looked nothing like the boys all the girls in my class wanted to be chased, caught, and love-tapped by. He was not a pretty boy. He had no freckles or pink lips or long eyelashes. No mole over his wide mouth. No copper complexion. He had eggplant-dark skin with scattered pimples and a thin Afro made big from a blow-out kit, patches of scalp peeking through like the ground beneath parched grass. Stuck in the back of his hair was a pick with a handle shaped like a fist. I thought it looked stupid to leave a comb in your hair.

Kimmie and Nolan switched places, and he leaned in toward her, talking to her ear. "Remember what I told you, now. One foot eases down on the gas as the other eases up on the clutch. Ready?" Kimmie turned around to me. "Rae Rae, don't say anything, okay? It'll make me nervous." I nodded, crossing my fingers. We took off. The car jerked and then cut off. "You've got to give it gas if you don't want it to stall," advised Nolan, levity lacing his words. Kimmie got going again, and we rode around in a circle. The car jolted badly when Kimmie shifted a gear, making it a horrible, jerky ride. Nolan kept telling her what she was doing wrong before she could figure out how to do it right. She'd get confused and hit the brake when she meant to hit the gas. After one particularly bad stop-start, Nolan yelled, "You need to pay attention!" He put his hand on her thigh, squeezed it. "I'm not playing, Kimmie; watch your feet! You're gonna ruin my clutch!"

Kimmie flinched. "Okay, okay."

Sitting in that little backseat, I knew Kimmie was far from a natural behind the wheel, not like I would become. I went out with them every day for the next two weeks. Driving a clutch never did turn into a smooth maneuver for her. She just didn't have the rhythm for it. Still, despite Nolan's impatient yelling, she learned well enough to get by. She failed the road test twice; Daddy teased her about it. "Tell me when you take the test again, so I can be sure I'm several blocks away," he joked. But she persevered, and by the time August was over, Kimmie

111

had a temporary Michigan driver's license. The permanent one with the photo of her smiling came after she was gone.

Now eight years later, I had my own smiling photo on a driver's license, undaunted by what lay ahead waiting for me—endless highways and byways, stretched out for hundreds and hundreds of miles, yellow diamond-shaped warning signs guiding me to safety.

Midnight wind peeled back from invisible sky, car headlights casting parallel beams of fuzzy whiteness onto the macadam as I drove along the Fisher Freeway—late for work and doing seventy-five miles an hour. Anticipation surged through my fingertips as I exited, drove along South Hill Road, then pulled into the sprawling complex of the GM Proving Ground and parked. I quickly clocked in and picked up my schedule. Tonight I'd be doing two hundred miles on the fast track, test-driving a diesel Cadillac. This was not my favorite assignment. Diesel Caddies were loud and clunky.

A few of the guys I worked with were gathered around drinking coffee, hanging out, squeezing the last few minutes out of their break time. I liked them despite their crude sex jokes, their pictures of naked ladies taped to their toolboxes, their cracks about my being jail bait. Fully macho, these guys loved their job at GM's test track, especially when they got to push their cars to the limit at top speed in flame-proof suits, maybe run over trees in the process. Yet they were harmless men who made twelve dollars an hour, thanks to overtime, and spent it on greedy women, overpriced liquor in corner bars, and poor hunches at Ladbroke Race Track. I relished their rough laughs, their shoulder bumping and backslapping, their sweet funk. I loved these men.

But most of all I loved my job.

Driving is like dancing. It's about listening for the underlying beat, the hum, and then flowing with it. Once you find your groove, you can go for hours, with the windows down and your arm hanging out, the rearview and side mirrors giving you a been-there view, sound of the tires' revolutions in your ears.

I said hello to the guys, poured black coffee, and headed toward the fast track. I slid into the driver's seat of the Caddie and started my run, turning smoothly onto the simulated road stretched out before me. If I could get my test drive done in under three hours, I'd be able to sneak in a nap before the next assignment. The only rub was that I wasn't allowed to go over the designated speed limit. If I finished too quickly, there'd be questions. I pushed in my Al Jarreau cassette, took off, and settled into the ride—coasting at sixty-five miles per hour.

The fast track was really the expressway of the proving ground. It had seven lanes, all dramatically divided by fresh white road lines. Along the embankments, manicured lawns with transplanted trees offered more simulated reality. Just as I turned the bend to finish my first one hundred miles, a Camaro and a Grand Prix flew by me, one on each side. It was Joey and Harold, racing each other on the outside lanes. And although racing wasn't officially allowed out on the fast track, a lot of the guys did it. Even Patty raced. She was the first woman test driver the company ever hired, and she'd been there for eight years. I didn't want this, even though the temptations were real. Everyone talked about how great the hourly rate and UAW benefits were, how much better it was to be outside driving rather than inside on an assembly line—as if those were the only two choices in life. Patty was lobbying hard for me to get a full-time position given that I'd graduated at seventeen from high school *and* was the youngest girl they ever hired. "I can do it for you, Rae, really," she told me, her frizzy blond hair covering her full face like a bonnet. "I fought these knuckleheads so women could get the good jobs. In fact, I got my eye on the real prize: traffic safety instructor!" She seemed thrilled over the prospect. "You stick with me, and I'll see to it you get hired on." I thought about that—settling into a life of driving cars for a living. "Getting paid to tear up the road," as the guys put it. But I wanted to tear up the road on a real highway, not one that circled around and around, going nowhere.

Once I clocked my two hundred miles, I turned into the little island in the center of the track and gassed up, then filled out my paperwork. My final assignment was to take the Caddie through the corrosion booth. I eased through the entrance of this sadistic car wash—fascinated as always by the concentrated rust and water that spewed out and pummeled the luxury car with malice—and thought about the waste, the idea of defacing a thing of beauty in order to see how much abuse it could take.

By four a.m., done with my assignments, I napped for two hours in the employee lounge, curled up on a hard plastic chair. I had a ragged dream about Derek gruffly wiping the lipstick off my face as he walked by me on a busy highway, his violated car left exposed and vulnerable on the road's shoulder. Rising out of that mini-nightmare with gratitude, I drank more black coffee, changed the oil in the Caddie, and waited to clock out.

Living the life of a night creature, being nocturnal, was like peeling off a layer of life that the rest of the world uses to protect itself. It divided me from the others, the day people. I left my house as the TV bellowed "Hereeeee's Johnny!"—rushing to get where I needed to be before midnight, like a reverse Cinderella. I slept with shades drawn against the sun and rose as children trotted home from school. A skim of clarity coated my brain, and I noticed things, minute things. But up against my body's out-of-whack biorhythms, my mind reacted slowly. In the end, I missed a lot.

At exactly eight a.m., I pushed through the front doors, hurried to the parking lot, jumped into Daddy's car, and tore out of there, hitting the freeway and rushing against rush hour—leaving behind Milford, Michigan, and its GM Proving Ground for what turned out to be the last time.

115

I was drifting into a soft, seductive sleep, the car's motion my lullaby when Daddy hit the brakes. My chest bruised against the dashboard. Neither of us had bothered to wear our seat belts. And we both knew better.

We were idling at the corner of Livernois and Puritan, barely two miles from home. Our plan had been to hit the freeway, make good time through Michigan, and at least be in Ohio by noon.

"Is the car okay?" I asked, worried that maybe Daddy had driven a lemon off the lot. He'd just bought this dark blue 1980 Cutlass Supreme from the Porterfield Wilson dealership. And now we were about to blow it out on the road—drive to the Grand Canyon and the desert, stop in New Mexico, turn around, come back home. The trip was in celebration of several things: my high school graduation, my birthday, and Daddy's miracle remission. Since the beginning of the year, he'd had no headaches. They just stopped. In gratitude, he stopped taking his Demerol. Cold turkey. "It's a good spell," he said. "I'm a run with it."

And he did. He and I went to the movies, saw *Ordinary People* and *The Shining*. And to my surprise, he went out a few times on a date with a woman. Those evenings, he dressed in his softly pleated black trousers and crisp white shirt, slicked his hair, and left the house smelling like aftershave. He'd slide into a turquoise Cordoba that picked him up out front, coming home many hours later, smelling like cognac. I never did meet her.

On his forty-ninth birthday, he prepared a huge dinner, cooking chitterlings and hot-water cornbread and string beans with salt pork. He invited over Mr. Alfred and his poker-playing and numbers-running buddies, and they all sat around playing ancient, scratchy 78s, each one an old blues or honky-tonk song. In our living room stood a pool table Daddy had recently won at a poker game. He and his friends played a few games on it, teasing one another about who always seemed

116

to be the one behind the eight ball. Later into the night, the men sipped on hard liquor and listened to raunchy Moms Mabley and Pigmeat Markham and Redd Foxx comedy LPs—slapping their knees while laughing so hard at dirty jokes, they nearly choked.

We started planning the road trip the day after Daddy's birthday party. Spring was a flurry of reading travel books and making motel reservations and packing carefully. Once I began my job at the proving ground, I immediately requested two weeks off at summer's end; I was beyond excited—having waited years for this.

"Let me drive first," he requested on the Day. "I'm bound to get tired soon, so you can pick up on where I leave off."

As Daddy drove, I leaned against the window, closed my eyes, and inhaled deeply. I've always loved the smell of new cars. And gasoline coming out of a pump. And burning tire rubber. Behind them, those aromas, lies the promise of mobility and with that, possibility. Every time I've pulled into one of those real service stations—the kind where the bell goes *ding, ding, ding* when the car rides across the threshold— all those smells come wafting out to me at once, and I get a little rush, a slight high.

"You gonna have to take the wheel," he said suddenly, out of breath. "Got black spots in front of my eyes."

He leaned his head into the steering wheel and rubbed the bridge of his nose over and over. *Damn it,* I thought. *This is not possible. He's healed!*

"What happened?" I asked, opening the door on my side. "Do you need to take a little medicine? You brought an emergency dose with you, didn't you?"

He shook his head. "This one's bad. Leaning on me extra hard all night. Can't see. Better take me to Vernon's office."

"You didn't tell me you were having an episode," I said, angry with myself for not noticing. The things I'd missed by sleeping all day.

"We been planning this trip, how long? Last thing I wanted to do was mess it up."

117

"You know better than that," I said, both crestfallen and touched as I slid out of the car, ran over, opened the driver's door, and guided Daddy out.

He groped his way around to the passenger side. The sight of him hunched over and helpless scared me, and I drove to the first pay phone I saw, called Dr. Corey's office. Ilene answered, still there. "It's Rae. I'm bringing my father in. He's having a bad one."

"Okay, Honey," said Ilene, her voice calm. "I'll tell the doctor. He'll be waiting for you."

With that, I flew down Livernois with no respect for the speed limit, whizzing by those colorful little flags waving outside first one then another and then another car dealership—factory-fresh vehicles poised behind every showroom window, each angled to shatter glass, collide with my hopes.

That summer of 1972, Kimmie really wanted to practice her driving so that the next time she went out with Nolan, he'd be impressed. We devised a way: stealing Daddy's car. I tiptoed into the den as he lay sleeping on the sofa, the spine of *I Know Why the Caged Bird Sings* fanned out at his side. Carefully, I eased the car keys from his pant pocket and slipped out the house, where Kimmie waited for me in the driver's seat of Oldie. I felt like Trixie Belden or Nancy Drew, off on an undercover adventure, my partner in tow. Kimmie turned the key in the ignition, and we took off, turning east on Seven Mile Road and barely whizzing along the curvy streets lining Palmer Park. Other cars passed us by as we plodded along Woodward Avenue in the reliable if aging Olds. Kimmie rode the brakes a lot at first, a little unsure of herself, but once we hit downtown the ride got better, smoother. We headed down Jefferson Avenue for several blocks, finally turning into Belle Isle Park, where we stopped at the giant water fountain with its changing colors, throwing in pennies for good luck. We rode past the picnic area, the Detroit River's fishy-water smell suddenly another passenger in the car, then parked close to the river's edge, where people sat on the hoods of their Chevelles and Thunderbirds and station wagons, enjoying the breeze. We got away with these joy rides several times.

This day, Kimmie turned up the volume of the radio, and we got out and hopped onto the car's hood, engine warm beneath our butts. We rested our feet on the front bumper as barges moved in slow motion across the river and Elton John sang "Rocket Man," the moon barely there above us.

"This reminds me a little bit of the Mississippi River," Kimmie whispered. "Gives you that same kind of feeling I always get when I'm sitting along the bank, like the world is so vast and you're so tiny up against it."

I studied the hypnotic dark waves of the water. "Why'd you run away from home?" I asked.

Kimmie looked up, up into the lazy night haze. My eyes followed hers, and there I found tiny stars, like twinkling connect-the-dots. "That summer was so bizarre," she said. "Papa said we could come be with him, but then he changed his mind. And that really hurt Mommy. And me. I was so miserable I just decided I'd go *get* him. I took a Greyhound bus, but I only got as far as Kentucky. Police pulled me off, made me go back to Detroit."

"But why'd you leave again?" I was confused.

"As soon as I got back, Mommy freaked out. Right in front of my eyes."

"What did she do?"

"She started sobbing and sobbing, and she tore out of the house in nothing but her underwear, ran down the street. Mean Mr. Green called the police, and after that they took her away. I just . . . I don't know, I just felt it was my fault. And I was certain Daddy Joe blamed me. He kept saying, 'This is the last straw. You hear me? The last straw.' When Mommy got out of the hospital, I heard him telling her, 'Get yourself together, because I got plans and they don't include Kimmie. Make that high-yellow nigger handle his responsibility.'" Kimmie shuttered. "It was ugly."

I could imagine my mother running wild down a street, wearing just a matching camisole and tap pants. Not that she'd done anything that odd around me before, yet I knew she had the capacity beneath her thinly veiled normalcy. But Daddy's harsh words surprised me.

"And then, I got to be with Papa after all," continued Kimmie.

"You wanted to go, right?"

She nodded. "The whole city was acting strange. Right after I left, folks tried to burn it down. People were dying. It was horrible. I swear I could feel it coming, like a rumble under your feet before a train approaches. I felt it coming."

"I remember the riot," I said. "That was the night Daddy left."

We gazed out at the Canadian skyline; it shimmered back at us. "But of course life down South had a few surprises," said Kimmie.

I knew nothing about how it felt to be "the child Cyril got out in the street," as they referred to Kimmie in that little stultifying Louisiana town where she and her father lived, but I did know that Kimmie had left me to go be with him.

"You got what you wanted," I pointed out.

"Sort of. At first, when Mommy sent me away, I was faking like I was thrilled, you know? If my mother didn't want me, then I'd go live with my papa, who did. But it wasn't at all what I had expected."

She got down there, this twelve-year-old girl going to live with her father, and discovered that his wife resented her very existence and certainly her presence.

"It was not fun," said Kimmie.

"You should've come back," I said, suddenly angry. "I don't know why you didn't just come back. Didn't you miss me?"

Kimmie closed her eyes. "I hated leaving you, Rae Rae. You don't know what a godsend you were to me when you were born. Before that, I was really lonely. Daddy Joe was never home, and Mommy was going on all these secret trips to see Papa, leaving me with Johnnie Mae of all people. It was crazy."

"I remember the day you left. I was sitting on the stairs, and you hugged me, then walked out the door." I shrugged. "And you never came back."

121

"I wanted to, but it was so complicated."

We sat for a while longer, watching dirty water slosh up against the rocks as Q93 played one top-forty hit after another from Daddy's car radio: "American Pie." "Freddie's Dead." "Saturday in the Park."

"I wish I could see Louisiana," I said as Sammy Davis Jr. sang "The Candy Man."

"You will," said Kimmie. She hugged herself against the breeze. "It's actually quite beautiful, in a slow molasses sort of way."

"Which do you like more? Here or there?"

Kimmie shrugged. "That's a toughie. I like being here with you, and I did miss Mommy, you know? All those years away from my own mother, that was rough. But to tell the truth, Papa has actually been good to me. And I have a couple of good friends down there." She paused. "Still . . ."

I looked over at my sister. "It's not like having both parents at the same time, is it?"

Kimmie nodded. "In the same house."

"Or in the same part of the house," I whispered.

Kimmie pulled me to her, and I leaned my head on her shoulder as she wrapped her arm around me. Mere seconds passed before Kimmie burped, ran to the side of the car, and threw up. Somewhere in the distance a tugboat tooted its horn.

On the way home, Kimmie drove fast and unsteady, not trusting her stomach to hold out. The car in front of us stopped abruptly at a yellow light. When we ran into the back of it, the impact didn't do much more than bounce off the other car's bumper. That didn't stop the driver—a squat, golden-headed albino—from jumping out of his souped-up Trans Am, bird wings spread across its hood, and examining his bumper with the care of a drug addict searching for a working vein. We both watched with fear as he headed toward Oldie.

"Look what the fuck you've done!" he bellowed, leaning into the window on Kimmie's side.

"Please don't hurt us, Mister!" I screamed.

"Ain't nobody gonna hurt you, little girl, so shut up!" He squinted his eyes as he leveled them at Kimmie. "You need to learn how to fucking drive that fucking old-ass jalopy!" He pointed his finger at her, gunlike. "Better be glad ain't no serious damage to my ride." And with that, he bent his finger back as though pulling a trigger, made a horrible sound like a bullet firing, marched back to his car, and sped off.

"Oh my God, oh my God," breathed Kimmie. "I'm never driving again." She turned to me. "You okay?" I nodded. She peered through the windshield. "Let me look at the car."

We both got out and inspected the damage. The car's front fender was bent pretty badly. "Uh oh," I said.

"Shit!" Kimmie cried. "Daddy Joe is gonna kill me."

For the first time in my life, I had no idea what Daddy would do. I'd never before been duplicitous with him. I crawled into the backseat and stretched across the upholstery, undone.

"We'll just explain what happened, right?" Kimmie took another hard look at the car's front end. "Oh, shit," she murmured. "Ohhh, shit."

We drove back home at five miles an hour.

Daddy was waiting for us. He'd watched from the den window as we pulled up to the curb, and now he was standing in the doorway, filling it up.

"What happened to my car?" he asked as we entered the living room.

"I'm so sorry, Daddy Joe," said Kimmie. "It was an accident. This guy in front of me stopped suddenly and . . ."

"And who told you you could even use my car?" He looked right at me, shame heating my face.

Kimmie shook her head. "We just . . . it was wrong. I'm sorry."

"I'm sorry too." My voice was so low, I could barely hear myself.

He pointed his finger at me. "You go wait for me in the den."

I left the two of them, crawled onto the den sofa, hugged a pillow, and listened.

Daddy's voice was even. "You need to make sure, as long as you live, 123 that you don't ever put my baby's life in jeopardy like that again, you understand?"

Silence.

"You wanna risk your own life, it's one thing. But not hers."

"It's just that that guy put his brakes on too—"

"You not listening to me. I don't want her riding with nobody who just learned how to drive two minutes ago. Understand?"

"Yes," she whispered.

"That's it," Daddy said, turning back toward the den. I heard Kimmie's footsteps run upstairs, where she would hug the rim of the toilet, sick again. Daddy looked over at me. "And you not no innocent here. You know better."

He grabbed my hand roughly and led me to the powder room, sat on the toilet lid, yanked me toward him, pulled down my shorts, and whacked me across my butt five times. I cried out. Within seconds, my shorts were back up, and he was pushing me away. "Now, go on and think about what you did." It was the first and last spanking he ever gave me. Even when I'd deserved one in the past, he hadn't hit me. In a rare show of mischievousness, I once wrote S-H-I-T on the sidewalk with chalk I'd stolen from school. Classmates saw me do it and decided to tell on me. "Mr. Dodson, Rae wrote a bad word on the sidewalk!" said the ringleader, Natalie Ford, as the group gathered on my front porch. Daddy looked down at them and said, "Didn't your mamas ever tell you never to stop off at anybody's house on the way home from school?" The girls left dejected, and afterward he cradled me on his lap, got me to confess. End of story.

I headed upstairs to Kimmie's room, but the door was closed, the telephone cord underneath. I could hear her by standing very close to the door. "Just come get me if you can, okay?" she said. "Yeah, now. Like *right* now. Please."

Within an hour, Kimmie would be running out the house to join Nolan.

I turned away from her closed bedroom door, my behind stinging. Suddenly, the door to the attic swung open, and Mama walked out.

"What's going on?" she asked.

"Nothing."

"Didn't sound like nothing down there."

Above our heads Mama had been dragging old boxes around for days and days as she rummaged through mementos, sitting cross-legged on the rickety attic floor, cobwebs sticking to her hair, cigarette burning away in a nearby ashtray. The front room was now cluttered with packed boxes—a bold step forward in her years-long sorting ritual.

She knelt before me. "We can share things, Rae. It's okay to tell me things. I'm your mother."

I bit my lip.

"Go ahead."

"We took Daddy's car and had an accident, and Daddy spanked me and Kimmie's sick, and everything's all ruined, and you never come out of the attic!"

With that I ran down the stairs, ignoring Mama's voice at my back pleading, "Come back, come back, Rae." I ran outside to the garage, where my bike was parked, and jumped on the banana seat planning to take off across the alley, maybe show up at Terrance Golightly's door. But it was already so dark that I lost my nerve. Instead, I got off my bicycle and threw it onto the ground with all the force I could muster. I picked it up, threw it down again. And again. Then I ran back into the house fast as I could.

That night, I slept under the dining room table. In the morning, I found myself magically beside Daddy in the sofa bed. I crawled onto his back, soon dreaming about what a perfect driver I would become.

D ays later, I was drifting in and out of the eleven o'clock news, half hearing of Shirley Chisholm's run for the presidency, Muhammad Ali's upcoming fight against Floyd Patterson, and a union activist named Coleman Young trying to become the city's first black mayor. Suddenly, a voice in the room was reciting the Pledge of Allegiance as Daddy roused me off his back, startling me awake.

"What is it?" I asked, barely focusing on the American flag waving seductively across the TV screen.

"Go back to sleep, Brown Eyes. I'm just going to the bathroom." As he got up, the slit in his silky boxer shorts opened, and I saw his penis. It was dark, thick. Crouching. I'd known for a while that he had one, that all men had one, but I'd never *seen* it. I lay there strangely nervous, listening for jingling keys or a slamming door until I heard Daddy's heavy footsteps traveling down the basement stairs. By the time I reached the hall door and peered from the top of the stairway, I couldn't see Daddy, but I could hear him.

"You best be getting out of here, young fella," he said. I prayed: *Oh God, please let Daddy have a gun.* I heard muffled voices. "Naw, don't 'wait-a-minute' me," he said, voice gruff. "Just grab your shit and get out my goddamn house, *now.*"

I heard scrambling and rustling, and suddenly Nolan ran up the basement steps, all big hair and bony arms, his shirt hanging out. Kimmie was right behind him, psychedelic bra in her hand and embarrassment across her face. Daddy followed, loosely holding a wrapped baseball bat, his breaths short and winded. Nolan scooted out the side door, and Kimmie pushed her way past me, turning back to say, "I see little pitchers have big ears *and* big mouths!" Her words fell over me like icy rain that attacks you in April when you've been praying so hard for spring to finally come.

After the basement incident, Kimmie ignored me. In retaliation, I took on daring bike-riding feats with Terrance Golightly. The frame of my bicycle was destroyed thanks to my slamming it against the ground, and in a valiant gesture, Terrance let me ride on the boy's bar of his bike. The most we could do was ride along tame residential streets, but I didn't care. I relished being near Terrance, who was more beautiful than ever with that lopsided Afro and his ashy elbows, his snaggle-toothed grin. I stayed out with him for hours and hours, until my pony-tail was stiff and nostrils wide with my own wild-girl musk. I headed home just as the street lights popped on, hungry for a peanut butter and jelly sandwich, satiated by my own little secret act of in-the-street defiance.

During those heady days, Terrance kept telling me I should ride on his handlebars. "I could go so much faster that way," he said. "Really fly down the bike path at Palmer Park." When I refused, he called me a scaredy-cat. Then he sang, "Such a girl, man. Such a girrrrl."

"I'm not scared!" I yelled.

"Then prove it."

"I don't have to."

"Scaredy-cat, scaredy-cat!"

"Fuck you," I said, running away, racing from the park, from his snaggletooth taunts. His voice trailed after me in the wind.

"Oooh, Rae said a bad word! Rae said a bad word! I'm gonna tell yo' Daddy, Rae of Sun!"

I ran with all my might until I was a dot to Terrance. I stretched my arms straight out, rushing against fresh-flying wind for block after block. I wanted to race across an imaginary finish line—where the reward was hugs of congratulations followed by dinner around the table with my mother and father and sister, our loving voices all talking at once, outstretched hands grabbing at freshly baked rolls, silverware clinking. When I got a cramp in my side, I stopped, plopping onto the ground to catch my breath before dragging myself home.

When Nolan arrived that particular evening and blew his horn out front, Kimmie walked down the stairs wearing a midnight blue halter dress in a clingy knit that came down to her ankles. I will never forget that dress, its silver threads covering the bodice, its silhouette of Kimmie's soft curves. There she found Mama sitting on the landing, blocking her path and smoking.

"I want to meet him," said Mama, her voice low, but strong.

"We have a big concert to go to tonight," said Kimmie. "Stevie Wonder and Azteca are playing at Pine Knob! We can't be late."

Her hair was pinned up, bouncy Shirley Temple curls escaping on the sides; she was wearing Rhonda's white clogs and looking like Barbie about to open the door to her mystery date.

"I know who's playing at Pine Knob, and I know you can spare five minutes." Mama took a short drag from her cigarette. "Stevie never starts on time. And he plays for hours."

Kimmie shrugged. "I'll see what he says. But you've got to let me by first." With her hair up like that, I noticed how Kimmie's shoulder blades jutted out, how wispy the baby hair was at the nape of her long neck.

"It's not for him to decide." Mama scooted out of Kimmie's way. "I said I want to meet him, so tell him to come in."

Kimmie turned back to Mama. "Vy, he's a grown man. I can't tell a grown man what to do."

"But you're not quite grown, and I can still tell you what to do."

Kimmie huffed, headed toward the door, swung it open, then

stepped outside, closing the door quietly but with force. I wondered if she'd bother to come back at all. But Mama waited patiently, taking another long slow drag, her legs crossed as one swung back and forth. Sure enough, Kimmie's key eased back into the door, and they walked in together. Holding hands. The fisted pick was gone from Nolan's Afro, which was now perfectly round and shiny and still see-through. Mama looked up at him, and I could tell she was startled. She hadn't expected someone so dark-skinned, so far from her idea of pretty.

"This is Nolan," said Kimmie.

"Hello, Mrs. uh. . . ."

"Dodson," said Mama.

"Mrs. Dodson. Nice to meet you."

Mama nodded. "Nolan, huh? What's your last name?"

"Bland."

"Your last name is Bland?"

Nolan smiled. "Yes, and I'm anything but!"

"Is that so? I'll bet you're not still in high school."

"Graduated a few years ago." He and Kimmie were still holding hands.

"How many years ago?"

"In sixty-eight. I'm twenty-two, in case you're wondering."

"And where do you live?"

"On Van Dyke."

"That's the east side."

Nolan half nodded. "Correct."

"I suppose you've seen some things."

"I don't see what the point of all this is," said Kimmie.

"Oh, there's a point." Mama put out her cigarette in the little cut-glass ashtray she held in the palm of her hand.

Kimmie shifted her weight.

"It's okay," said Nolan. "I'm not ashamed of where I live. Or anything else."

"Oh?" said Mama.

Kimmie sighed heavily, trying to appear exasperated rather than nervous. "Are we dismissed yet?"

"In a minute." Mama uncrossed her legs, gave Nolan the eye. "Take pride in this, Nolan Bland. If I ever hear about you sneaking into my basement again, I'm going to treat you like a burglar, blow your head off with my pink-handled forty-five, then call the police and tell them to come clean my carpet. Understand?"

Shock moved across Nolan's face as he nodded. Then he smiled, impressed. "I sure do."

Kimmie's mouth dropped. "I don't believe you said that! What is wrong with you?" She pulled Nolan toward the door. "I told you she was crazy!" Kimmie stamped past us both, Nolan at her heels.

"The pleasure was all mine, Mrs. D.," he said over his shoulder. "I like a strong black woman!"

"Just don't forget what I said!" Mama yelled as they rushed out. "Or else." Nolan slammed the door on her warning.

Once they left, I sat with my mother and listened to the sounds coming through the open window: Kimmie and Nolan running down the porch steps, the doors of his Karmann Ghia opening and closing, the ignition turning, the motor revving, then backfiring. We listened to the sudden burst of War singing "Slipping into Darkness" on the tinny car radio, their harmonic voices growing fainter as the car put-putted down the street, out of earshot. When the sounds of them were all but gone, still hanging like an afterthought in midair, Mama stood, turned without a word, and climbed the stairs. It was an elegant ascent, and I have it locked into my mind even now—the sight of Mama's long legs taking the stairs one at a time, both deliberate and defiant, until she disappeared around the landing and then, *whoosh*, closed her bedroom door. I sat there for some time, awed by my mother's audacity and never again more proud of her.

———

D ays passed. Kimmie still didn't speak to me. Bruised, I picked a fight with Terrance, finally putting an end to his teasing. "Scaredy-cat, scaredy-cat, where have you gone?" he sang. "Scared—"

I pushed him. Hard. He fell down, sat on the ground a full minute, dumbfounded. Apparently, his mother had taught him to never hit girls, and I could see him coming up with a substitute for the sticks and stones he couldn't throw to break my bones.

"Everybody knows your daddy is a bum with no job!" he yelled as he took off.

I chased him for two blocks, determined to scratch huge welts across his face before I got a stitch in my side and gave up pursuit. I limped home exhausted and angry.

By dusk, I was sitting on the back porch playing with my Paddle Ball, the repetitious *bonk, bonk, bonk* sound a type of sedative for my own naughty nerves.

Out of nowhere, Kimmie appeared. "Want me to comb your hair?" she asked. "It's a mess."

Miss Queenie hadn't been around all summer, let go in Mama's early throes of domestic exuberance—which ranged from cooking battered-covered dinners to shopping for groceries to hosting a card party—and as a result I hadn't had my hair combed in weeks. Instead, I just brushed it into a ponytail every day to mask the neglect. Gratitude flooded my scalp, and I nodded, hoping she'd find a little dandruff to scratch. Kimmie, big black comb in hand, sat me between her legs and pulled out the rubber band holding my hair together.

"I had a fight today," I said.

"Who with?"

I told her all about Terrance as she raked the comb through my tangled hair. It hurt more than I wanted her to know, but I had to finally grab her hand in self-protection.

"How'd you get to be so tenderheaded with all this kinky hair?" she said.

131

"Let me go get the Hair-So-New," I offered, jumping up from the torture of her comb, running to the powder room, returning with the bright pink bottle of de-tangler.

I got back between Kimmie's legs, and she sprayed so much Hair-So-New onto my hair that it was soon dripping wet. But the combing was painless, and I relaxed, leaning into her thighs. We sat like that for several minutes, the two of us saying nothing as she worked. What Kimmie did finally say hurt worse than any comb ever could.

"Daddy Joe sure has changed."

"Changed how?"

"Well, when he and Vy first got married, he was different. For one thing, he was slim and trim. Can you believe it? And he didn't just lie around in that den all the time. We used to do all sorts of cool things together. He took me to ride the bumper cars at Edgewater Park and to the Henry Ford Museum and the Michigan State Fair, and once we drove all the way to Mackinac Island. He even taught me how to shadow box! He was sooooo nice." Kimmie shook her head. "Boy has he changed."

"He still is nice," I insisted.

"Humph!!! Hardly. He threatened my *boyfriend* with a baseball bat! No respect for another man. I mean I had to really talk to Nolan. He wanted to . . . well don't even get me started on what he wanted to do. He says the older generation needs to be taught a lesson or two from the younger generation. That it's our *job* to question authority. Authority led us into Vietnam, you know? Anyway, I told him to leave Daddy Joe alone. He's just a sick old man."

I despised Nolan. He was the first person in my life I felt true hatred for, and it made me shake. I wanted him to die. "Well, you weren't supposed to be alone in the basement with him!" I shouted at Kimmie.

"And you're not supposed to be a tattletale."

"I'm *not* a tattletale!"

"Oh come on, Rae Rae. Everyone knows you tell your daddy everything."

"That's not true!!!"

"And I'll bet you keep all his secrets, don't you?"

"His secrets?"

"His secrets," repeated Kimmie. She paused. "Can I ask you something?"

"What?"

"Don't you think you're a little old to still be sleeping with Daddy Joe?"

"I'm going to stop on my next birthday," I said, hurt.

"I should hope so," said Kimmie. "You're about to be in the fourth grade!"

I fumed as Kimmie concentrated hard on creating a perfect part down the center of my head. When done, she gathered my hair on one side into a ponytail, began braiding it. Hiding beneath my wild mane, I fought with myself not to cry.

"Rae Rae?" she said. "Does he ever . . . touch you?"

"Who?"

"Him. Daddy Joe."

"What do you mean?"

"Well, I'm just asking if. . . ." She was pulling my hair tightly as she spoke. "Well, if he does anything that makes you uncomfortable?"

I tried to pull away, but her fingers were intertwined in my hair.

"I don't know what you're talking about."

". . . . Does he ever touch your private parts?"

"What are those?"

"You know. Your chest or your bottom."

"Why would he do that?" I thought about having seen his penis and wondered if Kimmie somehow knew this. Then something else occurred to me. "Did your papa used to touch your private parts?" I asked.

Kimmie sighed. "Of course not. But I didn't sleep with my papa every night either." She sounded strange, almost jealous. She took a ribbon from her own hair, wrapped it around my freshly braided ponytail. 133

"Fathers don't do that kind of thing anyway," I said, sure of it.

"No, they usually don't," said Kimmie. "Unless they're not really your father."

I jerked around so I could look into Kimmie's dancing eyes and ask why she was acting so ugly. But as I turned, I saw Daddy standing in the doorway, wearing a red silky undershirt. Even through the screen door, his face was scary—jet black eyes glaring hard, thin lips a straight line. Kimmie turned, let out a tiny gasp. The way he looked at her made my flesh crawl. He moved away from the door.

That night, Daddy insisted I sleep beside him in the pulled-out sofa bed. "You getting a little heavy for my back," he said. The mattress was cold, and it took a lot of tossing and turning before I could fall asleep. I didn't know then how much it hurt him to give up a simple pleasure he'd shared with his little girl, to have to discard it because her sister had sullied it. At some point in the darkest part of the night, I awakened to the sound of a motor turning over. I sat up. Daddy was gone. When I leaned out the open window, I saw him taking off in Oldie. This time, he hadn't even bothered to push the car to the corner. He revved the motor right there, flagrant in his escape. I had an urge to run after him, tell him to wait for me. But I didn't. Instead, I returned to the sofa defeated—my body no longer enough to keep Daddy from leaving in the night.

He returned, to my relief, later the next day. But he was different; something in him had shifted. As the days passed, I watched him closely. He didn't bother to circle ads in the *Michigan Chronicle*'s classifieds, didn't talk about "gettin' outta Dodge," didn't do much at all but read *Manchild in the Promised Land*, which he'd read a zillion times already. Worst of all, he had me sleep beside him every night, his back to me. Where had he gone that night? To the baby blue frame house with the flower boxes in the window? Had he banged on her door until she answered and insisted she and Josie run away with him? Had the new man stood between them and demanded he go away? Had there been heated words exchanged, a choice made?

Finally, I couldn't take it anymore.

"Daddy, have you picked a place for us yet?" I asked one evening as he turned a page of his paperback.

"I'm not going no goddamned where," he said. "I'm staying, and you're staying." He took a swig from his Pepsi-Cola, turning the bottle upside down so the pop flowed down his throat, Adam's apple bobbing. He drained the bottle, wiped his mouth with the back of his hand. "Why should I be forced out? Hell, let them leave. They planning to anyway."

I was not relieved by this news the way I would've been weeks before, when I was more naive. Now, I worried that Daddy didn't love me the same way anymore, couldn't love me the same way as long as we stayed in this house, where things had been said. I couldn't bring myself to unpack my suitcase. I left it as it was, hidden underneath my bed.

W hen she saw me, she jumped. I'd caught her staring at herself in the bathroom mirror. Her bright eyes, wet from tears, were like liquid jewels.

"What's wrong?" I asked.

"Nothing!"

"Why are you crying?"

"Get out!"

As Kimmie turned toward me, I saw purple blotches on the side of her face.

I gasped. "What happened to you?"

"Shhhh! Me and Nolan had a little thing, that's all."

"He hit you?"

"He just got upset because I was driving his car home and I had an accident in it. Not a big accident, a little one, but . . ." She sat on the toilet lid and held her hands out to me.

"But you said you weren't going to drive anymore."

"He made me. Said I had to get over my fear, and then, I don't know, he started barking orders at me, and I got so nervous . . . it's really okay." Her voice cracked.

I nodded, but it was not okay. Daddy had told me long ago what weakness for men led to.

"I was really paying attention, you know?" Kimmie blew her nose on a piece of toilet paper. "But he yelled at me, and before I knew it, I side-swiped a parked car as I was turning a corner." She snapped her finger. "Just like that."

"He can't do that to you! I'm telling Daddy!" I turned to run and

136

wake him, but Kimmie grabbed my arm, yanked me toward her, held me tight at both elbows.

"Listen, Rae Rae, you cannot say anything to *anybody* about this, you hear me? Huh, do you?" She shook me a little. "Do you?!"

"O-Okay . . . ," I mumbled. Her desperation stunned me. "But what's going to happen?"

"Nothing. We talked, and things are fine. Stuff like this happens when you both love each other so much. It was just a misunderstanding, and it'll never happen again. He promised."

I looked at her blotchy face. "Kimmie," I whispered. I had to know. "Why'd you ask me that question about Daddy?"

She paused. "Oh. Rae Rae, I'm sorry about that. Nolan put that in my head. He gets these wild ideas sometimes."

"But why'd you say it?"

She closed her eyes, opened them. "Nolan wanted to cool things off for a while after Daddy Joe caught us, and . . . the whole thing got me upset, 'cause I really, really love Nolan and I don't want to lose him." She looked over at me, her eyes dancing, skin aflame. "You'll understand more when you get to be a teenager." She grabbed my hand. "Now you have something on me, and if I ever do anything you don't like, if I ever say anything bad about your daddy again, you can tell on me," she whispered. "Until then, it'll be our secret."

She stood, gently eased me out of the powder room. "Let's both just go to bed."

And so we did—she to her bed upstairs, I to mine below, holding Kimmie's secret deep in my belly. To help me fall asleep, I thought about all the ways in which Nolan could die.

When Kimmie came out of her room the next day, her usually long wavy black hair was teased and stringy and limp, an obviously failed Afro that flopped around her forehead and cheeks—and covered the bruises on her face. She caught my eye and brought her finger up to her lips.

137

H ow dare that piece of east-side ghetto shit put his hands on you!" Mama yelled at Kimmie, trapping her inside her room a day later. As it turned out, Rhonda was the one who told Kimmie's secret.

"It's none of your business!" yelled Kimmie.

"Oh, it's my business all right. You're my business." Mama stood beside a poster of Jimi Hendrix, wringing her hands. "This is just something else to tear up my nerves."

"Who says you have to deal with it?" said Kimmie. "You haven't even been in my life for five years!" Kimmie's desire to protect Nolan had made her vulnerable and mean like a cornered bitch with newborn puppies.

Mama looked near tears. "That's how you talk to your own mother?"

"Look how you're talking to me," Kimmie whined.

"I am simply trying to tell you that you should never let a man dominate your life like this. It's dangerous."

"Excuse me? You should talk."

"What's that supposed to mean?"

Kimmie braced herself. "You sent me away because Daddy Joe didn't want me here. You think I don't know that?"

Mama shook her head. "You got it all wrong. I sent you away because I wanted you to be safe. I wasn't well enough to take care of you. And this city was too wild, Kimmie."

"Oh, yeah? Well, why didn't you ever tell me to come back after things calmed down? After you got better?"

"Because you always sounded so happy. I didn't want to take you away from that."

Kimmie flung her hair off her face, brandishing the remnants of her bruise. "Happy? Living with a whorish father and a jealous stepmother? Oh yeah, I was happy all right."

Mama winced. "He's still your father, and he didn't abandon you.

138

He took you in and cared for you. That's more than I can say about my own father."

Kimmie wasn't listening. "I waited and waited for you to call and say, 'Come home, Kimmie. I miss you.'"

"You ran away from home! To get away from me, right? So I sent you to the one person you were always begging for. Is that a crime?"

Whatever had gotten misunderstood between mother and daughter was too tied into knots to be straightened out now, tangled even more so by Kimmie's brewing resentment.

"You want to know something, Vy? I did more wild things down there than I could ever imagine doing in Detroit. You think southern folks are backward? Don't believe it." She smirked. "So what did you protect me from, huh?"

Mama sighed, giving up. "What do you want from me, Kimmie?"

"I want those years back."

Mama put her hands together, as if to pray. "So do I. But they're gone. All we have is right now. And right now we have a problem. One your papa needs to know about."

"Why can't this just be between us?"

"Because it's bigger than us."

"See? If you really loved me, you'd try to understand from my point of view."

"I'd never understand this, because I'm your mother. I'm not supposed to understand."

Kimmie sighed. "A lot of good that does me."

Mama folded her arms. "He's so big and bad, he can hit a woman. Now let's see if the ugly black fucker can stand up to another man."

With that, Mama left Kimmie's room, leaving her to roll over on her tie-dyed bedspread and punch fists into the matching pillows.

Nolan didn't take the news too well that Kimmie's father was en route to Detroit with plans to confront him. Kimmie tried to 139 convince Nolan that if he just apologized to her papa, everything would be back like it was. "He's a reasonable man," she said. "Just say that it'll never happen again."

"Fuck that!" Nolan sat at the wheel of his car as Kimmie sat beside him in the bucket seat. "You think I got time to deal with some bullshit like that? It ain't worth it."

And with all the bravado of the cruel little man he was, Nolan told Kimmie, *We better cool it for a while; I need some space, man, ya dig?* Still Kimmie pleaded. "Just give me a chance to work this whole thing out." *Nah, I am not having some uppity-ass bitch think she can intimidate me, okay? I'm a man, and I'm gonna get my respect. Anyway, don't need no girl who lets her mama all up in her business.* Kimmie rambled on. "She's not going to bother us anymore. I told her I love you!"

Nolan opened the passenger door and waited. Kimmie cried. *What did I say?* he barked, teeth gritted. Kimmie bargained. "You're upset now. We'll talk later, okay?" *I'm about to get real upset if you don't get outa my motherfuckin' car.* Kimmie reached for Nolan, who pushed her out onto the curb, where she landed on her ass; the Karmann Ghia screeched off, its door flapping wildly as Kimmie looked around frantically to see if Mean Mr. Green was watching.

For days and days on end, she locked herself in her room, while I sat cross-legged in front of her door. When she came out to use the bathroom, she stepped over me, then asked, "Anybody call?" I'd shake my head no, and she'd return without a word to her room, shutting me out. Thanks to the one 45 she played over and over on my red record player, which she'd blithely taken from Mama's room, the on-the-nose soundtrack to Kimmie's lovesickness escaped nonstop from under her bedroom door: *Everybody plays the fool sometimes / use your heart just like a tool / listen baby it may be factual it may be cruel / but I ain't lying / everybody plays the fool.*

"Leave her be," Daddy said to me finally. "She got a broken heart and can't nobody mend it for her. Just leave her be."

140

eluctantly, I did leave Kimmie alone, through those hot, muggy days of August, when it rained. Steadily. Our clothes stuck to our backs, and wide-open windows brought no relief. The next-door neighbor's grass was now knee-high. Daddy and I spent wet afternoons at Mr. Alfred's body shop, watching him repair the front fender on Oldie, fix the muffler yet again. The weather made the inside of the garage smell more than ever like gasoline and tire rubber and Mr. Alfred's cigars. Puddles of water formed on top of the gravel outside the garage door, little globs of green sludge floating across them while raindrops hit like Ping-Pong balls against the tin roof, accenting the men's words as they chatted.

"So you staying put," said Mr. Alfred.

Daddy nodded. "For now."

"That's the best thing. No sense shelling out money for no good reason."

"You got that right. Seem like every month by the time I get my check, it's owed out."

"Well, I'm a tell you now, one ten a month was too much to be paying for a flat. Too much."

"Good area, though."

"Not for long. Now that all the white folks done left it."

Daddy chuckled. "You got a point there, Alfred."

He took center stage again in the house, making breakfast food every day for dinner, using the black-handled knives he'd had since his days of mess hall duty in the army. His home fries were the best.

I sat on a high stool in the corner, watching him slice potatoes as I listened to random, profane yells waft through the flung-open back door. I loved the way the sweet smell of laden blackberries picked by me from our yard managed to endure alongside that of the frying home fries. When Daddy chopped the fat yellow onions, he let the tears fall for a while, then wiped his eyes with the back of his hand, winked at me, grabbed another onion. Sitting there nibbling on blackberries, listening to the rain, I watched him with joy, thinking all Daddies cried when doing what they loved.

Mama was feeling good—dancing around to "Superstition," wearing her chic wig when she had nowhere to go, chatting on the kitchen phone with Johnnie Mae. She was ecstatic that Kimmie and Nolan had broken up, and it showed in her upturned mouth, her live-and-let-live wave of hand. One evening, the aromas of the kitchen pulled Mama out of the attic and to the breakfast nook, where Daddy and I sat eating. I was so excited to have them there, my parents sitting across from each other, that I almost ran to persuade Kimmie to forget her broken heart and come join us. Would it have changed things if I had? I've since wondered, if we'd all sat around the table family-style, would it have fortified us from the impending doom?

"You always did know how to make some good home fries, JD," said Mama.

"Well, you better eat 'em while they're hot," he said. "They taste like a bad memory once they get cold."

They had formed an implicit truce. Mama thought Daddy was leaving soon. Then she would leave with Cyril, and the house would be rented out like all her other houses—become a home for some other hopeful family. That was her plan. She didn't know Daddy had changed his. And Daddy wasn't supposed to know about hers. He was supposed to believe all the packed boxes were just innocent offshoots of her ubiquitous spring-cleaning.

And so the three of us munched on home fries that long-ago summer evening, and they were delicious, full of pepper and salt and saturated flavor. I remember it vividly, that meal—as it was the last time I felt simple, unencumbered pleasure.

S low down, Brown Eyes," said Daddy, the back of his head sinking into the headrest. "You and your heavy foot. I don't go for all that fast driving, and you know it. Leads to no good."

I eased off the gas pedal, ever so slightly, just enough to make the green light as we crossed Davison Avenue, then accelerated a little more, imperceptibly. My hands were sweating, causing the steering wheel to slide under my grip. I kept sneaking glances over at Daddy. The skin just below his eyes had darkened. I leaned forward, tightening my wet grip on the wheel, reciting a New Age mantra in my head: *Eyebrows up. Eyebrows up. Eyebrows up.* I'd read it on a bumper sticker, and it made sense the way catchy phrases sometimes do, sounding all the more prophetic for its brevity, its simple directive: *Think positive, don't frown, allow good.*

When we got to Dr. Corey's office, he was waiting for us just outside the door. One look at his friend of twenty-five years bent over, struggling to walk, and Dr. Corey whisked us past the crowded waiting room. Ilene said, "Hey, Mr. Dodson. Bad one today, huh?"

Daddy sighed. "Yeah." We each held an elbow, guiding him to the examining room. "This one's trying to do me in."

Dr. Corey touched Daddy's burning forehead. "You've got to get to the hospital, JD. I can look at you and tell your pressure is way up, probably near three hundred. Dangerously high this time, Buddy. Too high to be playing around . . ."

"Just need a pain shot, that's all," said Daddy. "I'm trying to preserve what I got for the trip."

"Trip?" Dr. Corey folded his arms across his chest. "Did you hear what I said? You need to be administered treatment intravenously, get that pressure down right away. I can't do that for you here."

"You send me to the hospital, I'm a suffer in there and you know it," said Daddy. "They don't give a damn about nobody in pain. Treat you like chopped-up pig's pussy, you ask me."

Dr. Corey chuckled softly. "Don't worry about that," he promised. "I'll leave very clear instructions to make sure you get your pain medicine."

"Hell, they not gonna listen to *you*." Daddy rose a bit, turning his contorted face to his friend. "You my private doctor. In the VA, I'll be given any doctor don't happen to be busy. And he sure as hell ain't gonna wanna hear about my *special needs*. So I'm a be a sick colored man in pain, going through withdrawal. That's what you sending me to, Vernon, and you know it."

Dr. Corey's hand trembled slightly as he placed it on top of Daddy's. "JD, listen to me. You could have a stroke at any moment . . ."

"That's every day of my life."

"Well, I'm sure as hell not going to let you have one in here!!"

"Just give me the goddamn shot!"

Dr. Corey sighed, walked over to the counter of clear-glass jars, opened one, and took out a cotton ball as he spoke. "I'm giving you just enough to ease things until we can get you to the hospital."

"I am still in my right mind, far as I can tell," said Daddy. "And unless I agree to go, can't nobody make me. My baby and I got to hit the road."

Suddenly, these plans I'd made to travel cross-country to New Mexico, try alternative-medicine treatments to cure Daddy's hypertension—ideas grabbed from *Let's Go USA* and *Back to Eden*—seemed

145

silly and presumptive to me. As if I could change the course of a relentless disease by simply changing its scenery. I felt irresponsible and scared, certain now that Daddy had pushed himself too hard and all for me. I had chosen to ignore the obvious.

Dr. Corey searched Daddy's arms for a working vein and saw all were collapsed, his skin covered in tracks—tracks that led nowhere in Daddy's never-ending quest to ease his chronic pain. He had revealed his addiction to painkillers when I was twelve, on a frigid night as we sat watching *Chico and the Man*. It was deep winter, and heat blasted from the room's radiator, making it hiss like a mean witch.

"Go over there and look under the TV for me and pull out a bag," he'd said. "Bring it to me."

"Under the TV?" I repeated. It made little sense to me, and this was a really funny part of the show.

"Go on. You'll see what I'm taking about."

I got up, walked to the TV, and got down on all fours, trying to see underneath.

"Just put your hand in there. You'll feel it."

I did, managing to pull out the small, crumpled paper bag. I held it out to him.

"Bring it here."

He took the bag from my hand, pulling out a little glass bottle of liquid, a syringe, and a rubber band. "Here, help me tie this band around my arm."

I grabbed the thick rubber with my small hands. "You want a double knot, right?" I knew how to tie this particular kind of knot because Terrance had taught me once, that summer back when my bike was still new.

"Tie it tight now. That's it. Now tie it again, but not too tight. . . . Good. Okay. Thatagirl." He dipped the syringe into the little bottle and filled it, made a fist with the hand of his tied arm, thumped his lower arm a few times with two fingers and inserted the needle, right in the crook of his arm, into the greenish, snakelike vein. I winced.

146

"Doesn't it hurt?" I asked as I squeezed my eyes shut, unable to bear the sight of my father in self-inflicted pain.

"Don't matter, 'cause I need it," he said, pulling the needle out as a trickle of blood appeared; he opened the side table drawer, took out a bottle of alcohol and a cotton ball, cleaned the needle. With another cotton ball, he wiped the blood off his arm. Then he returned all his works to the bag. "Here, put it back now," he whispered.

I replaced the crumbled paper bag under the TV, and Daddy and I returned to watching *Chico and the Man*. He was soon laughing with ease at funny Freddie Prinze. Through the years I became a believer in the power of the dark liquid in the little glass bottle. Shooting up kept Daddy going—groggy but alive—long after the pills prescribed by Dr. Corey had lost their magic.

Now his doctor examined those cross-stitched scars all over his buddy's arms, sighed heavily, then jabbed the needle into Daddy's neck. The violence was startling. Dr. Corey turned to me, this man who had given me my pierced ears and my first pap. "You're his daughter, Rae," he said. "Talk some sense into him."

I grabbed my father's hand. "Please. You've got to go," I begged. "For me?"

Daddy looked over at me, his small black eyes beautiful wet marbles. Then he turned to his friend. "You just had to bring my baby into this, didn't you?"

"I'll go call an ambulance," said Dr. Corey. He moved toward the door.

"Wait!" I said, little horses fleeing their gate in my chest. "I'll take him myself."

"You know Veteran's is all the way in Ann Arbor?"

"I know where it is," I said, still holding Daddy's bear hand in mine.

As he led us out, Dr. Corey whispered in my ear. "Get him there fast as you can, okay? Fast as you can."

---

pen this window," Daddy barked. I fumbled for the button on the driver's side. "Need me some air," he said, sweat beads trickling down his hairline. "It's so goddamn hot."

I slowed down a bit, my road rhythm broken. "You want to lie down in the back?" I tried to keep my voice from trembling or rising.

He shook his head, eyes closed. "I wanna go home, that's what I want." He sighed. "I've lived a good life."

"We're getting you to the hospital!" I yelled. Then, more controlled: "This is just a setback, that's all. You always pull through. Don't worry."

"I'm not the one worried," he said, quietly.

I focused on the green direction signs that guided me along the Ford Freeway.

"You know, I ain't never been hung up on getting old. Nothing to recommend it, you ask me. All that gray hair? Ugly as hell." He ran his free hand through his slick, black mane. "Done outlived everybody's expectation as it is." I looked at his smooth face, the stubble on his strong chin. Tiny flakes of silver dotted his mustache. He looked too young to die.

"Let's not talk about this, okay?" I begged. We whizzed by the gigantic Uniroyal tire poised against the highway, Motor City beacon to visitors, landmark of comfort to me. Yes, I was going the right way.

"And if I do have a stroke, I do not wanna live through it, that's for damn sure. Face all twisted, speech slurred, body paralyzed. That's worse than death, you ask me. Anything happen, they try to make me linger, you honor my wishes." The Demerol caused the words to bunch up in Daddy's mouth, like cotton. "You a big girl now, can take care of yourself."

"Stop it, please!" I begged, my foot pulling back off the gas pedal as I exited the freeway. Signs for the Veteran's Administration Hospital greeted us. I followed them intently, certain now more than ever that time wasted on a wrong choice could prove fatal.

148

As the summer of 1972 wound down and Labor Day approached, Mama came up with the idea of a Going Away party; deciding to serve barbecued ribs, baked beans, potato salad, and cole slaw. She called Cyril to get his recipe for the rib sauce and taped the ingredients to the refrigerator door: *Worcestershire sauce, hot sauce, small onion, bell pepper, cloves of garlic, brown sugar, vinegar, tomato sauce.*

"Come on," Mama said, standing in the doorway of Kimmie's room, trying to coax her away from her bed. "You know I can't plan this party without you."

"I don't feel like it," said Kimmie. "I'm sick."

I stood beside Mama, my fingers crossed for good luck. I wanted Kimmie out of that room too.

"It'll be fun," she offered. "Wasn't the last one fun?"

"That was a lifetime ago," said Kimmie.

"This one will be even better. Rhonda can come this time."

"I'm never speaking to that blabbermouth again."

Mama stepped into the room. "You've got it wrong, Sweetie. She's the best friend you could ever have."

"Please, Vy, could you close the door when you leave?"

Instead, Mama walked into Kimmie's room, shutting me out. On the other side of the door, I could hear our mother's muffled, desperate pleas.

Days later, Kimmie finally opened her bedroom door. I promptly entered her room, sat down beside her. The four o'clock Million Dollar Movie was on. We said nothing to each other, the television screen flickering before us. Every day of that week we watched the afternoon movie together—inevitably a fifties or sixties tearjerker. I saw Elizabeth Taylor prostitute herself in *This Property Is Condemned*, Shirley Booth plead with Anthony Quinn not to leave her in *Come Home Little Sheba*, and Susan Hayward fight with her daughter over a man in *Imitation of Life*. In each of those tragic, bigger-than-life actresses I saw Kimmie. Perhaps she did too, because when we watched Natalie Wood in her white hat and white dress leaving Warren Beatty and his new wife behind in *Splendor in the Grass*, Kimmie cried.

I'm not surprised. He's that type. I saw that right away," Mama said as she and Kimmie stood together in the kitchen, the automatic can opener humming under her words.

"I can't believe it. I thought . . ." Kimmie's voice trailed off.

"You thought he'd own up to his responsibility. Not all men are like your father, Kimmie." Mama tossed the empty cans into the trash bag, and they clanged as they knocked against one another.

"You think he just needs some time?" said Kimmie.

"Time is not going to make him do the right thing." Mama opened the refrigerator door. "A man will only be with you if he wants you. No other reason. Trust me."

"I hate . . . his guts."

"Well, I could say I told you so . . ."

"Don't."

Moments went by as Mama minced cloves of garlic, sound of the knife whacking against wood filling the silence.

"Vy, you have to help me do something."

Mama tossed the garlic into the sautéing vegetables. She poured the sauce into a ceramic mixing bowl, added sugar, and stirred, her fork making a *ting, ting, ting* sound as it hit against the sides.

"I can't help you, not if it's what I think it is."

"Why not?"

"I don't believe in that."

"It's legal now. I talked to a woman counselor at this place here, and she said they could arrange everything once they get your consent. Airfare to New York is about ninety dollars, and then I just need another hundred and twenty five for the—"

"Everything legal is not right." The vegetables sizzled. "All kinds of laws set up against Negroes didn't make them right."

Kimmie sighed. "It's what I want to do. Mommy, please."

"Even if I did agree to something like that, which I never would, your papa is planning to come get us in just a few days. There's no time."

"We could postpone things, until I get this taken care of."

"That is out of the question," said Mama.

"But I've got to do something."

"Have it."

"I'd rather kill myself."

"Stop talking like that."

"I swear I feel like sticking a hanger up inside of me."

"Stop, I said."

"I wish I could fall down some stairs and lose it."

"No, you don't. I've lost one before."

Kimmie looked over at her. "I remember."

Mama slid the garlic and onions and peppers into a big pot, pouring the sauce in behind. "It stays with you. Even when God takes it away, it hangs over you." She tapped a spoon against the side of the pot. "It was a boy, and I always wanted a boy."

Kimmie nodded. "I was waiting for my baby brother to arrive. Why didn't you explain to me what happened?"

151

"You were six years old. What could I explain?"

Kimmie was silent.

Mama stirred. "This situation you're in, it's not what you planned, I know, but that's how life is. You accept things as they are until you can make a change." She paused to taste the sauce. "It'll be easier in Louisiana. There are plenty of old aunties around who could watch it for you while you finish school. It's not such a big deal down South like it is here. We'll just be a bigger family."

The pungent, sweet smell of the barbecue sauce drifted out of the kitchen, greeting me in the hall, where I was eavesdropping. "When I had you, it gave me something to live for!" I heard Mama say. "There you were, so pretty with your good hair and light skin and Cyril's ever-changing eyes."

I touched my bushy braids, pressed my fingertips into the lids of my brown eyes. Saw nothing but darkness.

Kimmie laughed a mean little laugh. "Yeah, a pretty little girl who had to slip and see her father behind his wife's back for the first five years of her life, and then not see him at all for the next seven."

Mama threw the spoon onto the stove. It landed with a thud. "That was a nasty thing to say."

"All I'm *trying* to say is I don't want that to happen to my daughter. I want to be married when I have children."

"I guess you should've thought about that before you did what you did."

"It's no more than you did when you were my age."

"I was *not* your age, Missy. I was older. In college. And at least I had the courage to live up to my mistake. Luckily for you."

A few seconds passed. "I'll get it done," said Kimmie, finally. "Even if I can't do it here, I'll find a way down there. There are old women who live behind the French Quarter, you know, who'll gladly do it."

"And you might die in the process," said Mama.

"Then that's something *you'll* have to live with, isn't it?" Kimmie stalked out of the kitchen, through the dining room. I chose the next moment to enter, through the hallway.

"Oooh!" said Mama, startled by my presence. "Lord, child, don't tell me those big ears have been spying on us again?"

"Is Kimmie going to have a baby?"

"It's not good to listen in on things you're too young to understand." She spooned out a little sauce, blew on it, pointed the spoon at me. "Here, taste this, tell me what you think."

It was yummy. Sweet, garlicky, a little spicy. "It's okay," I said, unmoving in the middle of the kitchen floor. "Is she?"

"That is nothing for a girl your age to be asking," said Mama. "And nothing for me to be telling you. That's Kimmie's business, isn't it?"

I supposed she was right and, feeling yet another shift about to occur in our household, left Mama alone in the kitchen standing over her cast-iron pot, stirring the barbecue sauce with her big wooden spoon. I moved toward the den, suddenly eager to play a game of gin rummy with Daddy, hold the spreads in my hand till I called "Gin!" and could hear him say, "You something else, Brown Eyes. You know that? You something else."

On the first day of relief from the rain, I finally let Terrance Golightly give me a ride on the handlebars of his three-speed.

"Dang, it's about time, Rae of Sun," he said. "I thought you were gonna be a scaredy-cat forever!"

"Just shut up and make sure you watch where you're going." The perfect size for his handlebars, I leaned back against his narrow chest as we took off.

I close my eyes, and we are moving faster and faster, flying romantically through the streets, our cheeks touching, my hands gripping metal, when I forget to keep my legs out to the side and my toe gets caught in the spokes of the front wheel. I feel a bone break, feel my ankle twist as the tires turn around and around. Suddenly, I am screaming hysterically, gobs of blood sprouting from my left foot. Terrance is dragging me to a grassy lawn, yelling for help, dragging me under my armpits, calling for help, when out of nowhere, Daddy appears. He gathers me into his strong arms away from Terrance and runs down the street to his car—panting, yet determined and elegant, like a cartoon hero in slow motion. Blood drips onto the floor mats of Oldie as he drives recklessly. At the hospital, the pain throbs as Daddy looms over me, my small hand held tightly by his rough, huge ones. I can feel the knife cuts along the meaty part of his palm. "You scared me, Rae Rae," he says, looking as though he's been chopping onions all day.

W hen he carried me up the walkway and through the front door—my foot in an ankle cast—both Mama and Kimmie were waiting for me.

Mama held her hand out to me. "You have to use better judgment," she said. "Boys never ride their bikes safely."

"The important thing is that she's okay," said Daddy.

"I got her," said Kimmie, who put my arm around her shoulders and directed me to lean on her as she headed to the porch. "I'm going to make you some lemonade," she said, dashing back into the kitchen and leaving me outside, where a ladybug landed on my knee.

My broken toe brought Kimmie back to me. And I believed that this would change things, slow them down alongside my own limping efforts to get around. It seemed to me it was the one surefire guarantee of love and connectedness—physical debilitation of one sort or another. The pain was worth it.

From that moment forward, Kimmie threw herself into the business of nursing me, which must have been right on time, as it gave her a focus in those waning days before Cyril arrived, with her maternal instincts bursting through, hormones overwhelming her. She promised to take me to see a Michael Jackson concert. And to the new movie based on his hit song, "Ben." "Soon as your cast is removed, we'll go," she said.

Best of all, Kimmie let me spend quality time in her room, no longer vigorously guarding it as her private fortress. Besides all the clothes and posters and the dog-eared copy of *Jonathan Livingston Seagull* at her bedside, there was her altar, built atop a low shelf. On it sat tall, ever-burning white candles, incense, colorful Mardi Gras

155

beads, photographs, glass bowls of sand and shells and stones, a mini-statue of a saint. "It's my offering to the gods," she told me. Sitting in the middle of the altar was a black-and-white photograph of Mama. In it, she was descending a staircase dressed in a dark evening gown, her hair pulled up, long elegant white gloves covering her arms. Her hand was extended toward a man in a suit waiting for her at the foot of the stairs. The photo caught him looking up at her lovingly. I was riveted by this glimpse of Mama's life when she was young and maybe even free.

"Who's that?" I asked, pointing to the man, even though I recognized the face.

"That's Papa," said Kimmie. "Back before I was born." She picked up the picture, touched it gingerly with one finger.

"They were in love?" I asked, envying Kimmie for memories she had of her parents together when I had none. Kimmie even remembered when *my* parents had gotten married; she'd told me the wedding took place downstairs in the living room, and that Mama wore an off-white short lace dress, à la Jackie Kennedy.

Kimmie studied the picture, smiled. "Papa says I was made from love." She sighed, put the photograph back on her altar. "But love is complicated."

It had turned out to be for her. Here she sat with two possible futures—returning to Louisiana and the risky visit to a back-alley auntie, or having a baby and the life of a teenage mom, thwarting her plans for Albuquerque. She couldn't have liked either option and that must have been a terrible feeling to have at seventeen—that both your roads lead to a dead end.

"Will you read my cards?" I asked, sensing her wistfulness and not wanting her to think about Nolan. "Since we never got to finish that first time?"

"Okay, but just one question tonight." Kimmie got her tarot cards from a drawer, and together we sat cross-legged on the floor. She

156

shuffled, held them in the palm of her hand as she sat quietly for several seconds, grounding herself, becoming one with the cards' energy. "Ready?" she asked as she held the deck out for me.

"I'm ready," I said, cutting the cards, then squeezing my hand closed as though the answer was inside for safekeeping. "Can I keep the question to myself?" I asked.

"Sure." Kimmie made a pile of cards, turned faceup. When an ace appeared, she stopped, made another pile, counting out thirteen cards. Then she made a third pile and again stopped once she got to an ace. "Ooh, the ace of cups and the ace of wands," she whispered. "Those are good cards. Cups hold your strongest desires, and wands provide the force to make them real. So the answer to your question is definitely a yes."

I was pleased with the tarot. I'd asked the cards if I'd ever see Kimmie again after she and Mama left.

"Can I do you now?" I asked, grabbing at the deck.

"You don't know how to read the cards."

That was true. "Can't you do it on yourself then, while I watch?"

"Well, I guess I could." She reshuffled the cards, eyes closed, and I felt I could see her forming the question in her mind. Suddenly, her eyes popped open, and she made three new piles. "Oh, shucks," she said as she turned over the last card. "Wow."

"What?" I looked at the cards, tried to make sense of what lay before me, but of course I couldn't. I saw three colorful figures, no more. "What is it?" I asked. "Is it about the baby?"

Kimmie put her hand to her mouth. "You know?"

I nodded.

"And you didn't tell Daddy Joe, did you?"

I shook my head.

" 'Cause I wouldn't feel right about him knowing."

"It's our little secret," I said.

She smiled with gratitude, pointed to the card in the middle. It had

157

an ominous image of a man dressed in a black robe, brandishing a scythe. "This is a powerful card," she said. "It overshadows the other ones."

"What's it mean?"

She never called it the Death card. "It means that one phase of my life is ending and another is beginning."

"Is that a good thing?"

Kimmie thought for a moment. "Yes, I think so," she said. "You have to let some parts of you die away, so other parts of you can live."

The morning of the Going Away party, Kimmie announced that she and Rhonda planned to watch the Labor Day fireworks along the waterfront at Metro Beach. Mama was not happy.

"I thought you weren't speaking to Rhonda," she said.

"We made up."

"How are you going to go out when I'm having a party for us?"

Mama and I were sitting at the kitchen table as I helped her make her shopping list. Kimmie rummaged through the refrigerator, looking for a snack. She finally settled on an apple.

"It's not our party, it's yours," she said, taking a huge bite. "Those certainly aren't my friends who're coming."

"Well, Rhonda is welcome to come."

"To tell you the truth Vy, she's not interested."

"Have you asked her?"

Kimmie took another bite, looked at Mama as she chewed. "Trust me," she finally said, her mouth full, apple juice dripping down her chin.

"Well, I know one thing." Mama pointed her ballpoint pen at Kimmie. "You'd better be back here at a decent hour."

"We will. The fireworks are over elevenish, so we'll be home by twelve."

"Twelve? I need you back earlier than that!"

"What for?" Kimmie held the apple midair. "Your friends will still be here, drinking and playing bid whist and carrying on, so what's the big deal?"

"Well, for one, Metro Beach is mostly white folks, and you just never know what could happen."

"What could happen?"

Mama grabbed a cigarette from the pack on the table. "I have a bad feeling about you being out like that on a holiday. You don't know how these fools in Detroit get. They start shooting off their guns and driving drunk and—"

"Vy, please. We'll be fine. God, you act like there's a bogeyman on every corner of this city."

"I feel like there is, to tell you the truth."

Kimmie sighed. "We'll be back home by eleven."

"You can't get home sooner? Fireworks out there in the suburbs are not gonna go past nine or nine-thirty."

"We'll be home by eleven, okay?"

Mama shook her head. "I hope this isn't part of some little plot of yours to mess up things, because if it is, I'm telling you now it won't work."

Kimmie shrugged. "Rhonda and I just want to hang out one more time before I leave. You're the one who said she was the best friend I ever had." Kimmie studied Mama's face. "Maybe you need a nerve pill, Vy. You're really hyper this morning." She tossed her apple into the trash can and sashayed from the room.

Mama sat there, her face slack. As she turned to me, I noticed the puffiness around her eyes. "Rae, run upstairs for me and get my pills out of the—" She stopped herself. "You can't run anywhere with that foot, can you?" The cast was coming off later that day. I couldn't wait because it had been itching unmercifully for the last two weeks.

"I can get upstairs easily, Mama." I had mastered a one-leg hop.

160

She shook her head. "Forget it. Forget I even said a word." She lit the cigarette she'd been holding, the flame from the lighter causing the slightest twinkle in her brown eyes.

I didn't know whether or not to believe Kimmie either. The night before, she'd walked into my room as I pulled out the money Daddy had given me to hold. I was thinking I should give it back to him, now that we weren't leaving.

"What's that?" she asked.

I told her.

"Is Daddy Joe expecting it back?"

"I think so."

"Do you mind if I borrow it?" Kimmie reached for the money. "I promise I'll pay you back right away. As soon as I get back to Louisiana, I'll send it to you. I have my own bank account."

"But, what if Daddy asks for it?" I said, feeling like this was definitely wrong, not quite sure how or why.

"Just tell him you can't find it, and before you know it, I'll be sending it back to you."

"What are you going to do with it?" I asked.

Kimmie smiled. "Start over, like the cards predicted."

I gave her the money, regretting it immediately.

"Remember," she said as she put her fingers to her lips. I watched as she folded the crisp one-hundred-dollar bills into small squares, sticking them one after the other into her hippie bra.

Kimmie was right about the party. It was still going strong by eleven o'clock that night. Everyone drank and talked and ate as Mama played a new favorite song, the soundtrack for her own drama, on the hi-fi record player. *Me and Mrs. Jones*. Cards flew across the folding table. Mama devoured her whiskey sour in big sips. *We got a thing going on*. I was hostess, Daddy stayed in the den, and Ernesto again sat

161

alone on the couch. *We both know that it's wrong but it's much too strong to let it go now.* Paper plates of half-eaten barbecue and baked beans and potato salad sat abandoned around the room. *We got to be extra careful that we don't build our hopes up too highhh . . .*

Lyla and Mama were card partners this time, playing against Johnnie Mae and Romey. Mama and Lyla were winning—they had the most books in front of them—but this seemed to be a critical juncture in the game because everyone was holding on to their last two cards, waiting. *You go to your place, I'll go to mine. . . . tomorrow, we'll meet same place same time.*

"I believe you women are about to be set," said Romey. "The moment of reckoning has arrived after all that wanton tossing away of trumps."

Johnnie Mae laughed. "Uh huh, 'cause I know what I ain't seen played yet, and if it ain't been played by now then I know who ain't got it."

"Shhhh, we are trying to concentrate here," said Lyla.

"Well, how long you need? It's on you," said Johnnie Mae. "Just play your hand, Honey. That's all you can do. You can't make something be there that ain't there."

Lyla played a card, a king of spades, and Mama moaned. "Damn, wrong suit, Lyla. Wrong suit."

Romey slammed a joker on top of Lyla's king, and everyone tossed their remaining cards into the center of the table.

"Well, that's that," said Mama. "We almost got 'em."

Lyla let go of her breath. "Yeah. . . ." *Meeeeee aaaaaand Mrs. Mrs. Jones, Mrs. Jones Mrs. Jones Mrs. Jonesssss.* The song ended in a crescendo.

Romey stood and shook Johnnie Mae's hand. She had on even more rings than before. "Well done, Madame, well done."

"Oh, sit your sweet ass down. I done told you I been playing this game since before you could wear long pants. You gon' believe me one of these days."

"Hey!" said Lyla. "We need Kimmie here to liven up the music. Play some more of her Funkadelic. I'm sorry, Vy, but I can't take no more of that Billy Paul. Song is *depressing* after a while. Whew." She gulped her drink.

"Amen," said Romey. "I miss your daughter's musical selections too."

At the last party, Kimmie had pulled the Funkadelic album out of its cover with flourish, each of us stunned by the picture of a woman's head sporting a huge Afro rising out of the ground, mouth open in a silent scream. She slipped the record onto the turntable, and suddenly we heard acoustic guitar strumming against heavy bass beats. Kimmie sang the first words of "Can You Get to That" as she threw her elbows out to the side, snapped her fingers. She sang in a melodic, mellow voice. And then she eased into a slow dance, winding her hips around as though there was a Hula Hoop we couldn't see. "This is how we do it down the way," she said.

"Well, all right *now!*" yelled Romey.

"That dance is a little *matoor* for you, don't you think?" said Johnnie Mae. She looked Kimmie up and down. "And that skirt is mighty short, mighty see-through."

Kimmie kept dancing.

"You just old-fashioned, Johnnie Mae," said Lyla. "Kimmie's outfit is *too* sharp!"

"Seem like something those fast girls up on Woodward Avenue be wearing, you ask me," hissed Johnnie Mae.

"Leave her alone," said Mama. "Kimmie's outfit is just fine."

"Maybe you just need another drink, Miss Johnnie," said Kimmie.

Johnnie Mae looked over at Kimmie, rolled her eyes a little. "Well, I just wanna know who's the mama here?"

"What's that supposed to mean?" said Mama. Johnnie Mae had known not to respond.

But this moment was different. "Where is that gal?" she asked. "Ain't she supposed to be leaving first thing in the morning?"

Mama nodded. "Her papa's on the road now. He should be getting

163

in around nine a.m. or so. We'll be there by this time tomorrow night."

"Chile, can't nobody get me back down to Louisiana," said Johnnie Mae. "Too many goddamn snakes in them bayous for me!"

"The bayou is beautiful," said Mama. "Especially at dawn."

"I don't need to be near no swamps, myself," continued Johnnie Mae. "I always wanted to live somewhere with pretty sunrises and beaches and wide, open spaces. Even as a little girl in Alabama, before I knew such a place existed, I wanted that. Somewhere I could just stretch out. That's why I'm gonna go on ahead and move to L.A. come the first of the year. Shit, what I got to keep me here?" Johnnie Mae sighed, sipped her bourbon. "I'm telling you, things just seem to go right when I'm in California."

"I know what you mean," said Mama. "I feel that way about Louisiana." She looked up at the huge clock hanging like art in the middle of our living room wall—it was just after eleven o'clock—then took a big sip of her whiskey sour. "It's where I belong. Not *here*."

"*Here* is your home," said Romey.

"So what?" said Lyla. "A woman's got to go where her heart feels welcome." She nodded slowly, turned down her mouth. "Wherever that is, you just got to go. That's what I believe."

"There are many places your heart may feel welcome in this country but *you* won't be," said Romey. "About ninety-five percent of it, to be exact."

"You just an old stuck-in-the-mud," said Lyla. "Don't like no kinda change whatsoever, do you?"

"I believe the term is *stick-in-the-mud*, and I like change just fine, thank you. That's my point. Enough hasn't changed around here for me to be venturing to little hamlets and villages in west Podunk, thinking my neighbors are going to call out the welcoming committee."

"Well, now, that depends, don't it?" said Johnnie Mae.

"On what?" asked Romey.

"On whether you show up with Ernesto on your arm, or you slip his fairy ass in through the back door."

Laughter filled the room as Ernesto smiled from the couch. Even Romey chuckled lightly, relaxing the air. "You are a mess, Madame," said Ernesto. "A total mess."

After one final round of bid whist they threw their cards into the center of the table, and Romey gathered them all, returned them to their little cardboard box. Ice melted in drinks, and Mama glanced repeatedly at the wall clock, peeping out the front window whenever a car rumbled down our block. I noticed too that she was smoking her cigarettes for a couple puffs and then squishing them out—long stubs tipped with bloody lipstick lying abandoned in the ashtray.

"It's getting late, Vy, Honey," said Johnnie Mae. "We was trying to wait to say bye-bye to Kimmie, but I for one am feeling a little lowly right about now."

"Ernesto and I can wait here with you, Baby, till she gets back," offered Romey.

Mama nodded. "I don't know where she is. That girl . . . I've tried to tell her how dangerous this city is at night, but she doesn't take me seriously. I can't wait for her to be out of here. It's no place for a teenager, really."

"She's all right, just defying your wishes." Johnnie Mae patted Mama's hand. "That's how young folks are, never listening to you, thinking they know way more than you do even though you the one done lived the longest." Johnnie Mae sat back in her seat. "And this ain't her first time doing this. You remember how she ran off once before. A few years back."

"What are you trying to say, Johnnie Mae?" Mama snapped. "That she ran away again?"

"No, Honey. I'm just saying she's a wild spirit. We all know that about her. The truth is the truth."

"Don't worry, Vy, she's just out having fun," said Lyla. "Shoot, I *hate* to come home whenever I'm out in the street with my friends."

"Yeah, well, that's because you-know-who is at home, waiting for your ass," said Johnnie Mae.

Romey chuckled. "Really, Lyla, isn't it time for you to leave *you-know-who?*"

"I can't. And you know why," snapped Lyla.

"Why?" Romey looked over the top of his eyeglasses at Lyla. "You said yourself that the factory pays you quite well. 'Making money hand over fist' is how you expressed it. Surely you're not staying around for somebody to pay the MichCon bill every month? You're worth a bit more than that, I suspect." Romey paused. "Certainly on your good days."

"Not that it's any of your business, but there are things that keep you around that have nothing to do with money!" said Lyla.

"What? Love? Loyalty?" Romey looked over at me as I picked up empty paper plates; then he turned back to Lyla, called himself whispering, "Or are we talking about *you-know-what?*"

"I'm talking about *things!*"

"Get outta her business, Romey," said Johnnie Mae as she rummaged through her purse. I tossed the paper plates into a big trash bag in the corner, perched myself on the steps.

Romey shrugged his shoulders in exaggerated befuddlement. "I'm just trying to understand why it is she feels she can't leave. He drinks like a fish. He's flagrantly jealous. The poor girl never wants to go home . . ."

"I'm planning to leave him, okay?" Lyla seemed not so young to me now, the way her blond wig sat too high on her head and her lipstick had all but disappeared, eye shadow creased. "You can't just pick up and go. You got to plan things out right."

"That's true," said Mama. "Planning is key."

"Now where the hell are my pills?" Johnnie Mae had dumped the contents of her purse onto the card table, revealing Kleenex, a crumbling red rubber makeup sponge, a stuffed wallet, and lots of little scraps of paper, ink pens, pennies.

"The inside of your purse looks like mine," said Lyla. "I thought

166

you'd have expensive-looking little gold things down in there or something like that."

"Hush up!" said Johnnie Mae. "I'm looking for my pills."

"You got a headache?" asked Mama.

"I got me a couple pains. Arthur is showing his ass loud and clear tonight."

"Arthur?" said Lyla.

"My arthritis, Honey." Johnnie Mae looked over at Mama, anxious. "You got anything I can take? Just a piece of something would help."

Mama nodded. "I'll be back." She stood and headed upstairs to her room. I moved out of her way as she passed me on the landing.

"Why is it that everyone feels compelled to take a pill at the first sign of a little pain?" said Romey. "Really, don't you think that's not so good?"

"Negro, please. I'm not gonna be in no pain if there's a pill out there that can stop it. Not as long as I got me some money." Johnnie Mae grabbed the crumbling sponge, looked into the tiny oval mirror of her compact, patted at her shiny skin. "I learned that from all those wealthy white folks living in the canyons in L.A. You know what they taught me? Taught me that suffering is easier if you rich." She powdered her broad nose. "Hell, even dying is easier when you got yourself some money."

Mama returned, handed two pills to Johnnie Mae.

"You sure you can spare both of 'em?"

"I don't need them anymore."

Johnnie Mae nodded, took the pills with her bourbon, draining her glass. "Wet this for me again, will you, Lyla Honey?"

"I wish she'd get here," said Mama.

I pulled the curtain back from the window on the landing, where I had a view of the side street. I crossed my fingers, hoping for Rhonda's car to pass, trying not to think about those one-hundred-dollar bills.

"So much is going on out there these days," added Mama, more to

167

herself than anybody in particular. The clock said five to twelve. Just the week before, a little girl had been kidnapped and murdered. And the week before that, STRESS (Stop The Robbers, Enjoy Safe Streets) police officers had killed a boy they thought was breaking into his own house.

"You take those every day?" Lyla handed Johnnie Mae a fresh bourbon and Coke on ice.

"I take *something* every day that I'm in pain."

"I'm kinda scared of that stuff lately," said Lyla. "Last Friday, my girlfriend Lucretia lost her baby brother to dope. He was only sixteen. He OD'd."

"That was from heroin, Lyla. Not pills. And look who's talking. I wanna see you go a week without your precious speed. What do you call them little capsules? Black Beauties . . ."

"Those are diet pills!"

"Since when you able to buy diet pills off the street?"

"Well, that's what I use 'em for."

"Uh huh."

"Should I call the police?" asked Mama.

"You don't have to believe me," said Lyla, her voice a pout.

"Should I call?" Mama asked again.

Suddenly, the den door swung open, and I saw him first from my spot on the landing as Daddy stepped out into the living room. Everyone turned to stare at him. His hair was slicked down and wavy, and he was wearing a crisp, white shirt rolled up at the sleeves, had on his good trousers, bare feet. I was excited and nervous. I wanted him to shine before Mama's friends, and yet I worried that his timing was off.

"How's everybody doing?" he said as he leaned across the den's doorway, his arm stretched out to support himself.

"Why we are doing just fine, JD!" said Johnnie Mae. "Ain't seen you in a many, many month of Sundays!"

"Yeah, has been a while," said Daddy. "I see life been treating you all right."

"Oh, fair to middling," said Johnnie Mae.

168

"From what I hear, you doing better than that Johnnie Mae. Hell of a lot better."

"I get by."

"Look to me like you've lost some weight," he said.

"You think so?" asked Johnnie Mae.

"Your eyebrows look thinner."

Everyone laughed. Even Mama smiled a little. Daddy chuckled ever so softly and made his way around, nodding a hello to Romey and Ernesto. "You two still make a cute couple." He turned to Lyla. "See you looking good enough to drive that husband of yours crazy."

Lyla blushed a little. "You ought to quit, JD," she said, flattered.

It was a scene from the past, from the days when Daddy and Mama were new and he took her to these card parties regularly, holding court as he kept folks in stitches, kept his cool.

"Well y'all excuse me, I'm just passing through." He made his way across the living room toward the powder room in the hall. Romey swished the ice in his glass. I could hear my own breathing.

"I'm calling the police." Mama stood, headed for the red princess telephone sitting on its marble stand in the hallway. I jumped up and stood beside her as she dialed.

"Now, Honey, don't do that. Not just yet," said Johnnie Mae.

"Kimmie probably just let the time get away from her," said Lyla.

"It's late," said Romey. "She *should* be worried."

"Think we ought to go out and look for her?" asked Ernesto-on-the-couch. Romey shook his head no, and Ernesto sat back, silent again.

"Yes, operator, get me the police, please." She paused. I put my hand to my pounding chest, to muffle the sound. "I want to report a missing person. My daughter. Well, she should have been home an hour ago and . . . Are you sure?"

Daddy walked back through the room, heading for the den. "Daddy!" I called out. He turned, looked my way.

"You ready to go to bed, Brown Eyes?"

I shook my head no, but Mama's voice filled the space before I could find the words to answer him. "Twenty-four hours? But if something has happened to her, by that time it might be too late!!"

"Who's she talking to?" asked Daddy, his voice carrying across the room. I moved in closer, stood beside the card table.

"JD, Kimmie's not home yet," said Johnnie Mae. "And Vy here is a nervous wreck."

"Where'd she go?" asked Daddy.

Mama slammed down the phone. "Out with Rhonda."

"She say where they were going?"

"To Metro Beach. She promised she'd be back by eleven." Mama squeezed her hands. "I feel like something's wrong."

Daddy rubbed his chin. "Let me put my shoes on. I'll see if I can find her. Maybe they broke down on the highway or something. You can spot that light blue car a mile away." When he said this, I wanted to crawl into his lap and confess about the money.

"I'll go with you," said Mama, heading upstairs. "Let me get my pocketbook."

"I'm going too!" I yelled out. Johnnie Mae leaned across the card table, caught my arm. "C'mere," she said, pulling my ear to her lips. "The best place for you is bed. It's late," she whispered, her bourbon breath hot on my neck.

I wiggled out of her grip. "I'm not sleepy!"

Romey stood. "It *is* late. And we should all leave, let these dear people deal with their crisis in private."

Lyla and Johnnie Mae and Ernesto stood, Daddy came out from the den with his shoes on, keys in hand, Mama ran back down the stairs with her purse, and I walked into the vestibule just as the front door swung open.

"Hey, Rae Rae," said Kimmie, nearly bumping into me as she checked herself in the closet door mirror. She then casually stepped into the living room, all eyes on her. As she passed by me, I breathed in heavy musk oil and beneath it the sick-sweet smell of marijuana.

170   I uncrossed my fingers.

L isten, Rae." Daddy's eyes were barely open, dark rings underneath like shadows. "I have another daughter," he said as we glided over speed bumps, now winding our way through the hospital grounds. The car eased along, its shock absorbers performing beautifully over the bumps, but I didn't understand my father's words, as if he was speaking Pig Latin and I was too slow to decipher. "She's a little bit older than you. Not quite two years," he added. "Your mama knew."

"My mama knew what?" I asked, furious that he felt compelled to tell me a secret, *now*. I wanted him to keep quiet, to preserve his energy, to breathe.

"About my other daughter," he said before making a weird sound in his throat. "You met her. You probably don't remember. I tried at first, you know, to . . . but Vy wouldn't have stood for it and I . . ." His voice petered out, he sighed, touched my hand with his. "Anything happen to me, you get in touch with her mother, okay? I got her number right here."

I nodded, stunned as Daddy carefully pulled a little piece of paper out of his wallet, right behind the old picture of me and Josie. I peeked a glance before his wallet eased back into his hip pocket, and there we were, young yet faded, the Polaroid Instamatic crackling at its folds, emulsion growing thin. One day the image, I realized, would disappear. Heat filled my face and burned across my cheeks as Daddy handed me the number and I took it into my unsteady hand.

I slipped the paper into the visor overhead, gripped the steering wheel with both hands, the way Daddy always did when creeping through a Michigan snowstorm. I remembered her. She knew who I was.

"And you ought to know this too, 'cause you're not a child no more." He looked at me, his face a double-dare. "I loved her mother. It wasn't some little something that just happened. I loved her. Almost chose to live my life with her too. Got real close a few times. Hell, you young and fool around, fall in love like that, you get all kinda courage. But came a point, I knew I couldn't go nowhere without you." He gazed straight ahead. "Ain't no man-woman love that strong."

I looked at him from out the corner of my eye, watched him lick dry lips, swallow—fearing what he'd say next.

"I did think about taking you with me," he said quietly, perhaps as an afterthought. "I really dwelled on that one." His face was shiny, distant. "But I figured that wasn't right, snatching a young girl away from her none-too-steady mama, running off, causing a bunch of commotion. . . . And when I was finally about to take you with me, when Vy seemed like she could handle it, well, you know what happened."

I did know. I realized I had been secretly yearning for Daddy's other woman, her soft bosom against my cheek. "I wish you'd taken me away," I said, wistful.

"What's done is done."

"Mama left me anyway," I pointed out.

"She did what she had to do."

"Did she?" I whispered, nine years old again and wounded anew.

A minute or two passed in silence as I slowly drove up to the hospital's emergency room entrance, parked near an ambulance, cut off the motor, turned to him. "We're here, Daddy."

He squinted, looking past me, breaking my heart. "I have my days when I wish things," he said. "Wish maybe if her and that man she married don't make it, if he don't treat her right, she'll come back to me in the end. He's the one got her, but I'm the one she wanted." He turned, reached for the door.

"What's her name?" I asked.

He paused, turned slowly back to me. "Selena." He said it with such love, I bit my lip.

"And her daughter . . . my sister. Her name is Josie."

His eyes lit up. "You remember? How 'bout that." He paused. "She was named after me."

"She knows who you are?"

Daddy shrugged. "She should. I was in her life from the time she was born until she was eight years old. I used to set her on my lap, give her little gifts, read stories to her. I taught her how to write her name, how to count to ten, say her ABCs. She called me Da Da." He paused. "I told Selena, 'Children remember. They deserve to know the truth.' But then her mama said it wasn't such a good idea, told me to stop coming around, so I did. Except for that once, when you met her. She's a young woman now, like you. Probably wouldn't recognize me if her life depended on it." He closed his eyes, leaned back. Tears slid down his cheeks. As I watched my father cry, I thought about Josie, with her magical string game and scary Barbie dolls and sad radio song.

An aide approached with a wheelchair. He tried to help Daddy into the chair, but Daddy wouldn't let him. "I can still walk, damn it," he snapped, his voice surprisingly strong. The aide nodded, grabbed underneath his armpits, and pulled Daddy up out of the Cutlass. Out of nowhere, a guard appeared at my window.

"You're going to have to move that car, Miss," he said. "Parking lot's right over there." He pointed west.

"Give me a moment," I told him. "Can't you see my father is sick!?"

"Miss, we have special emergency-room parking right over there, but you can't leave that car here . . ."

"I have to wait for him to get out first!" I yelled, thinking this man a moron.

173

Daddy leaned into the aide for support. "We got this covered, Brown Eyes. You go park the car. I'll be waiting for you."

"Okay," I said, exhausted. The guard, triumphant, disappeared. But I didn't move, just sat there in the driver's seat of Daddy's brand-new navy blue car and watched the back of his beautiful head as he lumbered his way through the automatic doors, away from me and into the bowels of the hospital for vets.

Passing

As a driver you have at least two blind spots (which) you cannot get rid of . . . but you can make them smaller by properly adjusting your mirrors. . . . If you and an approaching vehicle move into the center lane simultaneously, a serious crash could occur.

WHAT EVERY DRIVER MUST KNOW

That night before they left, I slept with Kimmie. Because it was her last night in Detroit, because I already missed her, I was grateful that I got to snuggle next to her warm body in bed. Daddy didn't mind. "I'll be right here when tomorrow comes," he said. "Go on and be with your sister."

We lay side by side in silence. I studied the way Kimmie's black light made her zodiac poster seem to lift away from the wall, how it added snowflakes to her eyelashes and an X-ray glow to my own hand.

"Want to play a game?" Kimmie asked, her teeth shining.

"Sure."

"I used to play this with Rhonda when we were your age and she'd have these pajama parties." She rolled onto her side. "Turn over," she ordered. "Face the wall." I did so as she lifted the top of my cotton pajamas. "Now tell me what this word is," she said as she wrote on my back with her fingertip. "Some letters are really easy, and others are hard to figure out," she explained. "You have to concentrate." Her finger moved firmly across my skin as she spelled out the letters *N-i-g-h-t*.

I spoke the word into the Day-Glo darkness: "Night!"

"Oh, I made it too easy," said Kimmie, lifting her nightgown and turning her back to me. "Now it's your turn."

I hesitated.

"What's wrong?" she asked.

"I'm thinking. I don't want it to be too easy."

"Well, hurry up, Rae Rae, before I fall asleep," she said.

I wrote *G* with deliberation, and then two swift *O*s, a *D*, a *B*, and before I could finish the *Y*, Kimmie whispered, "Good-bye." She turned over, kissed my forehead. "One more, okay?"

I nodded, turning my back to her. She wrote *H*, and then *O*, an *M* that tickled, and another letter I couldn't quite make out. Something about the way she formed it had me stumped. "Spell it again," I said. She did. "Is that last letter an *F* or an *L*?" I tried.

"No, silly rabbit, it's an *E. H-O-M-E*," she said. "There's no place like home." Kimmie clicked off her black light, tossing the room into near darkness except for the streetlights' soft haze outside her window. "Now let's try to get some sleep. Tomorrow's a big day."

Game over, we lay on our backs, heads sinking into the pillows, Kimmie with her hands behind her head. Tree shadows crawled with luscious slowness across the ceiling.

"Where's your home?" I asked. "Here or Louisiana?"

"Here," said Kimmie, with no hesitation.

"But if you've lived in two places, how do you know which one is home? The place you lived the longest?"

"No, the place where you're from." She thought for a moment. "Besides, nearly all of the people I love are here."

She brought her arms down to her side. I grabbed Kimmie's hand atop the tie-dyed sheet.

"Including Rhonda," she added.

"Even though she's a tattletale?"

Kimmie laughed. "Yep. Even with her tattletale self. She saved my butt tonight."

"How?"

"Kept me from running away again."

"But you're leaving anyway!"

178

"Yeah, but I was going somewhere else, Rae Rae. Somewhere new. Till Rhonda convinced me not to."

At that moment, Kimmie reminded me of a beloved glittery goldfish in Miss Miller's second-grade class. I was responsible for feeding it; sometimes I'd watch it throughout recess, my nose pressed to the fish tank glass. When no one was around once, I reached in to grab it. I touched it too, but it slipped out of my grasp, too fast and slippery to be caught.

"If this is home, why do you have to go back to Louisiana at all?" I asked, pushing the question into the darkness.

"Because I have to give this baby back to God."

"Why can't you give it back right here?"

"Because they're closer to God down South than they are up North."

"They are?" I still had my child's understanding of God, provided in large part by Kimmie, who'd taught me jingly prayers as a toddler. To me he was a Keeper of Souls ("now I lay me down to sleep") and a Shepherd ("I shall not want"). A biblical nursery rhyme figure. The way Kimmie now spoke of God made him instantly real to me.

"Yep, they are closer to Him down there," she said. "I totally forgot that fact till Rhonda reminded me."

Out there on the tough edge of the city, far from Metro Beach, Kimmie had tried to get Rhonda to drive her over the Ambassador Bridge to Windsor, Ontario. She had money now. And she'd heard that Canadians had legalized abortions for teenagers, no parental consent needed.

Rhonda told her that was crazy, to be sitting up in some strange doctor's office in a foreign country. What would she do if something went wrong? But Kimmie insisted nothing would go wrong, and her proof was that Windsor was an orderly place—no trash on the streets, two murders a year. But Rhonda was leery, convinced that black people from Detroit weren't welcome in Windsor. When Kimmie said she'd take the Jefferson bus down to the bridge and walk across the border,

Rhonda told her she'd look like a fugitive. Pulling over the baby blue Riviera, she turned to Kimmie, motor running, and convinced her oldest friend that just in case something did go wrong, she needed to be near those who cared about her. At least the aunties down in Louisiana could conjure up protection from the saints. Kimmie pondered. She didn't want to die alone on some doctor's metal table in a foreign country. She decided to wait.

As a bon voyage toast, Rhonda pulled out a nickel bag of reefer, and they smoked it with the car windows down, watching the dazzling lights of the Ambassador Bridge beckon against the night sky and nearly forgetting about the Going Away party.

"I'm coming back soon," Kimmie said to me, yawning as she eased onto her side. "I've been thinking, and I got it all figured out. Instead of New Mexico, I'm going to U of M next year. Rhonda is even thinking about applying there. Forget that dumb idea her father has about working in a factory! We might even be roommates." She yawned. "You can come visit me, Rae Rae, spend the night whenever you want."

"You promise?"

"I promise." Kimmie yawned again. "Cross my heart and hope to die."

I fell asleep that night picturing myself on a college campus with my big sister. I imagined it to be like Cranbrook Institute, where Miss Wheeler once took the class on a school trip—with sprawling expanses of landscaped lawn and castlelike structures made of stone and one primrose path after another, sturdy gates to keep you safely tucked inside.

But I soon lost my faith in the ability of places to protect, and now years later as I drove toward the Women's Health Clinic, feeling the fuzzy edges of a lovely narcotic high, I came to this realization: the idea of protection, of a reliable shield against fate, was a mean farce. With that insight, I turned right on Greenfield Road and stepped on the gas.

180

When I opened my eyes, Mama was leaning over me in full makeup.

"Get up," she whispered. "Come on. Get up."

"What time is it?" asked Kimmie, her voice groggy.

"Cyril will be here any minute," said Mama. "We all overslept."

Kimmie and I both climbed unsteadily out of bed, and Kimmie stumbled to the bathroom. I stood and stretched out my arms, yawning. Mama sat on the bed and watched.

"Remember when Kimmie arrived, and I promised you things would be different, that we'd be happy?" she said.

I nodded, rubbing the sleep from my eyes.

"Well now is our chance," she said. "You're coming with us."

I stepped backward. "I am?"

"You sure are." She smiled. "Excited?"

I might have said, *All this time that I'd been secretly preparing to leave with Daddy and then when I wasn't, all this time when I braced myself to say good-bye to Kimmie, you'd been planning to take me with you and didn't say so? How cruel.*

But I wanted to be flying down the interstate in a fast red car, Kimmie and Mama within arm's reach. After all she was my mother, whom

I revered, and I didn't really know *how* to say harsh things to her, even if I had formed the thoughts in my mind. I threw my arms around Mama's neck.

She gently pried me off of her, held me at arm's length. I felt her gaze pour over me as she touched my cheek with her palm. "Oh, Rae, wait till you see how much fun it's going to be," she said, her voice low. "Everyone down there is so friendly, and there are lots and lots of children to play with. Plenty of places to ride your bike . . ." Her eye caught something over my shoulder. She rose from the bed, went over to Kimmie's altar, picked up the picture of herself and Cyril. "Bless my soul," she whispered. "I didn't know she had this. Will you look at that?"

She was hoping, my mother, that this move to Louisiana with Cyril and me and Kimmie would give her a chance to erase the affair with a married man, the out-of-wedlock daughter, the years of slipping to see her lover behind his wife's back, her own failed marriage of two-way infidelity, the crucial years she missed in her daughters' lives. She was hoping she could start over and become a woman who really lived, pill-free and energetic. With cocktail parties and nights on the town and the same father for both her girls. But there was one person in her way. Or rather, two.

"What about Daddy?"

She put the picture back on Kimmie's altar, taking time to angle it just so. "He wouldn't want to come."

"But I can't leave him here." My excitement was escaping, alongside the air in the room.

"Don't worry." She looked over at me, proud of what she was about to say. "You can come back and visit him anytime you want. I promise." She gestured toward the door. "See how I let Kimmie go stay with her father when she asked? It's the same with you. Whenever—"

"But Daddy needs me!"

"Shhhh! You'll wake him up!" she said, finger to her lips. When she

182

spoke again, the tone in her voice had changed. "You want me to be happy, don't you, Rae?"

I didn't answer her. *I* wanted to be happy.

"Well, you want to be with Kimmie, don't you?"

Cornered, I nodded.

"This way, you can. We can be a family. Finally."

"But Daddy would be lonely."

She came over, squatted, putting our faces inches apart. "Your daddy has a special friend he likes very much," she said, her eyeliner suddenly scary. "I'm sure he won't be lonely."

"Yes, he will!" I cried, backing away from her. I knew more than she did.

"Shhhh!" Mama stood. "If you get down there and miss him too much, I'll send you back here. On an airplane, if you want. How about that? You've never flown on an airplane."

Kimmie walked into the room. "What's wrong?"

"Nothing," said Mama as she smoothed out her clothes. "In fact, everything is better than ever. Rae's coming with us."

Kimmie was as stunned as I was. "She is?" She looked at me. "You are?" She smiled. "Wow. That's great!"

It *was* great for Kimmie, who had grown attached to me again like when I was four. It was all working out—to have her baby sister nearby, to get an auntie in Louisiana to vacuum-suck every trace of Nolan out of her system, to finish school, then head to Ann Arbor a free girl, college-bound with a best friend in tow.

A car horn blew outside. "That's him!" said Mama. She moved to Kimmie's window, pushed the burlap shade to the side and looked down. "That's him."

I sat on Kimmie's bed. "I'm not going."

Mama turned back to me. "Rae, Sweetie, your daddy can't properly take care of you by himself. You know that, right?"

"But I know how to take care of *him*."

183

The car horn blew again. *Whonk. Whonk.*

"You'll finally get to be a kid, have some fun, instead of being his little private nurse."

"But I—"

"Listen, I'm your mother, and you have to do what I say." She turned to Kimmie. "Help her get ready, will you?"

With that, Mama rushed from the room.

"I don't understand why she's doing this," I said.

"Me neither," said Kimmie. "Not fully. But don't worry, okay?"

"Okay," I answered, believing Kimmie could make it all work out.

"Let's see what's going on," she said, grabbing my hand, leading me downstairs.

Mama had opened the front door, letting in the morning bird and traffic sounds. We watched as Cyril strolled up the walkway. He was wearing his lumberjack clothes—plaid shirt, jeans. He was tanned and still slender, still pretty. Kimmie ran to greet him.

"How's my Sweet Pea?" he said, giving her a big kiss on the cheek. Daddy always kissed me on the lips.

There, waiting magically in the vestibule, stood some luggage and a few of Mama's packed boxes. Cyril jogged up the front steps, across the threshold. "Let me just grab these, load up the trunk," he said, reaching for the bags.

Mama pointed to my little purple suitcase. "Those are your things, Rae. I found them under the bed." She looked at me. "Already packed."

I didn't know what part of this getaway plan of Mama's was spite toward Daddy and what part was love toward me. Either way, it was too much for my nine-year-old heart to take.

"I have to go say bye to Daddy," I whispered.

She lurched for my arm. "No. That is not a good idea, because he would be so upset he might do something crazy without thinking, you know?"

It was a hot, humid morning, the sticky air clinging to my thin Mickey Mouse pajamas.

184

Kimmie spoke for me. "Vy, I don't think you should make her leave without—"

"Hush! I know JD, okay? I know him, and I know what's best." She came over, grabbed my arms. "Now promise Mama you won't wake him up. Just go in, get dressed, and come out, okay?"

Cyril tried. "You've got to let the girl say good-bye to her daddy. That's a must."

I glanced at Cyril, liking him a little. "I won't take a long time, Mama. I promise."

"No!!" she yelled with a primal force that caused me to stumble backward. Cyril sidled over to where I stood. "Let's just do it her way for right now, okay?" he said to me. "We don't want her getting too worked up."

It was true that I didn't want Mama running half-naked down the street, so I moved toward the front door. Then something important dawned on me, and I stopped, faced them all. "Did you pack my record player Daddy gave me?" I asked.

"We can send for that later," said Mama, speaking through a long sigh. "There's no more room in the car."

"What about my drawing paper and crayons?" I pressed. "And my bicycle?" I didn't bother to mention that I'd ruined my bicycle.

"Rae, you can get those things later!" Her voice was high and sharp, and she must have thought I was crazy to want to take my things with me. In her mind, a child could start over with little or nothing. She had done just that as a young girl picked up from the orphanage, gripping one small paper bag and the hand of an unknown new mother.

"Just run upstairs and get dressed, please," she begged. "And no time for a full bath! Just a sponge bath in the sink!"

I walked into the house, anger propelling me to defy Mama. I got on my hands and knees below the front windows and crawled to the den. Daddy was lying down across the sofa. I couldn't tell if his eyes were open. I rapped on the glass French door, and he looked up. I waved 185 good-bye, then dropped down again, crawling fast across the living room and up the stairs.

When I returned dressed in seersucker shorts, Daddy was out on the porch, with Mama and Kimmie and Cyril each standing in the walkway.

"So this is what you gonna do? Sneak out your own house like a burglar?" said Daddy.

"It's not my house," said Mama. "Hasn't been for years."

"Well, it sure as hell ain't mine. You'd already bought the goddamned place when I met you."

"You know, JD, that just shows how you are. Here you had this beautiful home to live in and . . . you never even . . ." Mama paused, deciding not to go down that road. "I'm not going to put you out, if that's what you're worried about."

"Do I sound worried?" said Daddy, pride rising along with his blood pressure.

My parents' marriage, begun with a pregnancy that produced a stillborn child, was itself stillborn—a union formed with expectation and promise that never delivered.

Cyril turned to leave. "I think I'll wait in the car."

"Yeah, you best be doing that," Daddy barked at Cyril's back. "And get your fucking car out from in front of my home!"

Cyril stopped, turned, oh so calm. "Heyyy. No reason to get like that about it, Buddy."

"Just do what the fuck I said."

I'd never heard Daddy curse so. Cyril held up his hands, elbows jutting out, palms exposed. He glanced over at Mama. "I'll be waiting for you girls down the street." Then he walk-ran to his car.

"JD, don't make a scene," said Mama. "The neighbors."

"Maybe you should've thought about that before you decided to stage this little getaway in goddamn broad daylight." He crossed his

186

arms and spread his legs apart to steady his stance. "Here you are, trying to whisk Rae Rae off like she's one of your boxes you been packing up."

"It's not like that, and you know it."

"What do I know? You asked me to stay, and I did. Long as you needed me to. And then when you didn't need me no more, when you knew Kimmie would be coming, I agreed to go, didn't I?"

"But you *didn't* leave. I've been waiting all summer. If you had left like you were supposed to, we wouldn't be going through this right now."

"That still don't explain why you trying to sneak off."

" 'Cause I knew this would happen!"

"This is low-down, that's what this is," said Daddy. "You gonna be so bold-faced as to steal my baby from me? What I gave up to stay, you have no idea. And now you trying to take away the only good thing I got left? Just 'cause it suits you?"

"She was always going to live with me. That was the plan."

"Plans change, Vy. You know that. Besides, living with you in Detroit is one thing, and all the way down South is something else entirely."

Mama inched closer to Daddy. "Look, I know you waited around because I asked you to. I know that. And I'm grateful. But you're free now, so what's the problem? You're free, JD! Go on and be with your woman, and let me do what I'm trying to do."

Daddy shook his head. "I can't let you do this."

Mama dug her nails into the palms of her hands. "You just don't want to see me happy. That's what this is really about."

"You talking crazy, woman."

"Acting like you don't have options!" Mama yelled. "We both know Rae is not all you got."

Daddy sighed. He knew otherwise. "She's not going, Vy, so you can just get that notion out of your head right now."

Mama made a hollow, shrill sound. "Yes, she is. I'm her mother. She's going. We're going." Mama beckoned to us, her girls. "Come on."

Kimmie picked up my suitcase and moved toward Mama, but 187

Daddy held his hand out across my body, like a crossing guard on the corner at lunchtime.

"I said my baby's not going nowhere. Drop her bag, Kimmie."

Kimmie dropped the bag, and just in the way she let it plop to the ground, I knew she was on Daddy's side.

"Pick it back up!" yelled Mama. Kimmie picked it back up. Mama, who could go weeks sleeping on the same bedsheets, turned to Daddy, her eyes alive with mascara and ambition. "You're not going to fuck this up for me, JD. My girls deserve to be together."

Daddy smirked. "They deserve a whole lotta things, but that don't mean you been providing 'em." Mama's eyes lowered, her long, false lashes drooping in unison.

It was true. She'd tried to be a good mother, but there had been so much to manage: the two fathers, the depression, and the exhausting wait for Cyril to come and rescue her and her girls. Truth be told, it had all been too much. But now she was taking action to change everything. And for that she wanted full credit.

She looked up. "I'm not going to be made to feel bad." She glanced at Cyril's parked Volvo at the corner, making sure it was still there. "Not about this, because this is the best thing I could do for everybody concerned. And you shouldn't stand in Rae's way. Not if you're as crazy about her as you act."

Daddy must have quickly assessed himself, a barely-getting-by black man with a chronic condition about to lose his wife to a hazel-eyed, light-stepping college teacher with a fancy car. He looked over at me, those black eyes like little crystal balls.

"What do you want to do, Brown Eyes?"

I was silent.

"Just tell me what you want to do. Daddy will understand."

"I want us all to be together," I said, hopeless.

"Listen carefully now. Do you want to go with your mama and your sister?"

188   Shrug.

"Stay here with me?"

Nod.

"You sure?"

I nodded. No way could I choose anyone over Daddy. Not to his face.

Daddy took my suitcase from Kimmie. "She done said what she wants." He swatted at the air. "Now get the hell outta here, both of you."

Mama glanced again at Cyril's parked car, turned toward me. "I know you think you want this right now, Rae. But you're a child, and you can't really know what's best for you. I do." She grabbed at my arm and pulled me to her. Daddy grabbed at my other arm.

Kimmie screamed, "Wait a minute! This is crazy!"

Right there, in the middle of the walkway of our house on Birchcrest Road, on that sun-piercing morning, my mother and father pulled me in different directions. Kimmie ran to get her papa, and it was his words that broke through my parents' tug-of-war.

"Vy, let her stay," said Cyril, deep voice commanding respect.

Mama loosened her grip. "I can't just leave her here!" she gasped.

"You're going to have to. It's better than this fighting."

"But, Cyril, I thought *you* of all people would want her to come," said Mama.

"I want what's best for the child. Right now that seems to be keeping her where she is."

Mama dropped my arm, and Daddy quickly pressed me to him.

"Is this what you really, really want?" she asked me.

I looked into Mama's eyes. I have lived that elongated moment over and over through the years. Which was the right direction to move my head? I nodded and altered the course of everything that followed, as they say a butterfly flaps its wings and causes a storm on the other side of the earth.

She waited awhile before saying anything. We all waited with her. "You understand that I still have to go?"

"Yes," I answered. But I didn't understand any such thing. I had no idea on that hot August morning in 1972 what it felt like to pine over a   189 man for eighteen years and then be rescued from your deep longing at the ripe old age of thirty-six, now that he said he wanted you. Wanted you and the daughter you bore him.

Mama moved toward me, her eyes so filled with desperation I had to look at the pavement. She gave me a quick squeeze. Then she whispered, "I tried. Remember that, okay? I tried."

She let me go, and I watched as Mama and Kimmie walked away, the impression of her squeeze lingering. I noticed that across the street, Mean Mr. Green was peering out at us from his picture window. At the corner where Cyril was parked, Kimmie turned and waved. "Bye, Rae Rae!" she yelled. "I love you!!"

I tore away from Daddy's embrace, ran down the block to Kimmie. My hands grasped at the front of her embroidered shirt.

"I want to come with you," I cried.

"You're the best little sister in the world," she said. "But you have to stick with the choice you made." Suddenly, she snapped her finger. "I almost forgot!" She slid her hand into the back pocket of her jeans and pulled out the two one-hundred-dollar bills, easing them into my hand. Then she leaned right into my ear, touching the lobe with her lips, and whispered, "I'll be back. Remember that. I'll be back."

Mama turned to me, her hand gripping the car door handle. "You can come be with us at any time, Rae," she offered. "Just call when you're ready, and I'll send for you, okay?"

"Okay," I whispered. I stood there in front of Cyril's sporty red car and watched as they climbed into it, Kimmie in the front seat next to her papa, Mama in the back. As the car pulled into the street, Kimmie popped up magically through the sunroof and waved, her Indian silk shirt rippling in the wind. As I waved back, a song I'd heard recently, something about "jasmines" and a summer breeze, glided on smooth wheels through my mind.

Dizzy with emptiness, palming the money, I walked back to the house. Daddy was waiting for me on the porch. He placed his hand across the small of my back, guided me through our front door. "I don't trust those foreign cars for nothing," he said, slamming the door against the day. "Ain't worth a damn. None of 'em."

I believed him, and escaping many years later in my Mustang, I understood there was nothing Honda, Volkswagen, Mercedes, or Volvo could ever do for me.

After an incredible reprieve throughout the first half of 1980, several days before my high school graduation, Daddy had a migraine attack like none before it. It stretched him out on his back for forty-eight hours straight. We weren't prepared for this, having been lulled by his wave of good health in the prior months. By now, his endurance for excruciating pain had flagged. He tried lying dead still in the dark; I rubbed his forehead frantically. Nothing worked. Finally, in weak surrender, Daddy injected high milligrams of Demerol into his veins daily, sometimes twice a day, for over a week.

I wasn't alarmed. Having witnessed his self-medicating for so many years, I'd become adept at delusion, telling myself he was no different from a diabetic giving himself insulin. I was so intimate with Daddy's symptoms that I knew he was in a perpetual cycle of experiencing, recovering from, or fighting off headaches. This latest episode didn't alarm me, as it should have. I was desperate for Daddy to do whatever he had to do to feel better so he could make the cross-country trek with me. I believed this trip to New Mexico was going to save his life.

More to the point, I had a high threshold for drug use. Why I'd so far escaped becoming a druggie myself is one of those flukes of life. It's not like I hadn't tried. My first opportunity to smoke reefer came compliments of Mount Bethel Baptist Church, the year I was fourteen. Our youth group went on a daylong retreat to a hostel in Brighton, Michigan, where we had a discussion on "what it means to be a teenager today" and cooked huge communal meals and slept in sparsely furnished rooms with thin mattresses and no hot water. Maurice Franklin brought the joint. Five of us shared it during a nature walk, passing it back and forth between us. Despite elaborate puffing, I wasn't inhaling anything. Yet when the others talked about "feeling good, a little fuzzy man," I pretended to feel that way too. It felt like a distinct failure on my part, that inability to get high—a deficiency of some sort. I was convinced it was a sign, an indicator of what lie ahead for me: being on the outside of what's cool while pretending to be inside of it.

Later that year in her parents' garage, Lisa LaBerrie and I learned the correct way to smoke a joint; she'd gotten one from her big sister, Maria, who was a hip "nice Catholic-school girl" who hiked up her uniform to a micromini as soon as she was out of the sisters' sight, and who knew all the intricacies of petting, having mastered sexual pleasure without going all the way. Lisa and I smoked that entire joint, and afterward we were both so high we couldn't speak in full sentences. Terrified that her mother would discover us, we decided—because someone told Lisa your high comes down faster if you run—to sprint through the neighborhood. We ran and ran and ran across lawns and between houses and through alleys and stayed high, our hearts beating in our throats. Finally, way past both our curfews, we slipped into her house and sprayed hairspray all over each other (to mask the marijuana smell) before parting ways. Once home, I poked my head into the den and quickly said hello to Daddy, who scrunched up his nose, asked me, "What in the world you been doing got you smelling like sweet shit?" He looked at me with suspicion when I told him it was a homemade perfume Lisa and I had created. I ducked into my room and promptly slept off my high.

After that, Lisa and I knew better. Supplied by Maria, our joints now lasted for several days. She'd take a few languid puffs, I'd take a few, and we'd save the rest for the next time. The only thing I didn't like   193 about smoking pot was that it made me think a lot. One night while walking home from Lisa's in the throes of a sweet high, I realized a sad truth, one that hit me violently but with lucidity: Mama left me to be with Cyril. No one made her do that. She didn't have to leave me behind. She had a choice. And she chose to go.

I didn't smoke reefer again for a long time. Instead, I escaped into an illogical, teen fantasy played over and over in my head like a weekday rerun: *I have a little daughter who goes on joyrides with me in a sporty car, and I always, always put her needs first.*

I started getting high again in the late winter of 1979, when I was sixteen and it was cool to wear Jordache jeans, drive fuel-efficient cars, and disco-dance. Using those blank prescription pads stolen from Dr. Corey's office, I became an expert at "bustin' scripts." I researched the medical names—easily found knowledge in a pharmaceutical encyclopedia at the Sherwood Forest branch library—and duplicated Dr. Corey's unintelligible scrawl. For months I traveled to different party stores around the city, never going to the same one twice, filling fake prescriptions. It was too easy. I got the basic druggie stash—uppers, downers, speed—and carried the jumble of blue, yellow, and pink pills in a leather coin purse that once belonged to Kimmie. I spent much of my senior year in fraying peace-patch jeans and a wavy altered state.

Yet despite the parental influence, I did not have the heart for addiction. I couldn't muster the staying power. One day, tired of a dry mouth and insomnia, I gave up the pills, graduating to nickel bags of pot. I wanted to love marijuana because Kimmie had loved it. But I still found my highs too exhausting. Rather than relaxing or giggling or getting the munchies, I pondered and worried and regretted. I soon gave up the reefer for good.

I had one down thought often while high. If Mama had let Kimmie

194

fly to New York that long-ago August and receive a newly legal abortion, she'd never have been on the road that day headed to an auntie in Louisiana.

My number one teenage mantra: *Abortions save lives. Abortions save lives. Abortions save lives.*

I am still nine and dream we are all together, piled into Oldie as the silvery car, suddenly new again, glides through a brightly lit tunnel; Mama sits beside Daddy in the front seat, and in the back Kimmie quietly leans next to the open window. My head in Kimmie's lap, I can hear the oceanic sounds of her stomach growling. I am wearing the charm bracelet she's given me, full of lions, tigers, and bells on my thin wrist, and it tinkles as a warm wind gushes through the back window. Kimmie gently places her delicate hand on my head, entwines her fingers in my plaits; I am certain that only because of her hold on my hair do I not fly straight out of the window, like Tinkerbell. Suddenly, I am being shaken, and this shaking whisks me out of the car window, sucking me into the ether, beyond Kimmie's grasp.

Daddy was sitting beside me on the sofa bed.

"You having a bad dream, Brown Eyes?"

"No, it was a good dream," I said. "At first."

Daddy took my hand. "Sit up for me, okay? I got something to tell you."

I propped my pillow against the back of the sofa the way I'd seen Mama do in her bed. Daddy looked awful. He had heavy up-and-down lines in his forehead. And he was sweating. When I looked closer, I saw that his eyes were moist, and I imagined a yummy breakfast of hash and eggs waiting downstairs, as I assumed he'd been chopping onions this morning.

"I would give anything, anything at all, if I didn't have to tell you this," he said. He paused. "There was an accident."

"There was an accident?" At that moment he could've been reporting something that happened down the block, some tidbit of gossip unrelated to us. Maybe that crazy Elgernon had finally fallen off the roof and really hurt himself this time. Or perhaps Daddy heard something bizarre and remote on the eleven o'clock news the night before, and someone we knew was in danger. My mind was calm, nonchalant even. I was still ignorant of the possibility of personal tragedy. But my body was under no such illusion, as chill bumps popped out of nowhere and raced up my arms.

"Listen to me now, Rae Rae. They had a car accident driving on the highway."

"They who?"

"Your mama and your sister. And that man."

The chill bumps hardened. "Are they okay?"

Daddy shook his head. "It was a very bad accident. Your mama is in the hospital."

Reflexively, my hand pulled out of his and landed across my heart, where all my complicated longing for and resentment toward Mama gathered in a heavy ball of panic at the thought of losing her.

"Is she going to be all right?"

He nodded. "It seems so."

My hand dropped back to my lap, relieved. "She and Kimmie coming back here?"

He shook his head slowly. There was more. "Listen to me now. Kimmie didn't make it, Brown Eyes."

"Didn't make it where?"

He cupped my hands inside of his. "She didn't survive," he said, his voice firm, his eyes piercing.

"What?" I bolted up, and one of the pillows fell to the floor. I didn't   197 understand him, couldn't make out what he meant by that word. "What, Daddy?" Daddy and his big words. *Divorce. Survive.*

He grabbed me into his arms and held me tight—way too tightly for Daddy, as only Mama held me like that—and in my ear he said it. "She died, Brown Eyes. Kimmie died before they could save her."

I shook my head, chin resting against his shoulder. "But I just saw her. She kissed my cheek, and she said we would see each other as soon as—"

He stopped me. "Please, Baby. Try to understand what I'm saying."

I pushed myself out of his bear hug. "No! No!!" I screamed, right into his ear. "Noooooooo!"

As Daddy picked me up, I gripped myself around his neck, beating my small fists into his back.

"It's not true!" I screamed. "Tell me it's not true! Please, Daddy. Tell me it's not true." I grabbed his face in desperate hands, dug fingers into his cheeks and threatened him. "Take it back!" I screamed. "Take it back!"

"I wish I could," he said. "But I can't."

While no person I'd ever known had died before, I knew enough to know that death was ugly, its removal swift, and its cause traceable. I knew that that goldfish I loved so in Miss Miller's second-grade class had to be lifted from the fish tank one day because it was bloated and unmoving. Overfed, said Miss Miller. When Daddy let me have a pet hamster and I placed it too close to the radiator one winter night to keep it warm, we found it the next day, unmoving and bloated. We buried it in the backyard. Daddy rocked me in his arms, and I saw Kimmie curled into a ball, perfectly still and puffy. I cried hard, burning tears that tumbled fast as I choked on my guilt, snot running down my nose, tears flying off my chin until my head pounded and I held it for fear it would pound its way off my neck.

He touched my forehead. "You're burning up," he said. "Come with me."

Daddy gathered me in his arms, carried me to the big upstairs bathroom, and drew a bath. He prepared a basin of water and vinegar and placed that beside him on the tile floor. He helped me out of my nightgown and panties and eased me gently into the warm water. Down on his knees, struggling and groaning as his heavy girth got in the way, he took a sponge out of the basin of water and began bathing my body, just as I would bathe his years later. The smell of vinegar was pungent.

I closed my eyes, feeling the warm water against my skin as I sat there like a Raggedy Ann doll without bones, empty, tired, unable to lift my own limbs. Daddy grabbed an arm, sponged it, grabbed a leg, sponged it. When he let go of a limb, I let it plop back into the water with a splash, exhausted and uncaring.

"Can you stand, Brown Eyes?"

I shook my head. Daddy took a huge towel and wrapped it around my shoulders, then lifted me out of the tub, dried me off. "Be right back," he said.

I watched the back of him as he left the room, listened as his heavy footsteps moved through the house, causing the floors to creak under the carpet. I thought about Daddy dying, realized for the first time in my brief life that he could leave me sitting here on the toilet lid and not come back—get himself killed somehow from a stray bullet through the window or from strangulation by Nolan, who could be lurking in our basement, his mind set on payback. I realized then how risky love really is.

Daddy returned with Avon perfumed talcum powder taken from Mama's abandoned vanity top; he shook a little onto my chest and then slipped the nightgown over my head. Talc covered my feet, like white stardust.

"Hungry?" he asked.

I shook my head no.

"You sure about that? How about a boiled egg? With the yolk a little runny the way you like it. And some grits?"

"Can I have lots of salt and pepper?"

"You can have anything you want." 199

Daddy headed to the kitchen, and I followed behind, watching as he pulled out pots, ran water, turned on the stove. He then stepped into the living room, went over to the stereo console, and opened its glass door, where albums still lay stacked on a rack. These albums Mama never touched; they didn't get played at either of her parties. He pulled out one with Ray Charles smiling across the cover, all teeth and dark glasses, placed it on the turntable, gently dropping the needle onto the vinyl. Daddy held his hand out to me. "Come," he said. I stood, grabbed his hand as he led me to the kitchen. Ray's earnest voice wailed, *"I can't stop loooovvvvving you!"* Morning light spilled through the back-door window, a slender triangle on the burgundy linoleum. Daddy took my small hand into his huge warm one, grabbed me at the waist, directed me to place my feet on top of his and slowly guided me around the kitchen floor. Carefully, he picked up the pace, and soon I was soaring, my cotton nightgown billowing in the back, triangle of sun in my face, grits bubbling on the stove, and by the time Ray sang, *"I'll just live my life in dreams of yesterdayyyyy!"* and the gospel choir behind him echoed *"of yesterrrrrddayyyyy!"* the three-minute eggs were done.

How's that head?" Daddy asked after I'd eaten my grits and eggs. We were sitting together at the kitchen table.

"It still hurts," I said, because something did.

"Maybe you need to lie down, Brown Eyes."

"Maybe," I mumbled, fatigue glued to my mouth, hanging off my shoulders. He grabbed my hand and led me to the den. I slid between the sofa bed's fresh sheets, and Daddy placed a warm, soothing washcloth across my forehead. Next he opened his hand before me, and lying inside his soft palm was a tiny piece of a white pill. "Take this," he said. "For the pain."

"Are you sure it'll work?" I asked, because nothing was certain anymore and it seemed to me I could live with this pain forever.

200 "Have I told you wrong before?"

He hadn't. Like the night he used the closed end of a bobby pin to pull the mucus from my stuffed-up nose, he promised I'd be able to breathe. I could. Or the time a hangnail on my finger throbbed with pain, and he promised when I awoke the next morning, the hangnail would be gone. It was. I swallowed the little piece of a pill, feeling closer to Daddy than ever and at the same time feeling like a grown-up, Vy-type female with my talcum-powdered body, my sadness, my naughty nerves, and my own pill to make them behave.

I took one big gulp from the glass of water Daddy held out to me. My throat was raw. "Whose fault was it?" I asked, believing it was mine, that somehow my presence in that car would have prevented an accident; I didn't know then who had been driving or even if another car was involved; I only knew I hadn't been there and I could have been and that if I had, somehow things would have been different. I was well into teenage life before it occurred to me that if I had chosen to join my sister and mother in Louisiana, I most surely would've died too.

Daddy took back the glass, set it down on the little end table. "Bad things just happen," he said. "We want to blame somebody, but the truth is, sometimes bad things just happen."

I lay there, my eyes squeezed shut, envisioning a possible scenario: a highway, Cyril's car, another one crashing into it head first, turning it into an accordion, Kimmie squished to death on the passenger's side, no one's fault. I felt Daddy's presence folded within my thoughts like autumn leaves pressed upon wax paper.

"Feeling sleepy yet?"

"Not yet." I was afraid of what lay beyond the darkness.

"Tell you what. You can sleep on my back."

"But I thought you said I was getting too heavy for that."

"One more time won't hurt none."

He lay down, and I crawled over him into a ball, comfortable against his sturdy flesh. Behind my closed lids, I saw Kimmie and her funny-colored eyes. Kimmie and her warm-towel laughter. Kimmie and her whispered-in-my-ear promise: *I'll be back. Remember, I'll be back.*

"Daddy?" I asked thickly, the traces of Demerol beginning to work.
"Yeah?"
"Will you take me to the show tomorrow?"
"What do you wanna see?"
"*Ben.*"
"That the picture about the little boy and the rat?"
"Yes. Michael Jackson sings the theme song."
"Now there's a little fellow who got something special, don't he? Voice just like velvet."
"Can we go to the Mercury Theater and see it tomorrow?"
"Sure thing, Brown Eyes," he said. "Sure thing.

Moments passed in silence. Then, in a smooth falsetto I never knew existed, Daddy sang me a lullaby: *"And if that's not loving me, then all I've got to say God didn't make little green apples and it don't rain in Indianapolis in the summertime. And there's no such thing as Dr. Seuss or Disneyland and Mother Goose is no nursery rhyme. And when my self is feeling low, I think about her face aglow and ease my mind."*

Winding its way between the notes of Daddy's song, sleep came. And I dreamed. Fast, wild dreams pushed against one another. Dreams of back-porch Kool-aid, the put-put of Nolan's VW, the ace of cups, Belle Isle's connect-the-dots sky. And in every one of them, Kimmie lived. She lived.

I myself believe in flying," a strange woman was saying, her voice loud and husky. "I have *never* been one for long-distance driving. Now trains are a whole nother story."

Daddy's voice drifted back to me. "Hell, most Negroes can't afford airplane tickets. Got to get on the highway."

"Things are changing. It's the 1970s, for God's sake. I flew in here, didn't I? Got here in two hours, too. Can you believe it? Two hours. Had me a decent meal on the plane too."

"Well, Essie, you done always been ahead of your time," said Daddy.

I climbed out of the sofa bed, went toward the voices with hopeful steps. If people were talking about airplanes, then Kimmie couldn't possibly be dead.

When I entered the dining room, Daddy was there with a strange woman, sitting at the dining room table, which never got used. They stopped talking when they saw me. She looked at me with a long, sad face and Daddy's nose. I hated her for that because I wanted to believe everything was okay, and now I knew for sure it wasn't.

"How you feeling, Darlin'?" she said in a funny drawl.

"Fine, thank you." The trick was to be very polite, act like nothing was wrong. And then maybe it wouldn't be.

"Brown Eyes, this here is my big sister, your aunt Essie," said Daddy. "She flew in from down South to be with us a while," he explained. I went to sit on his lap.

"Pleased to meet you, Brown Eyes." She smiled.

"Hi" is all I said. Better to keep it simple.

"So, I'll bet you're hungry?"

I shook my head. I noticed she had a light mustache.

"Just a little bit? I got some catfish and a little collard greens and cornbread. How's that sound to you?"

"I don't want anything," I said, leaning my body against Daddy's. I wished she would just go home, leave us alone, this surprise sister of my father who had his pug nose and her own salt-and-pepper hair.

"Well you must've slept up an appetite," she continued. "You got to eat something. It's way past lunchtime. Suppertime, pert near."

"I'm not hungry!"

Silence.

"Okay, Darlin'. I'll keep a plate on the stove, just for you. It's a deal?"

I was starving. Sadness pressed down on me in thick layers; I buried my head in Daddy's chest, closed my eyes and kept very quiet, focusing on Daddy's heartbeat. *Boo boom, boo boom, boo boom.*

After a long while, Aunt Essie asked, "She sleep?"

I felt his body shift slightly as he nodded. I didn't move.

"What time is Vy expected in?" she asked.

"I don't know for sure. As soon as the hospital discharges her, I guess."

"Is he coming with her?"

"Hell if I know."

"He's gonna surely be here for the service? That was his child!"

"Who you asking, Essie?"

"Well, we'll all know in a little while. What about the arrangements?"

204

"Soon as possible, I imagine. I hope it'll be something simple."

"That's best," she said. "I for one don't go for those long, drawn-out services. Too much on the family. Just too much." She took a deep breath. "Never thought I'd be saying this, but my heart goes out to Vy. Lord knows she ain't done right by you, JD, but I don't never want to see a woman look down on her own child. Ain't nothing worse. Completely against the natural order of things."

"Ain't no such thing as a natural order in this world," said Daddy. "It's as random as all get-out."

"Not when God's in the picture."

"Hmph," said Daddy. "Guess he was busy in the wee hours of this particular morning."

"Can't question the Lord's plan, JD. It's not for human understanding. All you can do is pray. Pray for a young life lost."

"I'd like to know how prayer is gonna help me explain to this child what happened to her big sister. She loved her something awful, kept right at her heels. Sat by her door for days on end when Kimmie broke up with this no-count nigger she was seeing. Just sat there on the floor, waiting."

Aunt Essie sighed. "God will give you the words."

"Back off, Essie. You know me, and I haven't changed in that area. So back off."

"Well, if you can't trust in the Lord, then lean on your horse sense. She's a child, JD. Children bounce back. The one we got to watch is her mama. Lord only knows how Vy's gonna fare now. She ain't never been too stable in the head to begin with, as we all well know."

"Just be nice to her when she gets here."

"Now, what I look like?" she said, her voice rising an octave. "That woman will be carrying tragedy on her back. Imagine being in a car accident and you live, your daughter don't. I'm sure she wishes it had been her who went through that windshield. That's what any mother would wish. And besides," Aunt Essie paused for effect. "This here is

205

her house, not mine. She got every right to run things her way when she gets back."

"She's not really one for running things," said Daddy. "Ain't been for a long time. She tried a bit while Kimmie was here this summer. But that was all just preparation for leaving, as it turns out. And now this."

Now that both my parents had had their way—he kept me, she left with Cyril—neither was happy. Once again, a child's death had spoiled everything. Daddy sighed so heavily my body rose as he took in air and then fell as he breathed out. "Let me put my baby down," he said.

He carried me into the den and lay me across the sofa bed. "Rae Rae?" He'd seen my eyes flutter. I opened them as he sat on the end of the bed and leaned in, his face so close I could see all three colors of his inner lip.

He cupped my chin. "You hold on to every good memory you have of your sister, you hear me? That way, she'll be with you forever."

I stared at him, not fully buying what he was saying.

He let his hand fall, placing it on top of mine. "When my little brothers died, I felt like I shoulda been able to save 'em somehow. That there thing hit me so hard 'cause they looked up to me so. I was their big brother, their protector." He thumped his chest. "I still carry them right here. And you wanna know why? 'Cause I never let myself forget. I can tell you about the times I wiped their little behinds and when they rode on my shoulders and when I took them fishing. It makes me feel good to remember. You understand?"

I nodded, not understanding the bigger issue: why little boys and teenage girls had to die.

"I'm a ask you to tell me stories about some of the fun you and Kimmie had this summer. And every time I do, you gotta come up with a new story. Hear me, now?"

"I hear you, Daddy."

He rubbed my hand. "Okay, so tell me one right now."

206

"Right now? Anything?"

"Yep."

"Well." I thought for a moment, my mind flying over the whole summer, from the first time I saw Kimmie standing there in her crinkly sundress to the image of her waving good-bye from the sunroof of Cyril's car. I smiled. "One of those times we went to Belle Isle . . . in your car? We rode the Giant Slide over and over."

"Yeah? What was that like?"

"It's great, Daddy. You walk up a ton of stairs to get to the top. And then you get on this rug and you slide down. I was a little scared but Kimmie got on first and had me hold on to her waist, and then when she yelled, 'Ready!' the guy pushed us and we flew down the slide, and it was like being on a magic carpet and we went over these giant bumps and we were going so fast and flying and yelling and Kimmie had her arms straight up in the air and then I put mine up, and when we got to the bottom, we ran to the side with our rug and we started right back up the stairs." I took a breath. "It was so much fun."

Daddy squeezed my hand. "That's a good story, Brown Eyes. Now whenever you get ready to be sad—and the next few days are gonna have some sad moments in 'em, I'm not gonna lie to you—whenever that happens you come find me and tell me another story. Got it?"

"Got it."

"And if you can't get to me, you crawl to that spot you love so much up under the dining room table and tell yourself a story. All you got to do is go up under there when you need to."

I thought about that. "Yeah, you might be right, Daddy."

He chuckled, oh so softly. "Now, back to sleep. But when you wake up this time, you got to eat a little something. For Aunt Essie's sake, okay?"

"Is she staying?"

"For a spell. You gonna like her. Don't worry."

I lay there for a couple hours, listening to Daddy and Aunt Essie as they talked, their voices low. Heard her climb the stairs, heard doors

207

closing and bathwater running, heard all kinds of normal sounds brushing up against this abnormal day. When night came, Daddy joined me in the sofa bed. I scooted over to make room for his wide body and finally drifted to sleep. This time I didn't dream about Kimmie. This time I didn't dream at all.

I heard the song before I opened my eyes. *Da da da. Da da da, da da da. Mary wants be a superwoman, but is that really in her headdddd.* I leaped off the den sofa and followed the music up the stairs. *And all the things she wants to be she needs to leave behiiiind.* There she was sitting on her bed, suitcase propped open, the album with its gold Tamla label spinning on my little red record player. One arm was in a sling. She looked up at me. One eye was purplish, swollen. I was awed by her wound and halted by her bandage. She was so lovely to me and so tragic, I couldn't move.

Two days had passed since Kimmie died, days as thick and slow as the Alega syrup Aunt Essie poured on the Sunday morning pancakes. Nearly everything familiar to me was in those days replaced by Change. The phone rang a lot, coming at me like a plaintive wail for help. Each time I expected it to be Kimmie, calling from the road somewhere: *It was all a mistake. I made it. You guys just couldn't find me.* I realized I'd never heard her voice through a telephone, and that absence in our relationship pained me. As the years grew, I'd add many things to the list of what Kimmie and I never did together. Aunt Essie, on exaggerated bowlegs, would waddle toward the phone, tell every caller the same thing. "Thank you kindly for offering your condolence. Vy is expected in any day now. Call back, won't you?"

We waited for Mama to arrive so we could stop walking around Kimmie's death like it was a gaping hole in the floor. Aunt Essie wanted to cook food for the stream of company she assumed would soon be pouring through, paying their respects. She wanted to rush Kimmie's laid-to-rest outfit to the cleaners. She wanted to prepare the extra bedrooms for overnight guests and "get everyone situated" for the big day—do my hair and iron her silk slip and polish Daddy's shoes. But she didn't. Couldn't until Mama arrived. And so to keep herself busy, Aunt Essie did what she called her general cleaning.

She was agile despite the bowlegs, scrubbing and vacuuming and dusting her way across the distance of those first days with military precision. When I told her about Miss Queenie, she sucked her teeth. "I can't see a doggone thing she's done around here," she hissed, moving through the front rooms with grace and speed, attacking all dirt in her path. I was mesmerized by the rhythmic, circular motion of her arm, its loose skin jiggling as she cleaned glass-tops with balled-up newspapers and her own concoction of vinegar, water, and ammonia. Miss Queenie had always seemed distracted when she worked, her mouth filled with snuff, her mind on that pile of dirty clothes in the basement. Aunt Essie wanted to pounce on the den with her dust rag and scrub brush, but Daddy wouldn't let her.

"This here is my private space, and it's gonna stay that way," he said. "I don't want it smelling like a hospital."

Aunt Essie wrinkled her nose for effect. "That you won't ever have to worry about," she snapped. Daddy ignored her. "It needs a good wipe-down is all I'm saying."

"No."

"The whole room needs airing out, JD. It's so stuffy—"

"No."

She sucked her teeth. "Two human beings living in one little bitty room, it's bound to need some serious airing out." She paused, then pushed harder. "And anyway, why you got that child sleeping up against you like that?"

"Don't start, Essie. Do not start."

"It don't look right, is all."

"Then damn it, stop looking."

That ended that, and Aunt Essie turned her attention to the kitchen, which was a gold mine of smudge and grime and overlook. "I just don't understand folks who throw a rag around the place and claim they doing something," she complained. She peered inside the refrigerator and announced, "I am highly suspicious of anybody who takes money to clean another person's house," making Miss Queenie sound like an accomplice in a whole ring of conspiratorial cleaning women. "Certainly in this day and age, you got to be careful who you bring into your home," she noted. "Folks got options now. What kind of woman still doing day work?"

Mr. Alfred rang our doorbell late Saturday afternoon. He sat on the living room couch, with Daddy in the opposite chair. For a few years, Kimmie had lived as Daddy's daughter, and so JD deserved some respect-paying as far as his buddy was concerned. They talked about a couple cars down at the shop, European ones with tumbled insides that didn't work in any logical way and which kept Mr. Alfred "busy as all get-out."

I disappeared on my bicycle that evening, desperate to leave that house with its Mr. Clean aroma, its nonstop phones, its standstill quality. Out there on the sidewalks of the neighborhood, no one knew Kimmie had died. Men still mowed their lawns, and Jehovah Witnesses carried *The Watchtower* door-to-door, and squirrels leaped up trees. Yet I couldn't find Terrance Golightly anywhere.

On Sunday after the pancakes, Rhonda came. "I just can't believe it," she kept saying. "I just can't believe it." A hand clung to her throat as she talked. "Kimmie was so happy when she left. She had plans, you know?"

"To come back," I said. "She was coming back."

Rhonda's eyes brimmed. "She wanted to be closer to you, Rae Rae. She told me that, that she wanted to be closer to her baby sister."

"She did? She said that?"

Rhonda nodded.

My heart burned with fresh grief. "What else did she say?"

At that moment, Aunt Essie came into the living room and handed us glasses of orange pop. She offered food, but Rhonda said she wasn't hungry, thank you. Aunt Essie gave her a sad smile of understanding. "You and Kimmie were best friends," she said, as if she'd always known it.

"Since kindergarten, ma'am."

Aunt Essie sighed as she cupped her soft belly and waddled off, the space between her legs an oblong *O*.

"You want to go for a ride?" asked Rhonda.

I didn't know how much I wanted to until she asked me. I got Daddy's permission, and we dashed out. It was to be the first and last time I ever rode in Rhonda's baby blue Riviera, and I ran toward it with thirst as it glistened in the early September sun, beckoning like a backyard pool. She rode the Lodge Freeway with the confidence of a veteran, and before long we were rising up at Jefferson Avenue, past Cobo Hall and Tiger Stadium, headed for Belle Isle. She parked close to the river's edge, just as Kimmie and I used to do. She reached over into the backseat and pulled out a bouquet of flowers—a medley of orchids and forget-me-nots and lilies. Together we climbed out of the car and walked to the water, where we took turns tossing the petals out and watching as they rode the waves.

"I don't even have a picture of her," said Rhonda.

"Me neither."

"Not any at all?"

"Just the ones in my head."

We watched as the current carried the stems and petals and leaves.

When Rhonda dropped me off, I went upstairs to my room in search of the heaviest book I could find so I could press the petals of the flower I'd saved between its pages. There I caught Aunt Essie scrubbing down a wall in Kimmie's room, the same wall where a black-light poster of the zodiac wheel had hung. Kimmie was an Aquarius.

"Leave it alone!" I screamed, startling her so, she dropped the scrub brush.

"What??"

"Don't touch it!"

Comprehension moved across Aunt Essie's face, and she sat on Kimmie's stripped bed to collect herself. "Well, Darling, now I'm sorry. I'm just trying to bring some order to the house, that's all."

"It's not right for you to be in here."

Aunt Essie gave me a knowing look. "Come here," she said, patting the spot beside her. I sat, and she put her hands on me for the first time. They were like a varnished piece of bark, shellacked into softness. I could smell the Du Charm pomade in her hair.

"She's an angel in heaven now, you know."

"She is?"

"Yes, she's with the Lord. And let me tell you, that's a fine, fine place to be."

"What's so fine about it?"

"Well, Jesus is there, watching over everybody," said Aunt Essie. "And at the pearly gates is Gabriel and Peter. You know about them?"

"No."

"Well, I got my Bible, don't never go far without it, and I can read you some stories that'll make your heart sing."

"Can you read me the one about heaven?" I asked, mildly curious.

"I sure can, Darling. Whenever you're ready."

I never was. My experience had taught me that God had two purposes in the universe: to snatch your loved ones from you, and to take back babies you send his way.

When Mama arrived, she came through the front door carrying her square cosmetics bag and matching suitcase. Aunt Essie waved at Cyril before he drove off in his rental car.

"You remember my sister," said Daddy to Mama.

213

She looked at Aunt Essie with her good eye. "You haven't aged a bit," she said matter-of-factly. "Still strong as an ox."

Aunt Essie paused, took in her sister-in-law, whom she hadn't seen in a decade, since Daddy had carried his not-so-young bride to Tennessee and Essie saw through her, saw that her brother had married a woman whose heart was somewhere else. "What can I do for you, Vy Darlin'?" she said now, forgiveness and pity lacing her words. "Anything? I'm here to help."

"Get me some cigarettes, would you? Kool menthols," said Mama as she collapsed into the first chair available. "Somehow, I'm fresh out."

Stevie sang on and on until finally, Mama held out her unslung hand to me. I moved slowly to receive it. Her fingers were freezing. "You're all I have left," she said, looking right at me. "You're it."

Sitting gingerly beside Mama on the bed, I suddenly realized that I'd been waiting all these years for her to focus on me again, as she did those two riot-filled days long before—to reach out for me, call my name with urgency in her voice. Right then and there, I decided to accept the trade-off, accept losing Kimmie so that I could have more of Mama. I understood in that instant the basic principle behind loss: when a loved one dies, a void is created that must be filled. I assumed we would do that for each other, fill one another's void, and so I held her hand and waited, waited as Stevie asked: *"Where are you when I need you, like right now? Right now, right now, right nowwwww. . . . Yeah, need you baby, need you, need you baby."* Once the song ended, Mama and I sat there listening to the silence left behind.

She was restless, like a wounded animal lost in woods once familiar, wandering around, aimless, limping slightly. She walked through the living room and across the dining room and into the kitchen, where

214

she sat for a moment. Then she was up again and out onto the back porch. Then the front porch, back inside to the kitchen.

"Sit a spell, won't you, Vy?" Aunt Essie finally said, worry etched between her brows. "You gonna wear a hole in the carpet."

Mama looked over at her. "Can I have some water, please?" she asked, in a restaurant-customer voice. She was still standing, oddly balanced with her one good arm and one good eye.

"I'll get it!" I yelled, running to the kitchen for the water.

When I handed her the glass, Mama gripped it tightly. "I'm going to lie down," she said.

"You *need* to rest," blurted Aunt Essie, as though it had been her idea all along. "I put some nice fresh sheets on the bed. And I laid out your nightgown."

"Thanks, Essie," said Mama. "Thanks for being here."

Aunt Essie jumped into the opening. "No need to thank me. I'm here to help. I can help with the . . . arrangements, Darlin'. I know about these things. Done buried my little brothers and my own mother. Just tell me—"

Mama cut her off. "I'm going to bed right now. You want to come with me, Rae?"

I followed her, holding her slung elbow as we slowly climbed the staircase. Once in her room, I threw back the chenille blanket, pulled the top sheet out from its hospital corners, and watched Mama crawl into bed, fully dressed. The room was a hollow replica of itself now that her personal things were gone—like the vanity tray once full of cosmetics that sat on the dresser and the Naomi Sims wigs she'd kept propped on Styrofoam busts all over the room. But her smell was back. I handed her two nerve pills from inside her pocketbook, and she took them one at a time, chasing each with a tiny sip of water. The phone rang beside her bed. "Unplug it," she said, turning over and curling up. There she laid, chenille blanket pulled to her chin, for the next twenty-four hours.

With Mama upstairs and off limits, the rest of the day passed in a haze. Aunt Essie moved through the house like a tornado, scrubbing it with frantic attention—from the stove to the toilet bowls to the floors to the crystals on the chandelier. Cyril respectfully stayed away, tucked into his room at the Sheraton Hotel on Washington Boulevard, where he nursed a bottle of whiskey to numb his own devastation. Daddy and I passed the time leaning against the den's radiator cover, peering out at the street, holding each other around the waist. He had to tell his sister to *Hush up, Essie* when she strode into the den and started complaining that nobody was doing anything to get that poor child buried.

Truth is, we were immobilized, waiting for Mama to make the first move. What we understood intuitively was that hers was the grief that was greatest, and so we must defer to it. At first, we tiptoed around so she wouldn't be disturbed. But the adults' anxiousness grew as the hours did. Even I knew something had to be done soon. And that something loomed before us, a giant cloud of cruel detail waiting to open up and rain down on us with vengeance.

At nightfall, Aunt Essie sent me up to Mama with a tray of food. She wouldn't touch it. I turned to Daddy for help. He went to her room, gently closing the door behind him. She refused to talk to him. When Cyril called for the third time, Aunt Essie climbed the stairs slowly, gripping the banister as she hoisted herself forward, determination lodged in her grim mouth, a history of blood clots in her battered legs. She too came back downstairs defeated. "Won't budge," she told Cyril. "I'm worried myself." Finally, I plugged in Mama's phone by the bed and placed the receiver to her ear. She grabbed it, whispered, "I just can't," and hung up on Cyril.

When it was apparent that Mama planned to sleep her way through until it all went away, Daddy took action. He called Johnnie Mae, and she and Lyla and Romey soon arrived at our door. They marched right into Mama's room and propped her up against the pillows. Johnnie Mae threw off the blanket and threw open the windows, while Lyla rubbed

Mama's cheeks, and Romey made that all-important call on her behalf, using his best teacher's diction to talk to the funeral home director.

And then they talked to Mama about the business of putting Kimmie into the ground. They threw questions at her nonstop. *Will it be at a church? Which one? You need me to go with you to pick out the casket? Has anybody called the insurance company? Who can write the obituary? And do you have a nice picture of her? Start thinking about the service, Vy Honey. I know a woman who can sing. And Kimmie's clothes, do you have any with you? 'Cause if not, I can take you shopping. We need a reliable printer too, need to get the order in for the programs, can't wait too long. Same thing with the flowers. Who's gonna perform the eulogy, Honey? Now, come on, pick a day. I suggest Saturday. One week is long enough for a soul to wait to be buried. That only gives us three days. No time. I assume she'll go to Woodlawn Cemetery, right? Since it's so close by. And do you want a family hour the night before? We need somebody to cook. Can't JD's sister take care of all that? Ain't that why she's here?*

Out of nowhere, Cyril appeared in the doorway. Filling it with his height and hazel-eyed glare. "I'm much obliged to all of you for helping Vy through this," he said. "But I've got it from here."

Romey, Lyla, and Johnnie Mae rose, respectful, and filed out of Mama's room. Cyril went to her, leaned over, and said, "Let's get this behind us." Mama looked into Cyril's face and was surprised that she still loved him. She swung her legs over the side of the bed.

Death's pedestrian details reveal what your position is in the family constellation. As soon as Cyril stepped in, things fell into an orderly place. Of course he'd be the one to handle the details, not Mama. He was the one who knew Kimmie best. He lived with her those final five years as she evolved into the seventeen-year-old etched across our memories, the one that would be forever young and rebellious. To Mama, it was the way it should be—a father caring for his daughter.

Watching Cyril, you could understand why he never left his wife all

217

those years, even when Mama beckoned with his only child. He stayed married because he was ultimately a loyal man. And protective. Just to watch how he handled the funeral director was proof of that. "Don't you try to tell me what my daughter might need," he snapped at the man when he, businessman that he was, tried to suggest a pair of "resting slippers" with a matching shroud. And when Mama said she didn't want to see Nolan's black ass at the service, Cyril said, "That's the last boy she cared something mighty about. No matter what we think of him, he ought to be there if he chooses."

We had no family church to fall back on, and so Cyril chose Gesu Catholic Church on Six Mile Road, because he was Catholic. We learned that Kimmie had enjoyed lighting candles in one little church near their house in Louisiana. He added personal touches to the service, with a poem by Khalil Gibran that he found in her wallet and a recording of "Bridge over Troubled Waters," a song that reminded him of her. But it was hard without the cocoon of familiarity that other high school car deaths guarantee—no spontaneous shrines created by bereaved classmates, no long-faced teachers pointing out all her promise, no neighbors telling cute stories of watching her grow up. Kimmie had died between homes—rudderless and disconnected, just what she had been racing not to be.

Mama stayed in her bed as I sat guard at her side. But as the funeral drew nearer, I noticed a strange thing occurring. That message to me that I was all she had faded with each encroaching hour, like a fugue, and I wasn't sure that she'd ever spoken those words. She turned her back to the wall, as if done with me. On the morning of the service she said not a word, her face a stone. It was a necessary step, given what she had in mind. Unknowing, I stayed near, silently screaming at her to notice me.

What got me away from Mama's side was Aunt Essie's suggestion that Daddy take me shopping for something new to wear to Kimmie's funeral. "Need to get her out the house for a spell," I heard her tell Daddy. We drove downtown to Hudson's Department Store, where the

Thanksgiving Day parade we never attended was held. I was anxious for two reasons: I knew nothing about shopping for clothes outside of a catalog, and I knew all too well the importance of dressing right for the occasion.

Inside the store, with its perfect mannequins and bright lights and racks of clothes and white salesladies, I saw Daddy as others might— his wide, lumbering frame and frayed leather belt, his shirt growing perspiration stains like spilled motor oil under the armpits, stark against his milk chocolate skin. I rushed to make my selections quickly, raking through the clothes racks. A saleslady approached us.

"We have some nice summer dresses on sale over against that wall," she said, pointing behind us.

"We not looking for summer dresses on sale," said Daddy, in a talking-to-white-folks voice. "It's fall now."

"Well." She pursed her lips. "If I can help you with anything," she said, dashing off.

After walking around the girl's department a couple times, I chose a pretty polka-dot navy blue pleated skirt with a matching jacket. The jacket had a white, wide collar, and when I tried it on it made me think of Lois Lane, reporter. Kimmie would be impressed, I thought. We took it over to the saleslady.

"You're a lucky little girl to have your father buy you such a nice, expensive outfit," she said.

Daddy grabbed my hand inside his own and said, "She has a lot of nice, expensive outfits."

Our saleslady looked over her eyeglasses and asked, "Will you be putting this on your Hudson's charge card?"

"Nope. I got the money right here," said Daddy. "Cash and carry."

She rang up the sale in silence as Daddy handed over one of those one-hundred-dollar bills.

As we were leaving, Daddy pointed to a pair of off-white shoes with black polka dots. They reminded me of a Dr. Seuss book about a leopard with multicolored spots. "You want those?" he asked.

219

"Can I get them?" JC Penney's catalog never had anything like these shoes, with their black bow and wedged heel.

"Go find that lady, tell her we want to buy these right here," he said, settling into one of the seats in the children's shoe department. The chair was too small for him, and he looked stuffed into it. I found the saleslady, she helped me try on a pair, Daddy pulled out his wad of cash, paid, and within minutes we were walking out of the store— Daddy holding one moss-green Hudson's bag while I held the other. This shopping spree inside a store was the last one I would experience for many years.

O n the Day, Aunt Essie took care of everyone, helping me dress in my new suit, tying Daddy's one tie into a knot at his throat, and putting Mama's dress over her head, zipping it in the back. It was the first time Aunt Essie ever pressed my hair, a ritual that I endured every week for years, until the day I shunned her hot comb for an alluring Afro. She sat me in front of her and coated my hair with Du Charm, then took the metal comb that had been heating in its own little hollow oven and straightened my hair, one section at a time. From there, she slipped smooth blue-handled hot curlers into the little oven and curled my hair, click-clicking her way through the job with precision and rhythm. That smell of hair frying has always reminded me of death.

I was afraid to enter the church. I'd never been in one before. I stood at its threshold shivering, until Daddy prodded me along, whispering in my ear that it was okay. I remember how cavernous and ornate it was and looking nothing like the other important structures I'd been inside—the bank or the main library or the City-County Building. I assumed it was a place reserved for funerals.

When Daddy led me to the casket, my hand in his, I looked down at Kimmie, at the wavy hair flowing onto her shoulders, and I studied her smooth, Crayola-gold skin, her painted lips. I realized she was pretty despite her funny-colored, dancing eyes, not because of them. She was wearing her long, midnight blue dress that I so loved. Mama had let me select it. Her casket was draped in a spray of flowers, a little sash across it that read, "REST IN PEACE. YOUR LOVING FAMILY," and I wondered about that, about how peaceful a rest death could be. I would have stood there just staring at her for a long time if Daddy hadn't gently pulled me along. "Will we get to see her one more time?" I asked him when we were already at our seats. He didn't answer me, just looked down into my eyes, turned, and led me back to her.

"You can kiss her good-bye if you want," he said. I leaned in, kissed Kimmie's cheek. It was cold. And hard. I didn't trust my own lips, and so I touched her face with my finger, but it was still cold and hard. I jerked my hand away. Daddy grabbed it and led me back to my seat. We passed by everyone, including Nolan, his Afro a helmet, and Rhonda with her cupped hands full of tears, and Terrance Golightly, who boldly waved when our eyes met.

Cyril walked slowly to the front of the church and stood before us, his black suit transforming him from a confident lumberjack to a bereaved father. "I look out at all of you who didn't know my daughter," he said. "Maybe you knew her mother, maybe you remember her from her early days in De-troit, but you didn't know Kimmie like I knew her. And that hurts me deeply, to think you will stand up and file out of here and not really know who she was. So I'm going to tell you a few things that mattered to her, just a few things." He paused. "She liked that smell of sugarcane burning. And she loved the Mississippi River, everything about it. That and the big plantation houses. She just thought they were beautiful. 'Let's go riding by, Papa,' she'd say. 'I'll show you my favorite.' I can't tell you how tickled she was just to do that. And when we went fishing, it was nothing for her to catch a big one and throw it back in, laughing when the fish slapped against the water, tickled at how happy it was to be free." He shook his head. "And oh boy, that laugh. Like spring water trickling down a brook. That was some laugh." He paused. "I think I can say without a doubt that my Sweet Pea liked it down South. And neither one of us was sure what

221

would happen when she showed up." He smiled at a spot above all our heads. "The way she said, 'My papa,' it was like a prayer to my ears. 'My papa.' I guess that's the thing I'm going to miss most of all." He stood there for a few moments looking out at something only he could see. Finally, he shrugged, as if to say: *What's the use? You could never know her as I did, so what's the use?* Then Cyril left the sanctuary, slowly walking back to his seat, sound of his cowboy boots bouncing off the vaulted ceiling.

I sat stiffly through it all, unable to stop shivering. Daddy put his suit jacket around me. Mama's bruised face remained hidden by a black veil, and a fringed shawl hung from her limp shoulders. Aunt Essie sat gripping a handkerchief, the tops of her support hose peeking out from the rise in her black Sunday-go-to-meeting dress. My polka-dot shoes made me dizzy, and I closed my eyes. Throughout the rest of the service, I could think about one thing and one thing only: the stillness of all that beauty.

I found her sitting on her bed, still dressed in her black suit and black veil, which now hung like a bride's after the kiss, away from her face. She was staring at the record player, the album from days before nestled atop it. Wanting to show an understanding of what meant a lot to her, I carefully placed the needle onto the vinyl, at the front edge of the record. But just as the needle found its groove, Mama rose and snatched the record player's arm, the needle making an awful, screechy sound as it flew across the LP, scratching it mercilessly. Mama lifted the album and held it to her chest, rocking herself back and forth, back and forth. All at once, she moved to the open window, and with her good arm she hurled the circle of vinyl into the air, where it furled across the sky, a black Frisbee.

I have often asked myself just what it was my mother loved so about Stevie Wonder's music. I have tossed around many theories—that he was the perfect son she lost, that he stood for what could be full of life and visionary within a blinded, dying city, that knowing his mother lived nearby made her feel more connected to him. Maybe Cyril took her to a very early concert where Little Stevie sang and played his harmonica, and his distinctive voice forever connected her to a period of joy in her life. Perhaps it was some combination of all these things. And then again maybe it was as simple as this: my mother loved the feeling

Stevie Wonder's voice gave her, that feeling of beauty washing over her like a baptismal spray.

She returned to the bed and lowered her head into her hands. Her body convulsed, her back so fragile and bent that I couldn't see the stream of tears escaping through her fingers. I had not seen my mother cry since Dr. King's assassination, but I suddenly knew that she could not be what I needed. I knew that Mama wasn't like Aunt Essie. She wasn't strong as an ox.

She lay in bed after the funeral and thought about the people who would miss her. Cyril. He'd miss her, with his sloppy kisses and yummy loving, his fierce, strange loyalty. But he'd be able to live without her, just as he had all those years he refused to leave his wife. And JD? Nostalgia might make him feel sad for a little while, but he still had Rae. And what about me? She knew my attachment to Daddy would sustain me. She concluded that she was effectively alone in the world—no parents, no siblings worth knowing, just her own slender life and tiny, failed family. Death would be an exciting option in comparison—riskier and somehow more full. She thought of it as a place where all the others had gathered: her own flighty mother, her elusive father, her stillborn son, and now Kimmie. That configuration of family sounded so much more alluring. She started plotting that night and every free moment after—between the sad stares, the words of condolence, the interminable food, and Aunt Essie's ever-presence.

Two days later, an ambulance rushed Mama to the hospital. No one would tell me anything, not even Daddy, who simply said the funeral had "been too much on your mama." Once the ambulance left, Aunt Essie took a plastic bag into the bathroom and one-by-one threw away all the pill bottles she found in the medicine cabinet. But I knew that wasn't where Mama kept her cache. Her Valiums were tucked neatly in a Kleenex she kept folded in the side zipper of her pocketbook. I expected her to die in that emergency vehicle as medical technicians hovered, bruising her chest in efforts to bring her heart back. Today, all these years later, I still expect to get a call from Cyril, telling me of the accidentally lethal combination of whiskey sours and barbiturates found in her system. But because of how Mama attacked her beloved Stevie Wonder LP on that soft September day of Kimmie's funeral, I'll know it was no accident.

The very night after she came home from the hospital, Mama left with Cyril. She gave me a one-arm embrace as she guided my cheek into her belly, pressing her fingertips into my back. Her eyes were dry. "Are you coming back?" I asked.

"Not right away," she admitted.

My heart a laden water balloon, I begged. "Don't go. It's dangerous out there, on the road."

She took my little chin into her hand, tilted it back. "We're flying, Rae. Flying is safe."

I nodded my understanding, balloon punctured, vision so watery she seemed to float.

"Someday soon, you'll come spend some time with me in Louisiana, okay?"

"Okay." I forced the tears to stay put, refusing to blink.

She opened her purse, handed me a handkerchief. "Here," she said. "Hold on to this for me."

I took the handkerchief from her, brought it to my nose. It was white with a lacy macramé trim in a soft color others called ecru. It smelled exactly like Mama, like her perfume and menthol cigarettes, and I knew I was going to save it—but *not* sleep with it under my pillow every night like a lovesick girl, because as she left, a kind of resolve began taking shape inside of me. A protective layer grew over my heart that night, sheer as a membrane, and I willed it to quickly form its own crust and harden—become my personal shield against sudden good-byes.

225

In the days that followed, Aunt Essie prepared balanced meals: break-fasts with bacon and eggs *and* biscuits, hot lunches of soup and sand-wiches, and dinners with root vegetables and tender meats. These meals we ate together at the breakfast nook, woven place mats underneath our food. It was what I'd always longed for—all of us together at the table, having a meal. Only it wasn't the right us.

Aunt Essie also managed to get Daddy and me to sleep upstairs, in Mama's bedroom. She made her case to him as she stormed through the den, pushing past his protests, removing old newspapers and wiping down the TV. "It just don't seem right to me is all, you living in this tiny room like a hard-luck drunk," she said. "This is your house. You got four bedrooms upstairs. How come you can't use none of 'em?"

He resisted at first but actually seemed relieved to have a woman boss him around, take care of household things. He didn't really care where he slept, he said, as long as his baby was beside him.

I wished I felt the same way. Mama's bed was so much bigger, so much firmer, and less lumpy than our den sofa bed. And yet I didn't like it. I didn't like the largeness of the room, nor the vast space that existed on one side of me—the side where Daddy wasn't. It brought draftiness, and it reminded me of who was missing. Still I didn't think he'd ever kick me out of it.

That night, like so many others before it, I knelt beside Daddy and lay a compress across his forehead, gently applying pressure. I rubbed the back of my hand across his closed eyelids. He rolled over on his stomach. His breaths became steady. But as I began to climb into bed beside him he sat up.

"You'll do better now sleeping in your own bed," he said.

"Why?"

"Time to."

"Because Aunt Essie said so? What business is it of hers?"

"Just go on, do as I say. Gone to your room."

He meant it. She had finally convinced him that sharing a room with her father wasn't healthy for a girl my age. Now that I was his sole

226

responsibility, he had to think of these things, she pointed out. How did it look, she wanted to know, for a man's daughter to join him in his bedroom after his wife has left, taking over her mama's spot? And Daddy, for all his protectiveness, was a bit overwhelmed by this new role as a single parent. You have to worry about all manner of things with girls, Aunt Essie explained to him. You've got to think of the consequences of things later on down the road. He thought about it. She was a woman. Maybe she knew best.

And so I had to go.

I stumbled out of Mama and Daddy's bedroom, crossed the darkened hallway, paused at my own unused room, and entered Kimmie's. I flipped on the light and could see the rectangular spaces where the posters had hung, the spot on the wall Aunt Essie had scrubbed clean, and a thin layer of incense ash on the shelf where Kimmie's altar had been. I climbed onto the bare mattress, curled my body like an unborn baby's, rocked back and forth. But the flimsy membrane inside ripped loose, and without warning I was crying and crying circles of salty tears that slid sideways across the bridge of my nose and seeped into the naked pillow—nine years old and alone in bed for the first time in my life.

227

Part Two

Merging

Choose a safe space to enter. Then blend into traffic.

WHAT EVERY DRIVER MUST KNOW

W ith both my mother and sister gone, I connected them in my head as one lost love called KimmieMama. Believing their fates the same enabled me to lie to myself. They were both gone but alive, and we would hear from them soon. Kimmie's funeral I blocked out as some kind of ritualistic freak show that had nothing to do with reality, everything to do with adults' weirdness. I was adept at illusion, having practiced it all those years in that house when my parents lived up and down and didn't speak to each other and we all pretended it was okay. Mama and Kimmie were in some predicament they must escape from, after which they would call from a highway pay phone. This mental trick of denial worked well for a few days, days spent beneath the dining room table daydreaming about the reunion, plotting out what I would wear and would say, what it would feel like to once again hug KimmieMama.

In that time, Aunt Essie was there, caring for me and for Daddy. I told myself she and I were a team and it was our job to make sure Daddy had what he needed beyond his pills. I provided the warm compresses for his head, and she provided his meals and clean clothes. I still resented her for persuading Daddy to kick me out of his bed, but I knew enough to know we needed her. One morning as she washed my hair, my head bent over the kitchen sink as she poured a bowl of warm water along the nape of my neck, Aunt Essie murmured into my ear, "Surprised we haven't heard none from your mama yet."

"Maybe she can't get to a phone," I said.

"That ain't it," she answered. "She called and gave me her number soon as she arrived in Louisiana."

I lifted my head up out of the sink basin, letting the water run off my hair, down my back, as I turned to Aunt Essie. "You talked to her?"

"Put your head back in the sink, Darlin'. You getting the floor all wet." She guided my face to the running water, and I cupped my hand over my mouth as I listened in disbelief. "You and your daddy were sleep. Lord, she called about one in the morning must've been. Wasn't no sense in waking up folks at that hour. Ain't like any of us done got a lot of rest lately. I just took down the number and told her to call back later. Figured she would have by now."

Hearing this news pierced my fantasy. I cried into the kitchen sink, my tears flowing down the drain.

I kept dreaming about Kimmie and Mama. Different scenarios of the same thing: they were both in the Volvo, Mama sometimes in the front and other times Kimmie. The dreams always included the crash itself, and then I'd wake up. It was simple therefore to shift my thinking after Aunt Essie's revelation and tell myself they'd both died in the accident. I preferred that scenario anyway. *It's not that my mother never calls me; it's that she's dead.* Throughout that first year after she left, whenever the subject came up, I told people my mother was dead. Teachers, classmates, the Brownie troop leader.

It was easy to keep up this new lie for two reasons. First, I decided I hated my mother—for making Kimmie leave in the first place, for leaving herself, for being the one who survived, for not calling me. And besides, Daddy acted like she was dead. He never mentioned her name to me again, never spoke of her in the reverent tones he once did. And Aunt Essie only referenced her in the most disparaging asides.

234

Watching TV, she'd see some inappropriate behavior involving a mother and say, "A woman have a child, she need to act like she's somebody's mama," supposedly referring to a soap opera character or some neglectful event she heard on the news. But I always knew to whom she was referring.

With Mama dead in my heart, I missed Kimmie acutely. To escape my own grief, I spent every day after school and on weekends in my playhouse, where I created scenarios of family togetherness with the help of a couple dolls and Terrance Golightly. He'd come over, and we'd go down into the basement and play House. I was always the Mother, always in control, and he was always the Daddy, always sick and stretched out on the reclining lawn chair that substituted for a sofa bed in the playhouse. We easily graduated in our convoluted make-believe scenarios to "doing it." It was his idea, something he'd learned about from his big brother; I liked the dangerous nature of it. He said all Mommies and Daddies did it. We took off all our clothes, and he lay on top of me, rubbing against my smooth belly. I enjoyed the feelings it aroused in me, loved how it blocked out the pain of missing Kimmie and hating Mama yet gave me quick pleasure at the same time. I loved too the way his little taut body felt against my own, his chest angular and hard, penis like a Vienna sausage. His smell was a new one for me, that combination of bubble gum and wet dog, breath like sweet corn. And yet in the combination of all those new smells I recognized something familiar: the aroma of maleness. Playing house with Terrance got me through those early weird, sad weeks after the accident. I'd done the same thing all these years later, used a sweet guy as an ink blotter for spilled sorrow.

Meanwhile, in an attempt to draw me out of the basement—not that he ever knew what we were doing down there—Daddy began building the tree house for me in the backyard. For days and days of that Indian summer, he was out there pounding and sawing and sweating. Aunt Essie stood on the back porch with me as we watched. "Being a doggone fool!" she called out to him. "You got no business in your condition exerting yourself like that."

235

I thought her no fun and judgmental, and I began spending less time in the basement with Terrance, more out in the yard with Daddy. One day after Daddy had been working for hours on the tree house, he stood up against the tree trunk, wiping his forehead with a handkerchief and trying to catch his breath. He couldn't stop wheezing. Aunt Essie snatched me, pulled me aside. "You don't want him to have a stroke out there, now, do you?" she hissed, her mustache in my face. I shook my head no. "Then go talk to your daddy, tell him to stop that nonsense before it's too late."

"You tell him," I said, smart alecky.

She looked at me, shaking her head. "All right, Miss Backtalk, I will." She marched off, confronting him on the back lawn.

Before then, it really had not occurred to me that my father could die from his headaches. Riots and random violence I knew about. But from his own illness? Never crossed my mind. Once Aunt Essie corrected that oversight, it dawned on me that the pills weren't miracle drugs after all. I became terrified of what loomed as a possibility. As we sat in the den watching TV together one night soon after, I asked him right out, because I had to know.

"Are you going to die, Daddy?"

"Someday."

"Well, when you do, I want to die too."

"Don't talk like that. You gonna live a long, long time after I'm gone."

"I want to be buried with you."

"Don't you say things like that, Rae Rae. It hurts me to hear you talk like that."

I shut up, but I didn't stop thinking about Daddy dying, and my joining him.

What I did stop thinking about was Kimmie. As the days got shorter and colder, I didn't miss her anymore. It was as though she was a warm weather fixture, and it didn't seem odd at all to me for snow to be on the ground and no Kimmie. After all, by December more time had passed with her gone than had passed with her back in my life. I was used to her absence, used to not having her around. What had been different—a treat from heaven—was the sweet summer we had together. That was my first experience with the waning of grief. When she did cross my mind, I thought of her fondly and missed her in the oblique way I had before she ever returned. In fact, I decided Kimmie was a gift that had been given to me and then taken away. Twice. Even now when I hear that expression *Indian giver*, Kimmie's face, shiny Pueblo earrings dangling from her ears, moves across my mind's eye.

Christmas was filled with lonely abundance. In the past, it had been a time lacking ornamentation, apart from the little plastic tree Daddy put in the den window. There'd always been lots of nuts and clementines around because he'd made sure of that, but dinner was traditionally a simple capon that Daddy had roasted. I could always count on a few select toys—purchased by Daddy with money Mama left on the dining room table. I'd leave Santa Claus a slice of caramel cake and a glass of eggnog, go to sleep, wake up, play, and that was it. Quietly festive. Mama didn't seem to like the holidays—or rather she didn't know what to do with them. But this year, Aunt Essie decided to make a big deal of Christmas. She put up a massive silver-limbed tree that changed colors thanks to a little light with a revolving circular filter that threw red, green, and blue hues onto the tree's branches. She cooked and baked for two days and shopped for gifts that she elaborately wrapped and propped under the tree. "I believe in praising the birth of Jesus Christ," she said. "Rejoice in the Lord, and your days will be long."

Two days before Jesus's birthday, Daddy hit the number. "Praise the Lord!" he yelled when he found out. Aunt Essie wasn't amused by his "foul-mouthed sacrilege," but Daddy was so giddy it was infectious. We were all excited and Daddy and I went on a shopping spree for all times. He walked me into Toys "R" Us, gave me a shopping cart, and said, "Go pick out whatever you want. Hell, I'm your Santa."

237

On Christmas morning I found all my hand-selected toys under the tree alongside a bounty of surprises: board games, paint sets, books, winter sweaters, and a lamb's wool coat. We ate our big holiday dinner at the dining room table, went out that night to see the movie *Sounder*, and neither Daddy nor Essie mentioned the fact that December 25 came and went and Mama didn't call. To me it was confirmation that she was dead. That night as I sat amid my presents, overwhelmed and sad and grateful all at once, Daddy looked at my confused face and said, "I wish every day could be Christmas for you, Brown Eyes." And during the rest of his brief life, he tried to make that true.

The ultimate present from Daddy came after his death, in the form of my beautiful white Mustang.

I never saw Aunt Essie sleep. She was always the first up and the last to go to bed. She told me sleep held no joy for her. "Waste of time, dreaming a lot of mishmash from the past, making you want to look back when life is what's ahead," she explained. "You not gonna catch me turning to a pillar of salt." She preferred keeping busy, and she had a whole slew of ways to do that, besides cooking and cleaning. Even while she watched her "stories" on TV, she was knitting or shucking corn or sewing a hem in a dress. And she looked forward to getting out of the house. "I'm no homebody," she announced. She liked to walk to the grocery store every day for the fresh air. And by the winter, she'd already found and joined the nearest church within walking distance, Mount Bethel Baptist. That kept her busy on Sundays and a couple weeknights.

She also brought the community into our home, somehow knowing everybody within no time: the Arab couple who owned the party store on West Seven Mile Road and had just had a new baby, old men from down South who sold watermelons and fresh tomatoes and peaches from the backs of raggedy trucks, young men needing to cut the grass or do some handyman work (she was touched by the teenager who rang the bell, told her he was collecting garbage, and asked if she had any he might take down to the dump for a small donation). She gave away food, wrote letters to "incarcerated boys" with five dollars tucked inside. She lectured strung-out heroin addicts on corners, refusing to step over them as they nodded out. "When you're a missionary for God's work, folks will just talk to you. Open up and hand you whole pieces of themselves," she claimed. I guess for her it was true, because she was forever returning home with a sad story someone told her while standing in line at the bank or the bus stop or the grocery store. Now I see that her decision to leave her Nashville home behind and come take care of her brother and niece up North, that itself was a missionary act.

I guess Aunt Essie was just what you'd expect a solid, southern black woman to be, but I knew nothing about her type; she was so completely different from my mother, she was like a foreign country, and I studied her just that way, as though she brought with her a whole new language and locale, a different landscape across which to move through these odd days and nights.

She wanted everything respectable. That meant the house had to look like a woman lived in it. For the most part, she succeeded in making that happen. Plants in the living room, photographs from back home on the mantel, wax fruit in the center of the dining room table. But she never did convince Daddy to take the pool table out of the living room. She griped about it for weeks, begging him to put it in the basement, but Daddy ignored her until we all just walked around it as if it wasn't there. He never actually shot pool on it, except for that birthday party, and we began using it to hold things—umbrellas, magazines, my homework. It was his one defiant contribution to home decor.

Aunt Essie took over the never-used guest room as her own. On Sunday mornings, she let me watch as she dressed for church. I marveled at the squat, fleshy shape and heft of her body, how she prepped it for going out. First she put on her girdle, which took some work to get into, much pulling up and resting, pulling up and resting until the wayward flesh fell in behind its elasticized trap. Next came her support hose, a white woman's flesh tone two shades lighter than her own skin, with elastic bands around the thigh. Protection against the blood clots

240

she was prone to. And then came her long-line bra, which she put on backward, fastening a dozen hooks before sliding it around her wide torso. Her bras were always vividly white. The cone-shaped cups captured her sagging breasts and lifted them to stand-up attention. Nothing like Mama's wispy, ready-for-a-hot-date lace teddies and matching tap pants. I especially liked to watch Aunt Essie toss baby powder between her thighs and breasts. When she slipped her church dress over her head, it was always the same: a well-made, simply tailored shift in a modest print or solid like the kind on the plus-size racks in the women's department at Hudson's. I doubt that Aunt Essie ever ordered clothing from a mail-order catalog.

On Mother's Day, she demanded that I go to church with her. Finally. I hadn't been interested before, and Daddy had resisted on my behalf. But this day being what it was, she'd convinced him that I needed the distraction, so I joined her. She pinned a white carnation to her lapel, then gave me a red one. "Can I have a white one?" I asked. "Like you?" She paused, not bothering to tell me the symbolism of the colors—red if your mother is alive, white if she's not—and handed over the white one. "Might as well," she said. "Might as well."

It was a full two hours of singing and preaching and fanning. Afterward, I met new people, proudly introduced over and over by Aunt Essie as "my brother's child." Until then, I hadn't known what it felt like for another to announce your place on the family tree, declare your value by declaring whom you come from. Standing there with Aunt Essie, I felt awash in kinship, protection. Holding her hand as we walked home, I decided *she* was my new mother and I was lucky to have her.

When we got home, Daddy stood waiting for us in the doorway. "Your mama called," he said. "She's calling back in five minutes to talk to you."

I walked inside and stood looking at the Princess telephone in the hallway, afraid to touch it. I stared at the phone until it suddenly rang. I jumped. It rang again. I picked it up.

241

"Hi, Rae." Her voice sounded near, even as I envisioned the space it traveled through the phone wires to reach me. She asked about school. I told her it was fine. She said she hoped we could see each other soon, and that a package was on its way for me. It would arrive by my birthday, she promised. And then the conversation was over, but I kept holding the phone, letting the click sound hit me with its finality, letting the dial tone surge through the earpiece, until an operator came on to remind me that there was a receiver off the hook.

Just like that, Mama had risen from the dead.

It was hard to do anything but wait for that package. When the box finally arrived four days later with its Louisiana postmark, Aunt Essie helped me push it into the dining room, where she took a steak knife and slit it open. Inside the box lay piles of clothes. I recognized them immediately. They were Kimmie's.

"Well, I'll be," said Aunt Essie. "I have never . . . in my life . . . seen anything . . ."

I recognized the fringed vest and the palazzo pants and the patched jeans with the peace sign sewn into them. Aunt Essie tried to help me take the box upstairs, but I wouldn't let her touch anything. Instead, I carried every article of clothing up to Kimmie's room—which was now mine—and put each piece in my closet, one at a time. Some things still smelled faintly like musk oil Kimmie used to buy from the Muslim brothers selling it on street corners. It almost felt like I had Kimmie back, like the Indian giver had half changed his mind.

I called Mama that night. I made Daddy teach me how to dial the one, followed by the necessary ten digits. When she heard my voice, she sounded pleased. "Oh!" she said. "Rae!"

"I got the box, Mama. Thank you."

"I thought you might want to have some of her things," she said. "She had so many nice clothes."

"I love everything you sent."

"Take care of them, okay, Rae?"

"I will, Mama."

There was a pause, and in that silence Mama must have weighed a dilemma—whether or not to speak Kimmie's name. "She could really dress, couldn't she?"

"She sure could. I liked that outfit she gave you to wear for your card party. Remember? It looked good on you, Mama."

Then she let herself say it. "Kimmie just knew what looked good."

"Kimmie knew just how to match things together, the right colors and everything," I chimed in.

"She sure did."

And so it went. Mama and I were the closest witnesses to Kimmie's life that last summer, to the small moments and the big ones. Sharing that connection made ours a sweet, tight bond, we with our mutual memories. It was in its own way a perfect relationship—both of us getting a piece of what we needed from it.

Those intense telephone conversations lasted for three years, alongside Mama's ritual of sending me more of Kimmie's clothes for my birthday. Together these two events gave my life a steady reassurance that had been lacking even when Mama lived with us. The clothes were keepsakes of my big sister's, but more important, gifts from Mama. She was so stylish and sophisticated that I wanted to wear what she deemed worthy. I craved her advice, fashion or otherwise.

Most of the pieces I could get away with wearing because I simply pulled them tighter with belts or let them hang loose, and in that weird fashion moment that was the seventies, no one thought it odd. "That is *so* cool," girls would say to me about a pair of baggy bell-bottoms or a flowing maxiskirt engulfing my beanstalk body. "Thanks, this used to be my sister's," I'd say, keeping things vague so no one had to know she was dead. I wasn't even sure she was.

What I loved most about our talks was Mama's voice. She sounded exactly as she had that night before the funeral when she held me close and told me, "You're all I have left. You're it." We spoke in low voices, our lips brushed against the mouthpieces, ever so intimate, the smell of Jungle Gardenia permeating the telephone wires.

243

I felt something akin to happiness during those preteen years, with my mother a phone call away and my father at arm's reach. Only once in that time did an event impinge to upset my precarious joy: the psychic Jeane Dixon's prediction that the world would end on New Year's Eve of 1973. Mama said folks could mark their calendars based on what Jeane Dixon said. I didn't know how to prepare for the end of the world. That night shortly before midnight, I stood in the doorway of Daddy's room and held my breath until I was sure I saw Daddy's body rise and fall, rise and fall. And then I went to bed, reciting the prayer Kimmie had taught me: *Now I lay me down to sleep, I pray the Lord my soul to keep. If I die before I wake, I pray the Lord my soul to take.*

One day not long after Jeane Dixon's prediction Mama called, her voice broken up. "Stevie is in a coma," she said. "Car accident."

"Oh no!" I said, even though I hadn't gone near a Stevie Wonder song since Mama had left.

"I just don't understand," she said. "Why?"

I was silent, unable to answer her, feeling doom roll over our telephone relationship. So *this* was the end of the world.

She didn't call for a couple weeks, and I tried to accept this tiny Armegeddon, but then one day the phone rang, I answered it, and she simply said, "He woke up." I could hear "Boogie On Reggae Woman" playing in the background. She was quiet before she added, a note of envy in her voice: "Some folks attract miracles. Those are the ones to hang around."

I tried to think of someone in my life who had been lucky. I couldn't think of anyone.

The rift between Daddy and me came along with my entry into Hampton Junior High. I was twelve and wanted to hang out with Lisa LaBerrie and go roller skating at Northland Roller Rink, eat corned beef on rye with mustard at Lou's Finer Delicatessen, buy the top 45s at Mike's Record Shop on Avenue of Fashion and make up dance routines to our favorite songs.

Meanwhile, Daddy was negotiating with the monkeys on his back—one a searing pain, the other a potent drug. He was new to the Demerol injections, hadn't found the dosage that would, as he put it, "even" him out. Either he took too little and was controlled by throbbing headaches, or he took too much and nodded out. I didn't yet understand his heavy sleeping, nor did I understand his wide-awake irritability. I foolishly saw it as a rejection of me. Or maybe I used that excuse as an easy out. Either way, the bond we'd shared before was dissolving right alongside my preteen status.

Thirteen was by far the worst year of my life. First, for some reason I still don't fully understand, I was skipped a grade in school—snatched from my best buddies and thrust into classrooms with older boys and girls who didn't know me. My homeroom teacher only said I needed a more "challenging environment." I had recently begun hanging out with one of the "fast" girls in my school. Perhaps they were trying to save me from a life of ruin?

When my fourth birthday box arrived from Mama, included inside—sandwiched between Kimmie's old granny dresses and miniskirts and peasant tops—was a plane ticket. We had talked a few times about my coming to visit her "when the time is right," and I had been excited about the future. Now that the future was literally in my hands, I was terrified. When Mama called that Sunday, I announced that I didn't want to ride on an airplane. "But they're safer than cars," she said. "I'd take my chances in the sky over a highway any day."

What must have seemed irrational to my mother made perfect sense to me. I wasn't afraid of airplanes; I was afraid of their pilots. My fear of flying stemmed from my fear of accidents in general. I always believed Cyril was careless behind that wheel. And I felt that the best way to prevent an accident was to have complete faith in the one at the helm. Pilots were strangers I didn't trust.

The terror was real, but I misjudged its cause. It had been four years since I'd seen my mother. What if seeing me made her realize I was a poor replacement for Kimmie after all? Our weekly phone talks had stabilized me, taken the hate out of my heart, made me feel normal and worthwhile, a girl with a mother who loved her and would see her soon. Mama and I shared an intimacy that people can only have over a telephone or in the front seats of cars on long-distance rides, eyes focused on the road ahead. Distant love is pure.

And then there was Daddy, living life as though it were a part-time job, with his *this-day-I'm-asleep, that-day-I'm-awake* existence. I wanted to talk to him about the plane ticket and was trying to catch him on an "up" day when Aunt Essie said, "Don't go flapping that thing around JD. He don't need no reminders of that woman's conniving." She was certain Mama was plotting again to take me away from Daddy. "You got no idea how much that hurt him when Vy tried to pull off what she did that day," she told me. "She just gonna snatch you in broad daylight."

"You weren't even there," I said.

"Oh, but I heard, darlin'. Heard all about it."

"From Daddy?"

"Who else? That's why I know what I'm talking about."

"What did he say about it?"

"You don't want to know."

"I do."

She paused. "He said he felt like murdering somebody that morning."

"Daddy?"

"Watching them act like some perfect little family, and here he was a sick man and all, come that close to losing you."

"Did he really say that?"

"Said that and more. I says to him, 'Well now, JD, you wouldn't have done nothing crazy on account of Rae.' And he says, and I quote, 'Yeah, Rae saved a few lives that day, including her mama's.'" Aunt Essie raised her right hand. "As God is my witness, he said it. I got no reason to lie."

Naturally after that I stalled, pulled two ways. But Mama persisted. "I've arranged for you to have your own stewardess on the plane," she said. "She'll be with you throughout the flight. And I think you should stay for the entire summer. I've got it all planned out."

This spurred heartbreak, the image of my mother making "summer to-do" lists at the kitchen table of her Brady Bunch–style house, sipping instant coffee as a cigarette burned in an ashtray nearby, her feet clad in nylon slippers. *Louisiana.* Those lilting syllables, multiple vowels still held their allure. I thought maybe, just maybe, it was worth the risk after all.

But Aunt Essie protested. "What she wanna see you for *now?*" she asked, hands on hips in fierce protectiveness. "After all this time?"

"She misses me," I said.

"Hmph."

"And I miss her."

"Well, just keep in mind who been here all along, caring for you," 247 she said. "Just keep in mind what it would do to your daddy for you to leave him just like that." She snapped her finger.

I couldn't fully articulate my own dilemma because it was multi-pronged: I wanted to see Mama, desperately, but I was afraid my physical presence might disappoint her somehow. I also didn't want to hurt Daddy, couldn't imagine being away from him; yet I honestly didn't know what I would do if Mama asked me to live with her. And on top of all of that was Aunt Essie's intimation that the whole ordeal would surely kill Daddy—or make him kill. The best thing I could do was to develop a fear of flying.

But Mama threatened me, saying that her invitation wouldn't extend forever. She gave me a week to decide. Out of desperation I came up with a plan. I asked Daddy to drive me down South to see Mama. This was to me a perfect solution. It eliminated my need to get on an airplane; it got me to my mother; it included Daddy in the plans, and it gave me the chance to ride a long stretch of road just as I'd always wanted to do.

"I got to see about that, Brown Eyes," said Daddy. "Gotta see what Alfred thinks about my car going that far."

"He can tune it up," I said, more confident about my plan the more I thought about it.

"And where you think I'm a stay while you visiting with your mama?"

"You and Aunt Essie can visit family in Nashville. She's always saying how she misses home; you can stay there a while and then pick me up on the way back."

"You got it all planned out, now, don't you?"

I nodded, satisfied with myself.

"We don't actually have family left in Nashville."

"Aunt Essie has her good friend Lucretia."

"True. But you do know that Tennessee ain't nowhere near Louisiana?"

248   I shrugged. "It'll be an adventure."

Daddy laughed.

Plans went along better than I'd hoped. Aunt Essie's friend, it turns out, owned a boardinghouse in Nashville. "I'll just tell Lucretia to hold out a couple rooms for me and JD," she said. "That way, I don't have to disturb the folks who been renting my house." And Mr. Alfred put a new transmission in Oldie, as a gift. "Got it at a junkyard, didn't cost me nothing," he explained. Mama didn't love the plan, but she saw it as a decent compromise given that she couldn't convince me to fly. "Just make sure JD knows that I expect you to stay *at least* a couple weeks," she said.

On the morning of our trip, we all piled into Oldie and took off, Daddy driving carefully and methodically. He and Aunt Essie were arguing over the radio dial—whether it should be tuned to the blues or gospel—when the accident occurred. We'd barely gotten out of the city when it happened—hit from behind by an elderly woman driving an old Chrysler. It was just a fender bender like the one Kimmie and I once had, but Daddy's head rammed against the steering wheel, which gave him a searing, instant headache. Aunt Essie insisted we file a police report and have Daddy checked out at the hospital. And I was instantly enraged with my father. Once again, he was too fat to wear blue jeans and too sick to drive highways and byways. I could not *wait* to learn how to drive myself, which I saw as the solution to all these unnecessary accidents.

The hospital decided to keep Daddy for a couple days. As soon as an emergency room doctor took his blood pressure, the doctor panicked, awed by the high reading. We called Mr. Alfred to come tow Daddy's car, and Aunt Essie and I caught the bus home from the hospital. I made the painful call to Mama. She was not at all sympathetic once she realized we were all more or less okay. "That's what I've been trying to tell you about cars," she said. "But would you listen? It's like you *want* something to happen so I can have that on my conscious too."

Daddy's car never did run again. Mysteriously, after it got towed, the motor was gone, brakes shot. Mr. Alfred finally hauled it to an auto graveyard. Oldie was nine years old.

249

After the aborted trip, I called Mama as usual on the following Sunday afternoon. Her conversation was dry— more distant and perfunctory, too formal. She never mentioned my visiting her again. And within a month, she stopped taking my calls altogether. Cyril would answer the phone. Every time. And every time, he told me the same thing: "She's sleeping, Chicken. Call back later."

Hopeful, I continued to wear Kimmie's hand-me-downs.

A teacher's strike kept us from returning to school that September. It dragged on and on, into the end of October, and in that time I staved off boredom by reading books. Whatever Daddy was reading, whatever I could grab from the library, I devoured. When I got my hands on *Soul on Ice,* I read it voraciously, captivated by Cleaver's admission that he was obsessed with white women. By the end of the book, I decided I could no longer have straightened, "trying to be white" hair; I had to have an Afro. But Aunt Essie, who had washed and pressed my hair religiously every week since her arrival, thought an Afro was too "vulgar" for a girl my age. I ran to Daddy for permission.

"You and your aunt Essie should work that out," he said.

This infuriated me. I decided I didn't need to work anything out with my aunt. I proceeded to wet my hair, saturate it with lotion, and then tie sections of it with twisted strips made from a paper bag, so as to give it the right balance of curl and nap.

"Now, I told you not to do that," said Aunt Essie when she discovered me. "You call yourself not listening?"

I ignored her, kept tying my hair.

"I'm talking to you."

Silence.

"God don't like ugly," she warned.

I still said nothing.

"And while you thinking you too cute to answer me, remember this: God ain't so particular about pretty neither."

I sighed, wanting to seem bored by her idle God-fearing threats. I shrugged my shoulders for effect.

"You gonna listen to me one day," she promised. "Do hear me say, you gonna listen to me one day."

"I don't have to listen to you," I spat at her. "You're not my mother."

Aunt Essie caught her breath. I knew I'd stepped over a line, but I didn't care. I had Mama's telephone number committed to memory.

"Whatever you think of me, you gonna respect me," she said, her arms folded defiantly across her chest. "I didn't come all this way, give up my nice home and my friends, to be sassed by an ungrateful little heifer." Then she waddled off, her curved back boomeranging my shame back at me.

Thirteen was also the year I started my period. It was not at all how I pictured it would be. I'd been waiting forever and was certain I was the only girl in the ninth grade who hadn't gotten hers yet. It felt like a dirty little secret, my lack of a menstrual cycle. Poised for womanhood, I kept a box of Kotex and a Tampax tampon ready. When it finally came, I stared at this little red stain against my winter white pants and thought how with my blue sweater the combined colors were weirdly patriotic. It was 1976, and the entire nation was in a yearlong bicentennial frenzy. Truth be told, I had nothing to celebrate. Cyril still wouldn't let me speak to Mama.

Aunt Essie marked this rite of passage with one of her trademark one-liners of wisdom. "Keep your dress down and your panties up," she warned. Then she told me to go to the store, buy a box of Kotex, get some safety pins, and put a napkin between my legs for protection. "Don't go buying them tampons neither," she said. "Don't nobody but whores wear those. They the only women who got enough room up there for them to stay put." There was more advice. "You got to be real conscious of keeping your body clean now," she said. "A woman don't want to go around smelling like fish gone bad." I felt an overwhelming 251 sadness as I fumbled in the bathroom with my new sanitary belt and that bulky napkin. Fed up with the cumbersome pad, I secretly used my tampon in defiance. Still, I couldn't ignore that starting my period meant not only monthly responsibility but also womanly guilt.

Daddy wasn't much better. When I told him about my period, he mumbled something about being careful around boys from that day forward, abruptly stopped kissing me good-bye or hello on the lips. Rather than feel rejected by him, I felt guilty, as though I had somehow betrayed him by doing this thing called maturing. His actions made me miss Mama more profusely than ever. I was sorry I could no longer pretend she was dead. And yet I turned her memory into a living shrine. I built an altar in my room, where I placed a picture of her I'd found in a drawer. In it, she was sitting on the front porch, smoking, looking out into the distance. Next to that I put a bottle of her perfume and a note Mama had written for me once when I was late for school. I bought an old Stevie Wonder LP from Mike's Record Shop, and I spun one tune from it over and over on my red record player. *"The answer my friend, is blowing in the wind,"* he crooned while I stayed in my room for long stretches of time, feeling sorry for myself. I started to grasp the notion that Daddy and Aunt Essie had conspired to keep Mama and me apart. She'd wanted to take me with her that long-ago August morning when she left with Kimmie and Cyril; I believed that what she once told me over the phone was true: Daddy had stopped her because of his own selfishness. I thought that was the worst word in the world—*selfish.*

Throughout that school year, Lisa LaBerrie and I spent too much time in her parents' garage, experimenting with cigarettes and playing cards. I introduced her to Kool's menthols and taught her how to play Tunk. I tried to show her the art of shuffling but could never quite mimic Mama's lovely waterfall, that flutter and blur of the cards.

Lisa and I let hours peel away from one another as we played, blood-thirsty competitors keeping elaborate scorecards on who had won how many games in how many hours.

Meanwhile, I became obsessed with a boy in my junior high school. Beautiful Jesse Thompson. He was in my math class and already had a deep voice except for occasional cracks that I thought were unbelievably cute. He had a slight gap in his teeth, chipmunk cheeks, and dimples. A warm, delicious smile. He teased me a lot, so I knew he liked me too. But he was popular, and often I'd see him talking to a girl at her locker one day, walking another one home from school the next. "Jesse, Jesse, Jesse," I whispered while gripping my hall pass on solitary walks to the girls' bathroom, where I went to experience my obsessive longing in the privacy of a toilet stall.

I didn't actually want a relationship with Jesse. I didn't know what that meant anyway. Derek was still three years into my future. I just wanted to *think* about being with Jesse all the time, wanted visions of him to crowd out other thoughts, be obsessed for the sake of the obsession. He had once asked for my phone number and actually called me at home a couple times. That didn't last long because I was so over-whelmed by my crush on him, I could barely keep up my end of the conversation. In school, when we encountered each other, I was tongue-tied, completely unable to respond to his teasing with anything witty or honest. Terrified of rejection, I forcibly suppressed my burgeoning feelings, only allowing them to escape through my little blue diary. It was like a fever, my obsession for Jesse, but worse, because the high temperature was accompanied by sharp sexual desire. I couldn't stop imagining him covering my neck in tiny, puckered-lip kisses. And yet once in his presence, I would feign indifference. It was too much. Some days, I literally felt faint.

But now, Jesse had a fast girlfriend. They were inseparable. He seemed to be in love, even though she was the kind of "gal" Aunt Essie said boys didn't respect, with her tight clothes and wet lip gloss and

253

reputation for putting out. I secretly wished that Jesse would disrespect me that way.

It was a terrible year.

Daddy read my diary. I knew he had because it wasn't in the same spot where I'd placed it in my shoebox under my bed. I asked Aunt Essie first, and she looked at me like I was crazy. Then I asked Daddy.

"I'm not gonna lie to you, Brown Eyes."

"But why? That's my private stuff!"

He looked so sad it was hard to focus on my righteous anger. "So who is this Jesse?" he asked.

"He's just a boy a school."

"Don't seem like he's just a boy. He's all you write about."

"That's just make-believe."

"Oh yeah? Well, it's convincing."

I walked out of the den feeling, once again, like the guilty one. Daddy, who had always trusted me, had turned into a spy. I knew he didn't fully believe me when I told him I was going skating or bowling with friends. I knew he was leaning against the radiator, watching me closely from the den window as I left with Lisa to go to her house. I'd feel his eyes on me and think about how Kimmie must've felt that summer when we watched her like hawks.

Aunt Essie tried to mediate. She said I was all my daddy had in the world and now that I was getting older he was losing his little girl. All of this, I already knew. I still didn't know how to handle it.

Mr. Alfred was the one who saved me. He offered me driving lessons in his white deuce-and-a-quarter—an old Buick Electra 225 that he kept parked at the shop. Built to last, with its manual transmission, front-wheel drive, and power steering. Every Saturday, after doing our errands together and barely talking, Daddy and I would swing by Mr. Alfred's shop. He let me get behind the wheel, and there he'd coach me along the side streets, teaching me how to work the clutch, even briefly letting me drive a main street in the right-turn lane. I got more and more confident, loving the feeling of operating two tons of metal as it eased along the road, shifting gears, discovering what a balm driving could be. I didn't think about my problems while operating that battle-proof Buick. She was my salvation. After each lesson I was always sad, longing to be old enough to *really* drive. It made being thirteen even more intolerable.

H igh school wasn't all that bad: I liked most of my classes, had enough breasts to fill a B cup, and at fourteen was finally old enough to get a work permit.

No one ever said extra money was needed in the household. Daddy had his modest disability and veteran's checks coming in. Aunt Essie had her social security check from her dead husband, Mr. Bingham. But the recession was raging, Detroit's car industry rusting. Gasoline prices were sky-high. The little extras had dried up. Daddy didn't play poker anymore, and he hadn't been lucky with the numbers in quite a while. Aunt Essie began taking in laundry, claiming it gave her "a little something extra to do," and Daddy even tried cleaning up at Big Boy's after closing a few nights a week. I'd go with him as he swung the sprawling mop back and forth across the tiled floor, his transistor radio blaring Albert King or Lou Rawls against the echoing ceilings. He'd mop a section, stop, lean on the mop handle for a spell, pick up again where he'd left off. Aunt Essie, who heard how hard Daddy panted through the job, put a stop to it. ("Think about that child in there," I heard her tell him. "She needs you.")

When I wasn't job hunting, I spent nearly all my free time hanging out with Lisa LaBerrie and our fast friend Angie. At Northland Mall, we submitted job applications at clothing stores and shoe shops and fast-food joints and flirted with store managers—stopping for lunch at Elias Brothers', where Angie found more and more ways to shock us with her talk about boys and oral sex. Finally, I got hired at Red Barn and had to wear a ridiculous uniform that was supposed to resemble that of a milk maiden on a farm, with its white apron tied around a short gray dress. We sold burgers and milk shakes and fried chicken and wore plastic name tags. I liked it, liked the salty French fries and dealing with customers and having something responsible to do. Every night at closing, Daddy waited for me outside, while other girls who worked there slipped into the souped-up hot rods of their boyfriends.

I still had no boyfriends but now fantasized about a new boy. This one was named Antonio Snapp, and he walked the halls of Cass Tech High School with long strides and sly glances, his towering height and patted-down Afro adding to his aura. He had a coveted locker in the front hall, where he hung out every morning before the first-hour bell, along with other cool guys. With nine floors, and lots of obscure corridors, the school's physical layout nakedly revealed a student's social status. Choice locker locations were like prime real estate.

Once again, I lived out an entire relationship in my head, imagining many scenarios. My favorite had him storming the back hall of the third floor, where those of us relegated to Siberian lockers had banded together into a subset, turning our fringe status into a cool, antipopularity clique. He pushes past the motley group, grabs me in his arms, and French-kisses me in front of them all. Then he smirks, strides off into the crowded main hall, and the next day I am beside him near the front entrance, hanging out and giggling just two lockers down from Marjorie, the head majorette, and Resa, the back-flipping star of the cheerleading squad.

Somewhere in between my lonely days as a tenth grader at Cass Tech, my job at Red Barn, and my fantasy dates with Antonio, Mama began calling again—after more than a year. One Sunday afternoon the

257

phone rang, and there she was on the other end. She asked, "They treating you okay?" We talked for barely four minutes, just long enough for
me to learn that she'd begun an herb garden in the back of her house
and that the mint was growing fast and furious, taking over. She asked
about school, and I said it was fine, and then the call ended. After that,
she called about every month or so, and it was always the same—a perfunctory conversation about superficial things with a tidbit thrown in
about her garden. I never called her, understanding that she needed to
be in control of our contact. And I never offered up pieces of my life in
confidence to her. It was what it was, my relationship with my mother,
and I tried to finally accept that. Still, that protective skein instantly
grew back, stretching anxiously across my heart, protecting me from
feeling too much.

And no matter what, I would *not* become my mother.

It wasn't that I thought Mama was a weak woman. She had power,
ruling our household when she was there, even in her throne-away distance. She controlled the real cash flow. She convinced Daddy to abandon his lover and return home. She convinced Kimmie to go with her to
Louisiana. And for too long, she had me waiting by the phone, convinced we had a real relationship.

Yet I could never see Aunt Essie making choices for a man that hurt
the ones she loved. Aunt Essie despised women who sang the blues, and
I despised women who got them. Weak women, ones who cried over a
guy or fell in love constantly or dreamed of weddings in puffy white
dresses. I never wanted to get married. I decided no one man would
have my heart, no man other than Daddy. And once I vowed this to
myself, it was easy to stick with my vow to never have children. Children complicated your relationship, led you to love a man more than
you should, to abruptly push off from the curb with him.

In eleventh-grade social studies class, I wrote an essay based on the
book *A Baby? Maybe.* In strident language, my essay outlined how the
media hoodwinks women into thinking children are bliss, a covert ploy

258

led by Gerber's, Johnson & Johnson, and the slew of other advertisers who benefit from baby culture. On that one subject, I was a high school progressive—a radical.

And then I stopped bleeding. Because I ran track throughout junior year, competing and winning, and was very fast, I apparently chased my period away. At first, I was actually relieved. My period had spawned the awkwardness between Daddy and me, and it had prompted Essie to dole out God-inspired warnings about fornication. Besides, with no period, there could be no children.

But after a couple months I started to miss it, miss the rituals surrounding its painful presence: the heating pad across my belly, the sipping from huge mugs filled with Women's Cycle herb tea, the long bath to soak away the leg and back aches. I realized that my period was one of the few things that put me in touch with my body. During those five days every month, I actually felt a deeper connection to Daddy, felt a little more understanding of the pain he faced on a daily basis. And there was something else: my period was the one thing I had in my life not dependent upon whether or not my mother called, or whether or not my father felt good on any given day. It was reliable, and I didn't realize how comforting and rare that was for me, until it was gone.

When Dr. Corey wouldn't help me, I became obsessive. I counted every twenty-eight days and circled the date each month with a green ink pen on a wall calendar from Cobo Cleaners. And when the appointed day came, I rushed to the bathroom, said a little mantra of "yes oh yes oh yes oh yes," and pulled down my panties. Nothing. Month after month of nothing.

I believed God was rearing His ugly head, He whom I had ignored for years, despite all of Aunt Essie's admonitions and chapter-and-verse quotations. I guess I thought of Him as a father figure, and for me that meant a sweet and loving man who was well meaning but limited in power. Since I already had one of those in my life, I hadn't turned to

259

Him much. Now He was punishing me for vowing with my friend Lisa to never have children. I bargained with Him that yes I would have a baby *someday* if He just brought back my period. I crossed my fingers to add to the potency of my prayer. God ignored me and my pleas for seven long months, and in that time, dry between my legs, I gave up on Him completely.

Daddy started getting dark spots in front of his eyes. Because of that, he needed me to drive. Aunt Essie was of no help, as she had never learned how. The little piece of a car he'd bought since Oldie's demise stayed parked out front for longer and longer stretches. Sometimes, when he was "feelin' up to it," he'd still take the car out for a quick spin to do his errands or swing by Mr. Alfred's body shop. But that was now rare. In fact, Aunt Essie walked to the corner store for groceries when she couldn't get one of her church friends to drive her to Kroger's. Whenever I saw her coming back from the party store, I knew it was a trip born out of necessity. She'd vowed more than a few times to never shop in one of those "A-rab stores" because to her the places smelled funny, never seemed clean, and the "folks up in there treat you like they doing you the favor, when you the one whose people done been in this country from the get-go." Daddy had even asked me to find friends to ride home with from my job at Red Barn. "Not up to that night driving," he explained. I turned in my apron and name tag, because it was too hard to ask one of the May-belline queens if I could catch a ride home in her boyfriend's ridiculous car. I couldn't tolerate those silly girls, who squished up so close to Rod or Louie or Gino, the poor guys could barely shift gears. Besides, every single breathing female was a potential threat to them. Who needed the grief?

I wanted just two things in life: to get my license and to find a fun job. I thought about delivering pizza for Domino's or driving a taxi, even though I knew I was too young for either. Still, I had to find something that kept me in a car rather than behind a counter or a desk. And for weeks leading up to my sixteenth birthday, I studied that little booklet from the Department of Motor Vehicles over and over. I knew everything—how to steer out of a skid, when to yield, what the squiggly arrow on a yellow warning sign meant. On the appointed day, I waltzed through my road test—checking my mirrors as I idled, easing into traffic as I took off, passing responsibly on the right, coming to a complete stop at each stop sign. "Excellent!" the guy giving the test kept saying. "Excellent." To show off, I parallel-parked with perfection.

So when Derek and I met in line at the license bureau and he told me his father was a foreman at the GM Proving Ground, explaining what test drivers do, I couldn't contain myself. Why hadn't anyone told me this job existed? I flirted with him like crazy because I wanted that job. I would do anything to get that job.

It took an entire twelve months of begging, of prodding Derek to prod his father, of doing secretarial work in the front office to prove my commitment, of honing my road skills in Daddy's little piece of a car—but I did finally prevail at the Proving Ground. To pass the entrance test, all I had to do was show that I could both drive a stick shift and back a car up an incline. Easy.

I kept my entire relationship with Derek a secret.

I couldn't have chosen someone whose sensibilities were more unlike my own. He was what Mama's friend Romey would call *overt*. Nothing subtle about him. Why wear a black suit when an orange one gets more attention? Why wave at someone when you can yell, "Hey, what's up?!" across the room? Why develop one or two real friendships when you can be more popular by flirting with all the girls and biting your way into relationships with cool guys? He wanted everyone to call him "D-Dog." Imagine choosing your own nickname. He wore his false bravado and insecurity like one of those loose, ill-fitted suits he favored on Sundays at his father's church.

I wasn't too picky in choosing my first boyfriend because I had begun to think of myself as a young woman who would have many men over the course of my lifetime. I decided this was best. Otherwise, I might end up like Kimmie, driven to her death by her quest to correct a problem a man had created; or like Mama, who left behind her own child for a man who'd kept her waiting while he stayed married to another. Women with the love jones, as Aunt Essie would say. Women with a condition. I did not want to be one of those women.

Besides, I couldn't imagine what man was worth it, who among them could love me unconditionally like Daddy? Men, based on what I could see, were either weak or mean. They were either letting their women steal away in broad daylight or trapping themselves into sad marriages, or beating on their girlfriends à la Nolan. And according to Vy, only weak men hit women. Basically, men were pussies. And yet I've always loved so much about them, they with their deep-voiced, prickly-beard gifts that women do not, cannot possess. Daddy was the perfect man for me because I didn't care whether or not he was weak; I was his daughter so I got to take full advantage of all that gentle affection, all that yummy male energy, all that unromantic, pure love. And boys who were my buddies? Same thing.

Sex was another matter.

Intercourse with Derek was largely unpleasant. He was a heavy guy, and when he lay on top of me I felt claustrophobic. I was forever making him get off so I could breathe. Plus, his penis didn't work right. It was too huge, and given his vast inexperience, he didn't know what to do with it. He literally brandished it about. Once I asked him, "Have you had that weapon registered yet?"

"That's not funny," he said. 263

"I'm not laughing," I answered, pushing him off of me.

I had to settle for some little orgasmic trickle that came at the end of his flopping up and down on top of me for fifteen minutes. Since this made him sweat like a hog, I got drenched.

But the truth is that as soon as Derek and I started having sex, I got my period back. He got me flowing.

This fact meant we had to start using protection. Derek was crestfallen. "I don't think I'm going to like using rubbers," he said. "My boys tell me it sucks. They've been envying me a lot, you know, having a girlfriend who never has that time of the month."

I told him that was too bad and made him buy Trojan condoms. But we never got around to using them. I had this secret fear that whatever blocked the conception would block my menstrual flow too. Soon enough we got caught. I missed a period and was as terrified about its being gone forever as about the possible pregnancy.

I knew with an absolute conviction that I would not have the baby. Reasons tumbled out from all sides: Not wanting it, being too young, not even liking Derek, not being able to ever tell my father such news. Angie, whose mother's birth control pills had malfunctioned when we were in junior high, said childbirth was horrible. Finally, a baby would take me away from Daddy. And Daddy came first.

It was a frigid day in December, the streets slushy and covered with dirty snow pushed to the curb by cars with good traction. I wore one of my favorite pieces: a crocheted poncho from my Kimmie collection. I huddled beneath that poncho in the waiting room with Derek. He had pawned his clarinet and electric typewriter to help raise money for the procedure. Despite all my resolve, I was nervous. Derek put his arm around my shoulder to quell my shaking. We didn't argue once that whole day. Luckily, after the injection I felt nothing. I was barely twelve weeks along when the fetus was sucked out of me. I thought of it as the women counselors taught me to, as a dot atop a straight pin.

About two months after the abortion, Derek attacked me. I was stunned. I didn't know he had the guts. He yanked my hair in full view of everyone who cared to watch up there at the Top of the Tech, as we called the school's ninth-floor cafeteria. Yanked it so hard, he nearly dragged me across the room. I had made him do it, he said, because I was getting smart with him in front of his boys. And so, in addition to being a sorry lover, it turned out Derek was another weak man who hit women. He wasn't a mean guy; in fact he was a whiny crybaby, to tell the truth. But he had strength. He could punch his fist through a wall and lift the school's hall lockers from their sockets.

He thought all the self-inflictions of pain and destruction to property showed the extent of his frustrated love for me. I thought it showed how pathetic he was—to be incapable of articulating his needs, to have to resort to Neanderthal force just to make an unoriginal point.

The attacks continued. But I never feared Derek. All of his antics were like sucker punches: he pushed me down at a party, threw hot coffee at the chest of my white angora sweater, stamped my stocking feet on a dance floor with his shined shoes, sat on top of me in the driver's seat of his car, trapping me inside. And every time it was the same thing: *you made me do it.*

I believed him. Women, as my mother had demonstrated, were stronger than men. And besides, Daddy had often told me I was special, so maybe I was the kind of girl who could drive a man crazy. That's why it never occurred to me to think of myself as an abused girlfriend. I felt like the one in control—responsible for Derek's attacks maybe, but never deserving of them. It was Derek's character flaw, not mine.

Truthfully, the other reason I endured his attacks was because it gave me a sick pride to know that no matter what he did to endear me to him, no matter how many passionate outbursts, how many lockers ripped from their sockets, I kept my heart impervious.

Still, Derek really did become a pain in the ass.

Once, we parked his squat green Sunbird on a side street along the exclusive enclave of Sherwood Forest, supposedly to talk about "the relationship." But fed up with the stress, the burden of him, the secrecy about us, the unwanted pregnancy, I lost it. Right there, along those privately patrolled, tree-lined streets, I beat the shit out of Derek, punching him in the chest and the arm and on top of his hard head— hitting him until I grew tired. And it felt good to know what a boxer feels—that wonderful rush of adrenaline, the release of all your frustrations through beautifully physical, aggressive means. Throughout, Derek let me hit him. He covered his face, but he didn't swing back or yell or try to stop me. In fact, we were both silent except for the sound of my fists against his flesh, his grunts, and my moans. It is the one good thing I can say about him—that he sat there and took it like a man.

And he got me flowing.

I was number 632 in a graduating class of 928. Due to these massive numbers, the Cass Tech High grads of 1980 didn't get to walk across the stage. Rather, each of our names was called, and we stood at our seats. When the principal said my name, I felt I could hear Daddy's applause out there amid the throng of proud families sitting in the audience at Cobo Hall. I could see him in my head, if not in actuality, dressed in his cool black suit and crisp white shirt, hair parted on the side, gray fedora in his lap. Pride swirled beneath my gown.

Just days before, when Daddy had been laid out on his back from a massive migraine, and nothing seemed to be working, I feared he might miss my graduation. Aunt Essie had prepared me. "No matter what, he'll be with you in spirit," she said, which only depressed me further. But the night before, I caught Daddy digging out his one skinny, golden yellow tie. "You're going to be able to make it?" I asked.

"I'm gonna be there if they have to wheel me in on a stretcher," he said.

This convinced me that all things were possible, and I decided to be brave, to rally, like Daddy. So after the ceremony I met up with Derek as planned in the corridor outside the auditorium. Our tassels swung from our caps as we faced each other. "Listen," I said, feeling better than I ever had about the future. "This is it. It's over."

"What?" His eyes darted around, like those of a compulsive overeater seeking out a donut to stuff in his mouth. I knew he was going to try to bully away my decision. Push me hard or clamp down on my arm, not let go. "You're breaking up with me?"

"Yes." I turned away. "And don't try to come after me," I said over my shoulder.

Sure enough, he lunged, gripped my arm, dug his nails into my flesh. "You're just trying to ruin my graduation day, aren't you?" he said between clenched teeth.

And then, because I had timed this exchange, I said, "My father and aunt are coming."

There, making their way together down the corridor was Daddy, fedora in hand, and Aunt Essie, waddling beside him. Derek loosened his grip and stood there with me, watching them. As they approached us, I hugged each in turn before introducing Derek to them. "He's a classmate," I said. I thought Daddy's eyes flashed recognition, but he just nodded.

"You must be a very proud young man," said Aunt Essie.

"Yes, ma'am," answered Derek, in that voice he usually reserved for after-church fellowship.

"Well, see you around," I said, hoping I wouldn't, knowing I would. Daddy, Aunt Essie, and I headed toward the parking lot and a Chinese food dinner, leaving Derek to stare at our backs. Just like that, I was free.

That night, we sat together around the dining room table. Aunt Essie sipped her Lipton tea, Daddy his Pepsi-Cola, and me Red Zinger. Our first and only family meeting.

Aunt Essie touched my arm. "What's next, Darlin'?"

"I'm starting my new test-driving job tomorrow," I said. "I can't wait!"

268   "And after that?" said Daddy.

I shrugged. "We'll see how things work out at the Proving Ground."

"Don't want you getting trapped in something that don't take full advantage of your mind," he said.

"It's a really good job!" I reminded him.

"College is better."

"I'm going to go to college," I promised. "At some point."

I had this dream of going to the University of New Mexico. I wanted to see the Pueblo Indians and the purple sunsets and the vast, flat land just as Kimmie had described them. But I couldn't go. No way was I leaving Daddy behind.

"Just don't wait too long," said Aunt Essie. "Life's got its own timetable."

"I might take some courses part-time at the Center for Creative Studies," I offered. "They have a whole program in auto design." I had been imagining the kind of car I would design, one as comforting as a cocoon and whose exterior would change in color like the mood ring Kimmie used to wear.

That was the first time I ever spoke my dream out loud. Aunt Essie just nodded, and Daddy smiled. "You gonna be one of those firsts your whole life, Brown Eyes. The first female to do things in a man's world."

"Maybe," I said. And then I changed the subject, brushing the burden of the future off my lap. "What about you, Aunt Essie? Are you going back home?"

It had been her plan, when she arrived eight years before, to stay until I finished high school. Then she would return to Tennessee, to her big house with the wraparound porch and friendly neighbors.

"In due time," she said. "Might even convince your daddy to join me."

"Who? You not talking about me, I know."

"Well, how many daddies Rae Rae got?"

"Hell, Essie, you know better than anybody, when I left down South, I left it for good."

"The South has changed, JD. You haven't set foot in the place for thirty years, so you have no idea."

269

"Couldn't change enough for my taste." He took a big gulp from his Pepsi bottle.

"How old were you when you left home, Daddy?" I asked.

"Not old enough to be on his own," chimed in Aunt Essie.

"I was sixteen," said Daddy.

"And my mama grieved something awful about her only surviving boy taking off like that."

"Had to get out of there. Everywhere I went, folks pointing, whispering. 'You know them boys that drifter from Mississippi killed in the rock quarry? That there is the brother.' Who wants to live up under that?"

"I managed to."

"Well, Essie you got a strong constitution for that sorta thing."

"Wasn't that. Somebody had to look after Ma."

"And somebody had to go forward, make a way in the world."

"I made a nice life down home," said Aunt Essie. "Right nice."

Daddy leaned back in his chair. "And I can say the same. I created something here. I'm proud of my little girl, proud of this house. Proud of my marriage too, even if it didn't last. Hell, I wasn't even supposed to make it, and here I am staring fifty in the face. Proud of that too."

I should have said, "I'm proud of you too, Daddy," but I didn't. I was thinking about my new job the next day, thinking about my escape from Derek, thinking about the fact that Mama hadn't called to say congratulations.

Later that night, while walking through the dining room to the kitchen—I'd become a nightwalker just like Mama—I heard Daddy singing to himself in the den. A rarity. *"I was borrrrrn by the river, in a little tent and just like the river I've been running evvvver since,"* he sang, tearing up that Sam Cooke song with ferocity and tenderness. I stood by the den door out of sight and listened, my heart sinking a little more with each verse. *"It's been a long, long time coming,"* he sang, *"But I know a change is gonna come. Ohhhh yes it will."*

Because I worked all night test-driving and slept all day, after a few weeks on my new job, I became restless and anxious come three o'clock in the afternoon. After a game of gin rummy with Daddy and helping Aunt Essie with dinner, I was bored by dusk. There's something about driving for hours each day that made sitting still once I was off the road close to impossible. I paced around the house. Aunt Essie hated pacing. She gave me the idea that transformed my summer.

"Why don't you do something physical?" she said. "Get you some exercise."

She was right. I had run track in high school for two years and after graduation had abruptly stopped. After dinner, I put on my track shoes and took off for the track at nearby Mumford High School. It was deserted, which I loved. For one solid week, I ran five miles every night. And every one of those nights, jogging past the tennis courts alongside the track, I saw him out there. Hitting tennis balls across the net, practicing his serve. Dressed in white shorts and shirt, muscles of his long legs and taut thighs glistening in the night lights.

On the seventh night, I walked by the courts slowly, and as he saw me approaching, he walked over to the linked fence and waited.

"You're good," he said.

"So are you," I answered.

We stood at that fence talking about tennis and cars, life in high school, and with each passing minute I knew this guy, Kevin, was going to become my lover; he stirred in me the same feeling I'd felt during my days of obsession over first Jesse Thompson and then Antonio Snapp. Desire.

We made a date to meet at the courts the following night, and that became my life every day before heading to the Proving Ground— enjoying his lean arms around me as I learned how to throw my weight behind me on a serve, grip the racket with a two-handed backhand, volley defensively at the net.

271

On my off days, we went to backyard parties on streets in parts of town I'd never explored, to Canada for Chinese food, to tennis matches in the suburbs. And we went for long rides in Kevin's black Firebird, which was rigged with a CB radio and powerful antenna. He often broadcast to his CB buddies in not-so-distant places: "You got Dragon Fly over here. Come in. Come in. . . . Yeah, Roger good buddy. . . . smokies up ahead, watch out. . . . Catch you when I catch you. Ten-four." He gave me a handle, anointing me "Lady Sunshine."

And before long, we made love.

I was ripe for falling in love. Having finally gotten away from a heavy, tiresome relationship, I was newly graduated with a fun job. Possibilities abounded. It was summer. And for the first time in my life, I felt sexy. Kevin's way of rubbing my skin, of nibbling my ear, of kissing my wrists, his incredible passion overtook me. Feverish and lustful all the time, we clung to each other, having sex wherever we could: the backseat of his car at the drive-in, the park near the Proving Grounds, an empty bedroom during a friend's party, a telephone booth at a rest stop off I-94. And once in a motel room on Six Mile Road, where we paid by the hour.

Now I better understood what Kimmie must have felt for Nolan, why she seemed to give herself over to him so completely. It was the sheer force of arousal. My own desire had been driven by fantasy alone until Kevin showed me that a tongue on my nipple could be so unbearably good, that orgasms could just erupt, that a penis could feel good going in, moving within, coming out.

For my seventeenth birthday, Daddy bought me a giant road map of the United States, the kind that folds out and spreads wide across a lap. We sat together at the dining room table and trailed our fingers over crooked red lines and heavy dotted ones.

"When I left home, I took this road right here," he said, pointing along the path from Tennessee to Michigan. "I was jumping on and off

272

railroad tracks, hiding in cargo trains and whatnot. Young and wild and not thinking about danger. Stopped first in Inkster 'cause the train stopped there. Must've stayed there a month or so. Finally took a bus on into Detroit. Got me a job right off too."

Seemed like everyone that mattered to me had traveled the highways, taken journeys from here to there, been changed by it somehow. Mama, Kimmie, and Daddy each had hit the road in their late teens. I felt it a rite of passage that I be next. And I wanted Daddy with me. That's when I asked him to drive to New Mexico and back with me.

He didn't commit right away, just talked about how the little piece of a car he now had would never make it. I thought about when Oldie was shiny and almost new and we would glide along Woodward Avenue in it, listening to Ray Charles's *Greatest Hits* eight-track tape.

While Daddy and I both loved to listen to music while we cruised along a street or zoomed along a highway, it was not Aunt Essie's thing. She thought there should be silence when you were in the car, so as to concentrate on the road—or, as she loved to say, "Body can't hear itself think with all that noise."

She didn't bother to listen to music at all, in fact. If you wanted to see her go off, let a Billie Holiday or Dinah Washington tune pop up on Daddy's transistor radio. "Lord, spare me from those wailing women with their tragic lives," she'd say. "Why in God's name would you wallow in your own stupidity is beyond me. And why somebody wanna sit around and listen to you do it, that's a bigger mystery."

Her one exception to the no-music rule was her Mahalia Jackson records. I will never forget the command and frightful beauty of that gospel singer's powerful voice, the way her moans and full-out sound gave me chills as she filled our house with songs of praise those Saturday afternoons of my childhood. It seemed to me her heartfelt singing wasn't so different from that of blues women. It was all raw emotion and passion over men, one of whom just happened to be Jesus. But I could never point that out to Aunt Essie.

The summer evaporated. It was a whirlwind of test-driving, sex,   273 card games with Daddy, tennis, more test-driving, more sex, more card games, more tennis, much more sex. I loved not hiding Kevin, not feeling ashamed of him. The only strain came from Daddy's jealousy. It was subtle, but it was there. I felt it in his silences and slightest nods when I'd stick my head in, say I was going out with Kevin, would be back later. Aunt Essie told me this was normal, but I was saddened by it. And then one day, Daddy gave me the gift of approval: "Seems to be a nice fellow, Brown Eyes," he said. "And sure as hell smitten with you. The way it should be."

When Daddy drove up into our driveway in his new car, it was a stunning sight. Just like that, using his meager savings as a down payment, and paying high finance charges, he'd bought a Cutlass Supreme off the showroom floor—not even waiting for sticker prices to settle down. And this Olds was a beautiful deep blue with matching navy interior, stereo speakers, and cruise control. The most radical step I would ever see my father take—buying a late-model car the color of sapphires. At full price.

That car's automatic door locks and across-the-shoulder seat belts impressed me the most. Safety first. When I was twelve, I developed a plan for protection against further abandonment, a method by which Daddy would remain with me. I created rituals, recited self-made mantras, embraced superstitions to ward against harm. They included making sure not to step on cracks while walking to and from school every day, and saying, "He's okay, he's okay, he's okay" over and over upon approaching the house. I created my own form of fortune-telling, using a regular deck to substitute for Kimmie's tarot cards. ("If the nine of clubs shows up before a face card, it means Daddy will feel good today.") And my fingers were perpetually crossed for good luck.

But then Aunt Essie told me a story that shattered my confidence in these rituals. "You can never ask your mama about this, but I heard that what happened that day was Cyril got pulled over by the cops some-where in Georgia," she said to me one evening as we snapped green beans on the back porch. "Got pulled over really for driving that fancy foreign car. You know, po-lice always suspicious of a Negro driving a fine automobile on the highway. Anyway, if Vy hadn't been in the car with them, they might not of gotten stopped, 'cause from a distance you can't really tell what that Cyril is—and Kimmie having his color and all. But ain't no mistaking Vy's race. Anyway, they got pulled over and po-lice drew his gun and everything. Patted them all down, checked out the car, called in the plates—just plain ol' meanness like they do down South." She paused, snapped more beans, rubbed her nose with the back of her hand. "Then, when they finally let 'em go, Cyril decided Kimmie should drive for a while. You know, 'cause maybe a young girl would have an easier time of it with the highway patrol, right? Well, poor thing, she was so nervous—JD says she wasn't a good driver, as he recalls—anyway, she pulled out into traffic and ran right into another car going at least seventy miles an hour down the highway. Didn't have a chance, 'cause she got hit on the driver's side. That's why the others survived. They didn't get the full impact."

Even though too young when it happened to have been told the gory details, I didn't accept that version of the accident. Certain that Mama never would have discussed it with anyone, I decided Aunt Essie's tale couldn't possibly be from a reliable source. "Where'd you hear that?" I challenged her.

"Folks talk, Darlin'. News travels."

"If what you say is true, how come Kimmie's face looked so good at the funeral?"

Aunt Essie snapped away, working her wrists as though the string beans were knitting needles. "Morticians are like magicians. The good ones, anyway."

I shook my head. "Kimmie was in the passenger seat and she wasn't wearing a seat belt and the door wasn't locked, and she got thrown out the car when it happened."

276

"Who told you that?"

"Nobody had to tell me. I just know."

Aunt Essie sighed. "If you say so, Darlin'. We don't rightfully know for absolute sure what happened because we wasn't there. So maybe you right."

Truth is, once she told me that story, I secretly vowed that my new talisman against tragedy would be pure perfection as a driver, one who was self-assured behind the wheel, ready to react and able to merge evenly into traffic, drive the speed limit, avoid all collisions—never being in one and never causing one. But I broke my vow of safety when I drove Daddy that day to the VA hospital after our aborted cross-country trip, doing eighty miles an hour on the freeway, passing cars on the right, not bothering to use my blinkers. And still I didn't get him there fast enough.

Shifting Through

*Freeways are our safest roads. Traffic flows
in the same direction. There are no stops or
intersections. . . . The greatest danger is fatigue.
You can become hypnotized by the constant hum
of the wind, tires, and engine. Keep shifting your
eyes from one area of the road to another. Keep
checking your mirrors. Look at objects near and
far, left and right. If you feel tired, stop and rest.*

WHAT EVERY DRIVER MUST KNOW

endy, the morning-shift nurse, had braided Daddy's hair into the tiniest, neatest cornrows I'd ever seen. He gripped my arm and pulled my face to his. "Listen to me," he said, his eyes wild. "I've had two strokes since I been in here!"

"Shhhh, you need to rest," I said, afraid of his agitation and unable to know what to do about his claims. I was in fear of the head nurse—a heavy-footed white woman of middle age and bad temper with blue veins running through her cheeks. "He's very, very sick," she said when I asked her about Daddy's condition. "Didn't you ever think about encouraging him to lose weight?" she admonished. I shrugged hopelessly, not understanding how a man could walk into a hospital and not walk out of it. Hospitals were supposed to make you better than you were when you entered them. I felt bad for bringing him there in the first place and especially resented Dr. Corey for insisting that I do so.

It was Dr. Corey who told Daddy, way back in 1967, that his high blood pressure had gotten so severe it was like a loose cannon, could take him out at any time. Daddy recounted the story for me one night when we were packing for our cross-country trip. "I had left Vy to be with Selena, finally got up my nerve to leave for good, when Vernon tells me, 'JD, Go home and get your business in order. Things don't look so good.' Before I could figure out what to do, your mama calls me, got a pleading sound in her voice I never heard before. Says, 'Come home, JD. We need you.' More I thought about it, more I figured I *should* go on home, where I had a wife and a daughter and my name on the house. What could I as a dying man offer Selena?" He looked up at me. "Besides, you deserved to get to know your daddy in the little time I had left. So I came on home to die. But do hear me say, it was the hardest damn decision I ever had to make, walking out on the love of my life like that." He said, "Hmph," and added: "Whole thing woulda made more sense, woulda been more *noble*, if I'd a gone ahead and died like I was supposed to."

When doctors told us Daddy had taken a turn for the worse, Aunt Essie asked if they could move him out of intensive care to a quiet, private room where we could spend that time with him. The doctors nodded their heads in compliance and then filed one-by-one out of the little family consultation room, leaving behind Styrofoam cups of coffee for someone else to toss away. When they were gone, I asked Aunt Essie what she meant by *spending that time with him?* "JD just done got tired, Darlin'," she said. "He put up a good fight, willed himself to see you grow up. Now he just done got tired."

Only then did I realize he was going to die. After seventeen years of witnessing his illness unfold, I finally understood the gravity of it all— that a chronic, incurable disease is progressive, that it can be staunched but never stopped. Just because a man has lived with it for so many years doesn't mean he can keep living with it. Now I understood that a relentless illness such as his moves steadily forward to a crescendo, a climax with many variations but one ending.

Every night for seven days I stayed at the hospital with Daddy. Slept in the chair beside him, holding his hand, waking up at eerie hours of the night, watching the thin sheet softly rise and fall over his mountainous belly, now insanely comforted by that sight. When awake, he didn't talk, just lay there with his eyes open, staring out but not seeing. Occasionally, he'd look at me intensely and try to talk. But his speech was slurred, and I couldn't understand him. These moments were the

282

worst. I'd lean my ear in close to his lips, try to decipher the impeded words. It was torture because I felt he was telling me something profound, something to hold on to. Finally, he managed to make a coherent sentence. "Be a good girl," he said in a low, breathy voice. I kissed him all over his face, and when I placed my head on his chest, he lifted his hand and patted my hair.

During the day visitors came: Mr. Alfred, men Daddy played cards with, an old man from down the block who knew him way back when, a silver-haired neighbor he turned his numbers in to. I didn't want them there. They tried to talk to Daddy in loud voices, hovering over him and saying, "You gon' be just fine, JD" when their eyes shone with pity. They chatted awkwardly with me. Finally, after some uncomfortable minutes of holding their hats in their hands and shifting their weight from foot to foot, they'd leave. Nurses came regularly to check his heartbeat. Aunt Essie came every afternoon to pray over Daddy. She touched his temples with olive oil and left her Bible open beside his bed, pages turned to the Twenty-third Psalm. He wasn't an atheist per se—I'd found him watching Oral Roberts on TV on Sunday mornings more than once—but he'd shooed away the hospital minister in one of his lucid moments. This didn't deter Aunt Essie, who had many sayings about nonbelievers, such as: "God is thinking about you when you not thinking about Him. He answers prayer and forgives the cold shoulder."

Each day after Aunt Essie visited Daddy for a few hours, she took the bus home. It was a long way to go by bus—from Ann Arbor to Detroit, but she insisted it didn't bother her. "Gives me time to clear my head, think about this here ol' life of mine," she said. I understood what she meant. It made me love my job at the Proving Ground even more so, with its monotonous stretch of road and time.

Somewhere in those final days, I realized I was pregnant. Again. This time it hadn't been caused by lack of effort. I now had a   283 diaphragm, which the counselor had suggested after the abortion. Kevin and I used it several times. But our lovemaking was often so spontaneous, so furtive, that stopping to insert contraceptive jelly into a little rubber dome, and then insert *that* into my vagina, were improbable actions and wholly unappealing. Then again, I hadn't counted on being so fertile.

I decided not to tell Kevin. I was afraid that he might ask me to keep the baby, and I was not prepared for that possibility. I saw no neat symmetry in losing my father, gaining a child. It was one more complication in my life, and the only way I could process it was to handle it swiftly and efficiently. Telling no one, I made an appointment with the Women's Health Clinic for several days away, a Tuesday, a day that seemed as good as any for ending a life.

At home, neither of us talked about Daddy dying. Not directly. But Aunt Essie dealt with her anxiety the way she knew best: she cleaned the house. She even had the windows washed by professionals and ordered new carpet for the entire downstairs. The beige carpet Mama had chosen umpteen years before was so bare that threads hung from it, the wood on the steps flagrant as it peeked through. I came home from the hospital one day to gather a change of clothes and found red shag carpet snaking through the house like a brush fire. "Everything needs replacing at some point," explained Aunt Essie, usually so frugal with her money. I imagined her someday transforming the entire house into a showcase of cool antiques against warm color.

One evening after I'd driven Aunt Essie home from the hospital, just as I was about to return, I found her still dressed in her too-light support hose and iron-shine brown dress, sitting at the dining room table with a cup of sugarless Lipton tea. I made myself a cup of herbal and joined her.

"Did your mother live a long time?" I asked, suddenly wanting to know more about Daddy's history, things I had failed to ask him when I had the chance.

Aunt Essie sipped her tea. "Well, let's see. She was fifty-eight when she died. That was a long life back then for someone with my ma's condition. She had what they call the drinking disease." She rubbed her knees. "Shoot, we were lucky. Wasn't but one colored doctor making house calls. I know folks, lost their parents before they were out of short pants. Ma hung in there. And she went through a lot, you know. Losing her babies and all, the way she did. I tell you, us Dodsons are survivors." She paused. "But even the strong get tired."

"Tell me about the little brothers," I said.

She shook her head. "I can't rightly speak on it much. Still pains me." She pressed her lips together. "One was seven, other one ten. I told them not to go down by that rock quarry, but they were boys. Hardheaded." She looked into her teacup, was quiet for a minute. "I still owe them a spanking," she whispered.

On that final morning, Daddy's breathing was suddenly labored and loud. Rattling. And he was unconscious. The head nurse came by and examined him. "What is it?" I asked, terrified by that horrible, racking sound.

"It's phlegm. We need to drain his esophagus, so he won't drown in it."

"How do you do that?"

"Tube down his throat, suctions it all out."

"Is that painful?"

"It's a little uncomfortable, but he'll feel better afterward," she promised.

I had my doubts. "Maybe we should just let him be."

"It's better to clear it away," she insisted, blue veins slashing across her cheek.

While she left to get the necessary equipment, I rubbed Daddy's forehead, letting my hand glide across back and forth as I'd always done. His skin glistened. Daddy used to tell me I had "healing hands." When he returned to me that day after the city's riots, he'd left behind a woman who had cared for him once the headaches got severe, rubbing his forehead every night. It made him feel good, he said, to see me instinctively pick up where she'd left off.

When the head nurse returned, she told me to step outside. "This is not something family members feel comfortable watching," she explained. I called Aunt Essie. "He's been making this loud, hawking sound all morning, and they're about to drain his throat," I reported.

"Oh Lord, a rattling sound? I'm on my way. But it'll take me a good hour and a half." I was about to hang up when Aunt Essie called my name through the phone.

"Yeah?" I answered.

"You be right there with him. Don't leave the room." She rushed out the next words. "And if the time comes, let him go, Darlin'. He'll try to hold on for you, so you got to let him go. He's suffering."

I hung up on Aunt Essie, not meaning to.

The head nurse came and got me out of the waiting room. "You can go back in now," she said. "I'm done."

"Is he okay?"

"He'll rest better." Then she added, her face full of efficiency, "You have any other family members you want to be here?" I didn't answer, rather rushed back to Daddy. As I stepped into the room, the silence was much more disturbing to me than the rattling sound had been. His eyes were shut, and he was working his mouth—opening it and closing it over and over—gasping for air. I knew he was suffocating. Thanks to that bitch of a head nurse.

I couldn't bear to watch him this way. I grabbed his hand, leaned in, and whispered, "It's okay, Daddy. It's okay. You can go."

He grasped my hand, stunning me with his strength. He gripped tightly, squeezing and squeezing as though riding the wave of a bad pain. Suddenly, the grip loosened and his mouth fell slack. I eased my fingers out of his hand and put my ear to his chest. Nothing. Put my hand before his mouth. Nothing.

Nothing.

Slowly, methodically, I washed Daddy's body: arms, legs, belly, feet. Next I removed those tiny cornrows, one by one. Afterward, his hair   287 standing on end, I worked Vaseline into it. I started to comb it back, but I stopped, unable to go on, suddenly wasted. When Aunt Essie found me, I was sitting beside Daddy, holding his skinny fine-toothed comb in my hand, looking into space.

A fter doctors had recorded Daddy's exact time of death to be 7:20 p.m., and we rode back home from the hospital in silence, I left Aunt Essie alone to go venture into the basement. I dug through the cedar closet, unearthing a box of Daddy's old albums, then sat cross-legged on the cold cement, flipping through them. I was dazzled by their worn jacket covers, by the initials *JD* scrawled in black Magic Marker on each. Now that they had become documents, singular pieces of proof of one man's existence, it stunned me—the reality that a near destructible object—a circle of vinyl—can long outlive you. When I found the Stevie Wonder *Greatest Hits* album, my assumption was that Mama had left this one behind. Yet there were the initials written across the cover in black Magic Marker: *J.D.* You never fully know anyone.

I chose carefully from the pile and taped one tune off each album onto a blank cassette. The music jumped in time and style from the Ink Spots to Jackie Wilson to Al Green. A taste of B. B. King and a splash of Sam Cooke. Ray Charles, of course. Thinking suddenly of Kimmie as she waved from the sunroof of Cyril's Volvo, I was sorry I never got "Summer Breeze" on a 45. Everyone, it seemed, was covering that song these days.

S elena answered on the first ring.

"This is Joe Dodson's daughter Rae," I said. "He wanted you to know if anything happened to him." I paused. "It did."

Selena sucked in air, moaned softly. For a few seconds, neither of us said anything. "How are you doing, Rae?" she finally asked.

"Okay. I was with him when he passed."

"Was it . . . ?"

"A stroke."

"Yes, well." She paused. "You were everything to him. His little girl."

"Apparently not the only one," I said, wanting to be cruel because Daddy was dead and other people weren't.

Selena absorbed my blow. "I'm really sorry about your father," she said. "Deeply."

"Thank you," I mumbled before hanging up. Whatever I'd wanted from her in that moment, whatever it was, it made me feel suicidal not to get it. I went into Daddy's bedroom, grabbed one of his big white shirts from a chair, and lay across his bed, burying my nose into the cotton. Aunt Essie's competent voice drifted back to me from another room as she made her calls. "Hello, is this Alfred? This is JD's sister, Essie, calling. We . . . yes, well not too good, not too good at all. We lost JD today."

Soon, the house would swell with people bringing food and flowers and the brisk determination to "do something." The funeral director would show up—a tailor-suited black man with a mustache and a practiced, somber look, there to spend the insurance money on "putting Mr. Dodson away as he would have wanted." A different undertaker from the one used for Kimmie's interment, but the same kind. The kind who lived in an apartment above his funeral parlor and sat in the dark every night in an overstuffed chair and drank until

290

he was full of his liquor, stumbling past embalmed bodies to an empty bed.

Before all that began, before the onslaught of death's details, I lay there rocking back and forth, Daddy's shirt my pillow, and replayed Selena's soft voice: *You were everything to him.*

But was I enough?

Mama showed up.

As people strolled in to view Daddy's body, she walked up to me where I stood beside the casket.

"Wow, Rae, you're so tall!" she whispered. It seemed improbable to me that her voice could remain the same all those years and her face could change against it. The skin around her high cheekbones was puffy, and beneath her eyes lay permanent dark crescents.

As I stood at my father's funeral, staring at my mother whom I hadn't seen in eight years, my brain kept saying, *Remember this. Remember this*, terrified that I wouldn't. I took her hand. Age spots covered the back of it, and her palms were rough to the touch.

She licked her perfect full lips and took a deep breath. "This isn't easy for me. Being here," she said. "Just to have to be in Detroit at all is hard. But I wanted to do this, for you."

That she had done the hardest thing imaginable, for me, caused the protective skein I'd grown back across my heart to slacken. Suddenly, I wanted to tell her about the pregnancy, hoping she'd invite me back to Louisiana—where we'd hire some auntie to help raise the baby and all live together family-style.

I moved near her. "Mama, let's talk after the service, okay?"

"Cyril and I are not staying. Our plane leaves at two."

"But I want to discuss something with you."

"Rae, please don't ask me if you can come back with me." She shook her head. "It's just not the right time."

I stared at her, stunned by her mind-reading ability but more so by her bold rejection.

She inched a little closer. "We tried; it didn't quite work out. Let's just do the best we can now, okay?"

"The best we can?" I repeated.

She sighed, as though disappointed that more explanation was needed. "What I'm trying to tell you, Rae, is I can't risk it again. I cannot risk getting close to another child who might die on me."

"But what about now, while I'm still alive?"

She met my eyes with her own. "I feel bad that I don't feel bad."

Someday I will be grateful to my mother, for that gift of liberation she gave me. Someday I will accept what she told me to be true and understand that life had reduced her to taking Valium from the edge of a king-sized bed. But in that moment at Daddy's funeral, I could only swallow my fantasy and try not to choke on it as I pressed a palm against my belly, silently telling the unborn baby this: *You are lucky you will never know the sting of sudden good-bye.*

"I'll call you," she said, like it would be the most natural thing to pick up again with our telephone relationship. She moved to take her seat among the mourners.

"Mama?" Her black suit was swimming on her bony frame. She turned to me. I was dry-eyed, dressed in a brand-new sapphire blue silk dress, the only piece I owned not a hand-me-down. I'd worn my dead sister's clothes for so long, I didn't know my own style, didn't know what I might have become on my own. I held her gaze. "I won't be home tonight."

Mama looked away before focusing her pooled eyes on me. She nodded, turned, and slowly walked not to her seat but to the exit, right out of the funeral parlor door.

293

They are all the same. Orchestrated torture dressed up to look solemn and respectful. Cloying words about the loved one being back in God's arms, God who knows best and never makes a mistake. The sight of cheap red and white carnations, the rows and rows of mourners—some in respectful black, others in bright colors meant to suggest a celebration of life amid the obvious end of one. Gut-wrenching sobs of regret and sorrow. Wobbly organ music played out of tune. A dead body in a box, its lid closed dramatically at the end. The slow march to somber chords out the back door. Torture.

At the cemetery, just as the minister ended his ritual of "ashes to ashes, dust to dust," Selena stepped away from the small crowd forming an arc around the grave and tossed a white flower onto Daddy's metallic blue casket, whispered to him, then walked my way. The narrow heels of my pumps sank into the late summer soil as I watched her coming toward me, strands of coifed hair escaping their bobby pins, swelled breasts all but peeking out from where the flower had just been. She moved closer to hug me, and her grasp was strong and warm and soft, like it had been that day when I was a little girl and she had offered me her yielding flesh. I regained my balance, the smell of apple candy hovering.

"Thank you for coming," I said.

Eyes rimmed with empathy, she said, "Do you know about your sister, Rae?"

I nodded. The fading Polaroid of Josie and me was now in my car's glove compartment. The kind-faced nurse had handed over Daddy's meager possessions, and I'd dug hungrily through his wallet, finding a worn love letter I'd written to him when I was seven, his disability papers from GM, and the peeling photo.

"He didn't want to keep it a secret," she said. "That was my idea."

I shrugged, deliberate in my indifference. "It doesn't matter. It's not like I ever really knew her."

"I was wrong," she said. Then she grabbed my hand and placed into my palm a folded piece of paper, closing my fingers around it. "I was wrong," she repeated before turning away. I watched her leave, remaining hypnotized by the sway of her soft wide hips until Mr. Alfred came up to me, blocking my view.

"JD looked mighty fine," he said. "You put him away nicely." He stepped back, shaking his bowed head, looking down at his deacon-in-church shoes. "I'm gonna miss him something awful," he said in a low voice, his best buddy in the ground. "Something awful." I patted his hand as my eyes searched for her. She was gone.

Later, I sat exhausted in the back of the limousine. I rolled down the window, and as we moved away from Daddy's fresh grave, I craned my neck to stare at the soft, dark earth surrounding his plot, little mounds piled high like rich black coffee grinds. Aunt Essie, face streaked with wet grief, placed her hand firmly on my thigh, holding on as we moved along the cemetery road. I looked at the rows and rows of somber tombstones and thought how comforting it would be to crawl into that grave with him, curl atop his back. But then I realized that was impossible, as Daddy had been buried faceup.

When I ventured to read Selena's note, we were already on Seven Mile Road, crawling through the red light at Fairfield, the limo's headlights bouncing off the midday sun. I squinted and slowly opened the little piece of paper. There I found penmanship so small and fluid it stung my eyes.

That night, Aunt Essie and I sat at the dining room table as she rubbed her swollen knees, sipped her Lipton tea. I couldn't help thinking of her infested bowlegs, of the sneaky, invisible blood clots that lay in wait to travel languidly to her heart. Daddy had left us both the house, which Mama had long ago signed over to him. "I'm thinking, I been here all these years, no count in my going back down South. Nothing left for me there really," said Aunt Essie. "Thinking what with 295 this big place, all these rooms, I might take in boarders. Help me out, what with Mr. Bingham's pension check being so meager." She referred to her long-dead husband seldom and each time with a courtesy title of mister. "It's your house too, Darlin', so what do you think?" she asked.

"I think that's fine," I said. "I'm leaving, anyway. First thing in the morning."

"Leaving? Where to?"

"To drive cross-country like me and Daddy were planning to do," I said with incredulity in my voice, like it should have been obvious.

"You going with Kevin?"

"No."

"Alone?"

"Yes."

"I don't know about that now. You got to be careful out there on the road, a young girl in a fancy car," she warned. "Something could happen."

"What could happen?" It seemed to me the safest place I could be was on a stretch of tarmac in the driver's seat of a new car, automatic door locks clicked, seat belt fastened.

"You know," she said.

"Know what?" I snapped, impatient with her forewarning, needing her to just say it.

"Accidents happen, Darlin'. We both know that."

"Not if you're careful," I said. "And a good driver."

Aunt Essie stared at me. "Some things can't be avoided."

"And some things can."

"Darlin'," she purred. "Listen to me. It's too soon. Why don't you wait a little while? We can comfort each other through this—"

"Daddy and I planned this trip. I'm going like we planned."

She sighed. "What you hoping to find out there? Your daddy is not down the highway somewhere, waiting for you. He's gone."

I pushed back my chair, absorbing the impact.

She tried to put a warm compress across my grief. "Well, if being on the road is what you want, why don't you drive down to Louisiana and visit your mother? She left so fast, you didn't really get to spend much time with her, did you?"

"That's not in my itinerary." I said. Twice was enough. I was never going to be abandoned by mama again. Of that I was certain.

"No?"

"No. Anyway, I'm like Daddy. There's nothing the South can do for me."

"Oh." Aunt Essie's mouth stayed pursed in that O for an eternity. "Well," she finally said. "Family is everything, Darlin.' Don't I wish my two little brothers had lived?" Her eyes filled. "I wouldn't be alone right now, would I? No next of kin."

"I'm your next of kin," I said, kissing her square on her forehead. Then I left her there, her tea grown cold.

The double stench of cigarette butts and sweet carnations hung above us as Kevin thrust himself into me, my buttocks melting into the den's deep red shag carpet. I arched my back and moaned quietly. We were compatible, ever in sync lovers. But tonight especially the sex felt raw and urgent and perfect. In her room above, Aunt Essie snored softly; in the room beside hers, an old army buddy of Daddy's named Sam lay his tired body across my father's bed, and in the living room his sons slept across makeshift pallets on the floor—the guest room's mattress deemed too soft for their backs. Above us, a door creaked open and heat rose through my body. As I wrapped my legs tighter around Kevin's, my mind's eye saw only a huge dark blob—not unlike the raised hood of Daddy's new Oldsmobile, flown open as I'd driven the car down Roselawn a day before. Suddenly unable to see in front of me, attracted to a danger I could only feel, I kept moving. Covering each other's mouths, we came together. For the first time. It shocked me, the way physical pleasure had broken through my numbness, without my permission.

Kevin and I slid out of each other's sweaty grasp. Despite the sanctity of Daddy's den, I felt surrounded by remnants of the occasion—dishes seldom used on lamp tables, ashtrays overflowing, bouquets of flowers reeking. I dozed off with semen dripping from my thigh, awoke hours later—the morning upon me, my tongue heavy, cum dry and crusty. I wanted to have sex again, just to be entered and filled, but that was impossible. Kevin lay beside me flaccid and dead asleep. The house would soon be swelling with watchful, waking visitors, and I needed to slip Kevin out before Aunt Essie found him. Besides, I had an appointment to keep, the road to hit.

I woke up Kevin, nudging him gently. "You have to go," I whispered.

He nodded, groggy. He had given me a fruit basket with yellow pears and shiny apples by way of condolence. And himself.

I walked him to the door. He kissed my cheek, demure given where his lips had just been the night before.

"Send me a postcard or two from the road," he said, joking but meaning it.

"Sure," I said, meaning it back, wishing he could come and not wanting him to.

"You really should've let me hook up a CB radio in your car, so we could talk while you're on the highway," he said.

"Next time," I promised.

He nodded, smiled at me. "Next time, Lady Sunshine."

We kissed good-bye. A real deep, tongue-thrusting kiss. I didn't understand really why I was leaving. Compelled to go and already longing to be back.

I cooked breakfast, using one of Daddy's gleaming, black-handled kitchen knives to slice vegetables for omelets. I cut the red peppers and scallions with precision, thinking how many times I'd watched him do this. As the sautéed peppers sizzled, I threw in the scallions and thought about these sharp knives with their smooth, worn handles. I knew I would cling to them with outsize attachment, like Kimmie's old clothes. It startled me anew, that recognition that possessions can far outlive their possessors.

Daddy's old-time buddy and his sons rose, bathed, wandered one by

299

one into the kitchen. Sam coughed a lot, his chest filled with emphysema, asked for coffee only, please. Aunt Essie took care of everyone, ushering them in and out of the kitchen as soon as they'd devoured their eggs.

Once the men had eaten, said their good-byes, and piled into a long, old car en route to Kentucky, I headed for my room. There I took from under my pillow Daddy's Demerol pills I'd found stashed in his end table drawer. I wanted to feel mellow, vaguely aware of my own sadness but not riveted by it—like I had felt as a child when Kimmie was newly dead and Daddy sang to me about little green apples. I swallowed a pill dry and headed toward the kitchen, where I found Aunt Essie staring out of the little window over the sink, washing dishes. Her gray hair was parted down the middle, two thinning plaits pinned on each side. I would miss her, she who had stepped in and raised me when my mother stepped out; she who had told me "You can't miss what you never had" as a way of warning against sex when I entered adolescence; she who had concocted a tea of ginger and yarrow and sage to help bring down my stolen menses. All these years I had relied on Aunt Essie even as I secretly tried to resent her for ripping me off Daddy's back. I now understood what she had done for me. Made this moment possible.

"I'm about to go," I said.

She turned to me, drying her hands on a dish towel. "You sure about this?"

I nodded.

She squinted at me. "You call me from the road, now."

I hugged her thick body as she wrapped her arms around my waist, her head barely reaching my chest. "I just hope he knew I loved him," I said into the top of her head.

She squeezed me tighter. "How could he not, Darlin'? How could he not?"

"I just hope he did."

She rubbed circles into my back and whispered, "God be with you." I finally let go. "I love you, Aunt Essie."

300

Her face contorted as she waved me off. "Go on, now. Call me. And be safe, you hear me?"

I walked out of my childhood home and slipped into my new convertible Mustang, where it sat waiting in the driveway. It was so beautiful, humming beneath me with power and grace. Aunt Essie waved from the kitchen window, and I waved back. Daddy had taken out a special insurance policy that paid for the new Olds in the event of his death. "He bought that car for two reasons," explained Mr. Alfred. "One, to try to get back some of the good feeling he had when he bought that first Olds way back when, and two, to make sure you had a little extra something just in case things didn't work out as he planned." Dr. Corey was in on it too. He'd approved the necessary medical forms Daddy needed to qualify for the insurance. They all expected me to sell the Cutlass and use the cash for college. Instead, I bought this creamy-white Ford Mustang. Daddy would call it "sporty and low-riding." I felt no guilt over my betrayal of brand loyalty to GM, because I knew Daddy had once been equally disloyal. This impulse purchase marked my entrée into a world of individual choices made without consideration for loved ones—a place filled with exhilarating unaccountability. After I drove it off the lot, Mr. Alfred immediately rust-proofed my new car against erosion and time. "That job will last you a good many years," he predicted.

I bought all new clothes for this trip, took nothing old with me, save a few talismans of protection: Kimmie's charm bracelet, the ecru-toned hankie Mama long ago gave me, and one of Daddy's billowy white shirts. Since the funeral I'd taken to wearing as household slippers his old shoes with the backs down. On impulse, I threw those, heavy and worn, into my suitcase too. My packed bags sat in the trunk, beside the spare tire.

I pulled into the clinic's parking lot, suddenly realizing I'd forgotten the homemade music tape full of Daddy's songs. I quickly glanced over my shoulder, hoping to find the tape in the backseat, and in that time another car, a painfully lime green–colored Pinto I never saw coming, cut into a parking space before me. I rammed into its tail, my car's front end up against its mammoth rear window. Nothing moved for a few brief seconds, the hushed sound of metal against metal drifting like a bad rumor through the air. Upon impact I felt a tremor run through my body, spine-tingling in its pursuit, causing goose bumps to sprout across my arms and a quiver of deliciousness to escape between my thighs, my mind a broken record as I burst into a silent chant of *Eyebrows up. Eyebrows up. Eyebrows up.* My hands gripped the steering wheel, and I suddenly, irrationally longed for Aunt Essie and her succor, for her own talisman against misfortune: salt. She had sprinkled it around the house, left it in a bowl of water on Daddy's nightstand, and when need be tossed it over her shoulder. Once she read in *Ebony* magazine that salt was a culprit of high blood pressure in black folks, and she decided with alacrity that keeping it away from Daddy would keep him alive. She solicited my help, and together we threw away the blue Morton box with the little girl in the yellow dress holding an umbrella, and hid the saltshaker from the kitchen table. She stopped cooking with it. Daddy railed that his food was "bland as all get out," and he didn't believe that medical nonsense anyway. He made me sneak into the kitchen and retrieve the saltshaker, bring it to him in the den at night, where he ate his meals with stealth after Aunt Essie was in bed. He swore me to secrecy.

The driver, a thirtyish woman with hair as long as Cher's, jumped out of the Pinto. Our two cars were rubbed up against each other.

"Didn't you see me!" she screamed.

I looked at her, woozy. *Eyebrows up. Eyebrows up.*

"Well, at least back up!"

I put the car in reverse and inched backward, then for some reason I pulled up the emergency brake and turned off the motor. Suddenly, she was at my window.

"I guess we're going to have to exchange information," she said, running fingers through her endless mane.

Sitting there, looking up into her thin face with its harsh angled nose, my brows ridiculously arched, I realized I had failed at something profound. Out of my gut came agonizing, wrenching moans. Loud ones.

"Oh my God, don't do that!" she yelled, appalled. "Listen, listen, is this like not your car or something? It's okay. It's not that bad. It's just got a little dent. And mine, it's really old anyway."

Tears fell. Unable to see through blurry vision, I irrationally turned on the windshield wipers.

"Uh, are you all right?" she asked.

I shook my head no as she handed me crumpled tissue from a huge   303 macramé purse with an owl's face on it. I wiped my eyes, turned off the wipers. Burst into tears again.

"God, you are a mess."

"I'm sorry. It's not you . . . it's just that . . . it's not you."

"That's obvious." She looked around, as if to ensure no one had seen the crime occur. "Listen, I don't mean to just leave you like this, but I have an appointment I cannot be late for. A very important one." She dug around in that voluminous purse until she found a pen. She dug deeper and, unable to find a piece of paper, opened a stick of Juicy Fruit gum, popped it in her mouth, and scribbled onto the back of the wrapper, thrusting it at me when she was done. "Here, call if you want to. But you should know now, I got no-fault insurance."

I took the gum wrapper as she disappeared through the clinic door, her Cher hair swinging. I could barely read her chicken scratch, yet the sight of it made me think of Selena's neat, lovely, schoolteacher's cursive. I stumbled out of the car, headed for fresh air and the trunk. I tore into my Samsonite bag, looking for that little piece of folded paper, unable to find it, such a little bitty piece of paper, desperate to find it, that little tiny scrap of paper. . . . Rummaging, I tossed aside the clinic appointment card and found myself holding Daddy's obituary. His picture stared out at me. It was my favorite photograph, and taken by me on an autumn day as he leaned against the den radiator, sun streaming through the stained-glass windows. I kissed his image and got back into my car, locked the doors, reclined the bucket seat all the way back, and lay there, letting the bodily symptoms of grief encroach: burning sinuses, stinging eyes, aching chest. When I couldn't bear my own pain, I sat up and gripped the steering wheel, shaking it ferociously and screaming: *"How could you leave me? What am I supposed to fucking do now? What am I supposed to do? Daddy. How could you? How could you, Daddy?"* I raged and cursed at my father, feeling betrayed, left in agony by a hit-and-run. Then I cried.

When it was all over, with my forehead throbbing as it pressed up against the steering wheel, I found it. The little piece of paper. Right there, in my lap. Fallen out of Daddy's obituary. It read: *Josie D. McHenry, 722 Barnett Street, Atlanta, Georgia.* I slid Josie's address into the sun visor. Yanking open my glove compartment, I pulled out my new road map, and the Polaroid of me and Josie fell to the car floor. I studied the map. Atlanta was directly below Detroit. A straight shot down I-75 South. I picked up the picture of us, examined it. There it was, smack dead in the middle of Josie's face. Daddy's beautiful pug nose. I tilted the rearview mirror, caught a peek at my profile—saw cried-out brown eyes and a Creole's nose.

I turned the key in the ignition. As I shifted through neutral into reverse, the car purred. I pulled away from the hot green Pinto—its bumper dotted with white paint—shifted into first, wheeled out of the parking lot, and made a bold U-turn on Greenfield Road. Within minutes I was sliding onto the entrance ramp of the Chrysler Freeway. I pushed the stick past third into fourth and once out there in the full flow of traffic, crossed over to the fast lane, easing into fifth. My fingers turned on the radio, punching through stations until the song leaped out at me. *Brandy you're a fine girl what a goooood wife you would be but my life my love and my lady is the sea!* I leaned back against the headrest and buckled up for safety. Random, familiar tunes coming through the airwaves like prophetic messages would guide me through Michigan, that long stretch of Ohio, across the Mason-Dixon line into Kentucky and right through to Georgia. My foot heavy on the gas, and with somewhere to go, I drove.

I dream that I am sitting in the quasi-funky intersection of Atlanta's Little Five Points neighborhood with its vintage shops and old record stores and alternative newspaper bins, my sister, Josie, across from me at an outdoor café with the back-to-nature name Eat Your Vegetables. She is telling me about her memories of Daddy, and I am breast-feeding little Kimmie as I cradle her in the crook of my arm, intoxicated with my own escape. Southern sun shines.

I have sold my car, in love with mass transit.

ABOUT THE AUTHOR

Bridgett M. Davis is an associate professor of English at Baruch College, where she teaches creative writing and journalism. A graduate of Spelman College in Atlanta, and Columbia University, she is the director of the award-winning film *Naked Acts*. She lives in Brooklyn, New York, with her husband and son.